Warren Lee Goss, Richard Wilmer

Jack Alden

A Story of Adventures in the Virginia Campaigns (61-65)

Warren Lee Goss, Richard Wilmer

Jack Alden
A Story of Adventures in the Virginia Campaigns (61-65)

ISBN/EAN: 9783337340926

Printed in Europe, USA, Canada, Australia, Japan

Cover: Foto ©Raphael Reischuk / pixelio.de

More available books at **www.hansebooks.com**

"I saw one of our men run forward to the rebel color-bearer."
— Page 151.

Frontispiece.

JACK ALDEN

A STORY OF ADVENTURES IN THE VIRGINIA CAMPAIGNS
'61 - '65

BY

WARREN LEE GOSS

AUTHOR OF "JED," "TOM CLIFTON," "RECOLLECTIONS OF A PRIVATE," ETC.

———

NEW YORK: 46 East 14th Street
THOMAS Y. CROWELL & CO.
BOSTON: 100 Purchase Street

TYPOGRAPHY BY C. J. PETERS & SON,
BOSTON.

DEDICATED

TO

THE BOYS AND GIRLS

OF A

REUNITED COUNTRY.

PREFACE.

THIS book is the third, perhaps the last, of a series of historical stories of the war for the Union.

In it, as in "Jed" and "Tom Clifton," the author has endeavored to teach the new generations born since the brave "Army of Northern Virginia" laid down its arms at Appomattox, the story of that conflict, together with lessons of patriotism and endurance for the right, and a broad spirit of national charity.

Many of its scenes, which may to the present generation read like romance, are unexaggerated recitals of real occurrences.

The incidents of the passage of the Sixth Massachusetts through Baltimore in 1861 were narrated to the writer by him who is known in these pages as Colonel Grim.

The escape by tunnel from Libby Prison is, with little change, the thrilling experience of a comrade and friend.

There is, the author believes, not a description of a battle or scene of the war in this story that is not true to history or to real army life.

If it be objected that the actors in this story are too young to have participated in great events as described, the reader has only to count backward from the age of many living veterans of the war, to show that this objection has no foundation.

With this brief introduction, I dedicate these pages to the children of the new generation.

W. L. G.

Norwich, Conn.

CONTENTS.

LIST OF ILLUSTRATIONS.

Drawn by Frank T. Merrill.
Engraved by John Andrew and Son.

JACK ALDEN;

A STORY OF ADVENTURES IN THE VIRGINIA CAMPAIGNS.

CHAPTER I.

"NAP UP."

SMASH went my new ball through the window of our dining-room, crashing like a bomb among the crockery on the table.

"Oh!" exclaimed my mother, " the new cups and saucers! The set is ruined!"

My father, who was at home ill for a few days, came into the dining-room, whither I had been dragged as an offender, and where my poor mother, tearfully wringing her hands in dismay over the broken crockery, cried out as my father came in, "Just see what Jack has done! It does seem as if everything in this house was going to rack and ruin!"

Father looked ruefully at the wreckage for a minute, and then said with a forced smile, "Well, mother, if we have children we can't have every-

1

thing else. Didn't I tell you we were always 'nap up' in this family?"

My father in this remark referred to an incident of the previous week, when the material for new suits for my two brothers and myself, which had been sent to the tailor's to be cut, had been returned with the garments cut the wrong way of the cloth. At first father had been much vexed; but on being told that in consequence of the mistake nothing would be charged for the cutting, his face lit up with a smile, as he remarked, "I don't know that it makes much difference. It seems to be the natural condition of a large family to be 'nap up,' and I expect to go through life so."

What is sometimes known as "a good old-fashioned family," such as was my father's, is not so common now as in times past. I believe, however, that it is one of the best training-schools that a child can have. It was here that I learned, early in life, to fight my own battles, and to estimate myself, if not others, at my proper value.

My father, if not a poor man, was at least not regarded as a rich one, even at a time when in New England ten thousand dollars was considered a fortune.

He was a small contractor in masonry and stone-building during the summer months, and in winter taught the district school, at a time when masters were as important in the schoolroom as teachers.

In the coast town of Centerboro' robust young

men, who served as first and second mates of
coasting-vessels, often attended district schools
during the winter, to learn navigation, and to
write, and cipher as far as "the rule of three."

My father was a graduate of a well-known
New England college, and, as a master, was such
a complete success that none of his unruly pupils
had ever succeeded in their attempts to turn him
out of the schoolroom, or in any other way to get
the better of him. He ruled with a rod of iron,
and punished unmercifully all who attempted to
dispute his sway. Such were the methods of those
days. I mention this fact, because his government
in his own home was in direct contrast to his
schoolroom methods. In his own household he
did not exact that strict discipline which is, I
believe, too often a mistake in family government.
I have heard him remark that a large family was a
miniature republic, in which the members, if not
governed too much, would the sooner learn self-
government. That if children are governed too
strictly, they lose that spontaneous and full enjoyment of life to which they are as much entitled
as their elders.

I have since observed that young people who are
too much restricted and hampered by prohibitory
rules become either unhappy or priggish, and lose
that joyous quality of mind which contributes so
much to their buoyancy in after-life.

Is it not also true that when restricted by tyrannical rules, children, like older people under such conditions, develop hypocritical and cringing syc-ophancy, or break out in open revolt? I believe it may be laid down as a rule, that as a river runs most smoothly when least obstructed, so he who is least hampered by small restrictions is least liable to break beyond bounds.

Be this moralizing true or false, it is true that in our family of many children, our father seldom in-terfered with innocent and often noisy amusements, though he reasoned with or censured us when guilty of injustice to one another.

It was in this "go as you please, if you injure no one," method of government that I was reared until twelve years of age. I also realized, in this democracy of the family, that the world was not for me alone, and learned to show a proper con-sideration for others. I observed that here, as in larger spheres of action, the tendency of con-flicts or strong rivalry was to leave things "nap up."

But the happy days of our family were num-bered. The family circle, soon after the incident I have recorded in the opening of this chapter, was broken by the death of our dear father, after an illness of only a few weeks. During the last few days of his illness he was visited by his younger brother, who executed some papers, the nature of which none of us understood, though we believed them at the time to be my father's will. This uncle Richard was reputed to be a sharp business man and a money-getter.

To my mother's surprise, after father's sickness and burial she discovered that my uncle Richard held a heavy mortgage, but lately executed, on the house and farm, on which depended the support of her family. What had become of the money received on the mortgage?

Several freshly receipted bills were found; and my uncle exhibited memoranda of his own, of moneys that he claimed had been loaned my father, sufficient to make up the sum named in the mortgage.

A council of relatives and friends was convened to consider the future support of the family. After due discussion they advised that the boys and girls too young to work should remain with my mother, while Robert, the eldest, managed our little farm for their benefit and support; the other. children were to be distributed among relatives and friends.

It was my misfortune, in this distribution, to fall into the hands of my uncle Richard, who agreed to take me into his family, and treat me as his son, he having no children of his own. I was to receive my board, clothing, and six months' schooling each year, in return for my services until I was eighteen years of age.

At that age, not much over twelve, a boy knows

little of life, and dreads nothing which is not
tangible to him in some unpleasant form.

I remained at home for a few weeks after this,
while my scanty wardrobe was being put in order.
Then, accompanied by my mother, I was driven
fifteen miles to the railroad station, to be sent to
my uncle, feeling none of those forebodings which
seemed to oppress my sorrowing mother.

I had never before seen a railroad, or any of the
wonders connected therewith, and was bristling
with curiosity.   Naturally visionary, and not a little absent-minded, I heeded but little the parting
admonitions of my pale-faced mother.

The railroad cars, fine with gilded decorations
and red plush; the hoarse whistle of the locomotive; the creaking brakes, and the clatter of the
train in motion,—seemed to my fancy as wonderful as a scene from the " Arabian Nights."

My attention was so taken up with these wonders, that after I had changed cars at Myric's for
my destination, I found to my dismay that I had
left my satchel on the seat of the car from which
I had changed.   On my arrival at Shoeboro', I
could at first see no signs of any one who would
conduct me to my uncle's.

I had not regarded the loss of my baggage as a
very serious matter, and walked the long platform,
asking questions of every one I met, like a living
interrogation point.   I soon encountered a boy
about my own age, with light curling hair, and

"I soon encountered a boy about my own age."
— Page 6.

large mirthful blue eyes, his soft hat on the side of his head. He held a whip in his hand, which he occasionally cracked in a most wonderful manner as he talked, exclaiming, "Say! can you do that?" and then after a moment added, as if it were secondary to that performance, "See here, are you the feller that's goin' up to Alden's?"

"Yes," I said, not surprised that a stranger should know me. "Have you come for me?"

"Yes," replied my new acquaintance; "where's your baggage. "I'll help you up to the Corners with it, where the team is." Then he added, "I've just brought in a lot of shoes, — killed two birds with one stone, you see."

I explained that I had left my satchel in the car when I changed at Myric's.

The boy whistled a long, melancholy note, looked at me as if with wonder at my announcement, cracked his whip, reflected as he said, "Won't the old man just be mad! Well, come along."

"Who," I inquired, "is the old man?"

"Why, I mean Richard Alden; we always call him the 'old man' behind his back. He's a tough customer — a driver, I tell you!"

After reaching the team at the Corners, I said, as if in continuation of the conversation, "My uncle is a deacon of the church, and I'm told is a prayerful man."

Now, I confess it did not interest me whether
my uncle was either a deacon or prayerful; but
being away from home, and having on my Sunday clothes, I thought it the proper thing to im-
press my acquaintance with a few stately company
remarks, as I had heard my elders do.

The boy winked, cracked his whip again, and
laughed as he said, " Yes, Deacon Alden *is* mighty
prayerful; but during haying-time and other busy
seasons he runs prayers and business pretty close
together, — time is money, you know."

" What do you mean," I inquired, " by running them together? " For reply, the boy said,
" Amen — Add, hitch up the horses," in sharp,
nasal tones so like my uncle that I laughed heartily.

" So Add is your name? " I said inquiringly.

" No; my name is Addison — named after some
big man; but they call me Add for short — han-
dier in haying-time," said the boy with a wink.

I was still laughing when the team halted before a house situated on a grassy knoll at a fork of
the road, and where Add, jumping out, exclaimed,
" Here we are! "

I had arrived at my uncle Richard's.

In addition to the house, there was a weather-
beaten barn, and between the house and barn stood
a low framed building, with a pile of fresh leather
chips in front of it.

" That," said Add, with a snap of his whip

towards the low building, "is the shoe-shop; plantin'-time is just over, and the teams will start up to-morrow."

Seeing that I did not understand, he continued, " A team is a gang of men for making shoes, in which each one of 'em does a part. I last and peg 'em; Jim Dean, that feller you see coming out of the shop, trims edges; the old man fits outer soles and puts on heels; and Elbridge Mason, that boy you see coming down the road, works mornings and nights and Saturdays, when out of school. You'll get into it as soon as you want to. Here's the old man."

At the sight of my uncle Richard, Add's whole manner changed; he drew down his face, and no longer cracked his whip, whistled, winked, or talked.

Richard Alden came out as we were unhitching the horses, spoke sharply about one of the traces that was hanging in the mud, taking no notice of me, until I explained that I had lost my satchel, when he stopped short in adjusting the traces, and looked at me with his fishy light-blue eyes; and though he made no remark, and there was nothing in his manner out of the ordinary, except his cold, harsh voice to imply anger, yet I felt in some way that I had not heard the last from him about the loss of that satchel.

"Well, come and get your supper," said my uncle, as he walked briskly towards the house, looking back once or twice as if to hurry the rest of us.

My uncle's wife was a pale, overworked woman, with a patient, pleasant face ; and once as she touched my hand in passing food, in some indefinable way I felt that I should find in her a friend.

After the blessing, my uncle ate in silence, and over the table there feel a chilly reserve — not unusual for the family tables of New England working-people, but in marked contrast to the chatty, pleasant one to which I had been accustomed.

That night I was shown to an attic room by my aunt, from whom I once more received a comforting intimation of friendliness and sympathy, though there was hardly a word spoken between us.

Before I went to sleep I had remarked to Add, who occupied the room with me, that I didn't think I should like living with my uncle Richard.

CHAPTER II.

LEARNING TO WORK.

THE morning after my arrival I took my first instructions in bottoming shoes, as it was called.

The workshop was some twenty feet square. Around its walls were what were called, "stand-up benches," at which a dozen men and boys were at work. The centre of the shop was occupied by a machine for rolling leather, to which was fastened a skiver for thinning the material, and a machine for cutting welts. There was also a low tub near by half filled with water, called a shop-tub, and used for wetting leather.

Such were the simple equipments of the shoe-making industry thirty-five years ago. The great shoe-manufacturing system of the present day, with the machinery for sewing, pegging, trimming, and lasting, had not then been invented. The bottoming of boots and shoes, however, had already become a standard industry in Massachusetts towns; and little shoemaking shops dotted the country, and were a part of the environment of the farms and villages within thirty-five miles of Boston.

Richard Alden had taken up this work ; and his
economy, calculation, and energy were such, that
he was known the country round as "a driver"
and "money-getter," qualities for which the average New Englander has so great respect, that of
such are reverently made its deacons, selectmen,
and members of "the Great and General Court,"
even to this day.

Uncle Richard had what was termed "the
faculty" to run his farm and shoe-business together, making "one hand wash the other," as
New England people call it, and making both
occupations profitable. In this manner he was
reputed to be "laying up money."

I took my place under his directions at one of
the benches, by the side of a device known as a
"jack," by which the shoe was firmly held with the
sole upward. I was instructed how to drive pegs,
and then left to learn the rest by experiment. I
first drove the awl into the leather, and tugged
hard to get it out. I was shown how to hold the
handle loosely, with the hand pressed to the sole
of the shoe, while I struck it with my hammer,
then suddenly to tighten my grasp, which would
bring the awl out easily.

In attempting to follow these instructions, I
caught the fleshy part of my hand, next to the
little finger, between the iron hasp and the shoe.
It hurt me so sharply as to bring tears to my
eyes.

This flurried me so, that I became nervous, and began to break awls almost as fast as I could fit them into the hasp. Richard Alden soon detected this fact, and, coming to my bench, angrily exclaimed, "Why don't you work as I told you to?" I replied that I had hurt my hand. Whereupon he struck me with the welt he held, exclaiming, "I'll learn yer to destroy property!"

The workman at the bench next to mine said sympathetically, "It's too bad to strike a little fellow like that, Deacon." Whereupon my uncle struck me twice more with the welt, exclaiming, as if I had made the remark, "I'll learn yer to give back-talk!"

William Reed, the workman mentioned, flushed, and turning his back to his bench said indignantly, " If you strike that little fellow again, Alden, I'll never do another stroke of work in your shop. The boy ain't to blame. Can't you see that the leather is too wet?"

My uncle turned pale, hesitated, then went to his bench, saying, " The boy is a good-for-nothin'. He lost his baggage comin' down, and it's goin' to cost me no end of money to find it."

I had never before been struck in my life; and I could scarcely keep from crying, not so much from pain as from homesickness and humiliation. I did not then understand why my uncle had yielded to his workman so abjectly, but afterwards learned that William Reed was the best workman in the

shop, and was a man of some property; and I suspected that my uncle owed him money.

After this Reed became my instructor, and
quickly taught me my work. So that in a short
time I was able to do my part well and quickly;
yet I could not seem to do enough to win a pleasant word from uncle Richard.

That winter I attended school, working in the
shoe-shop mornings and evenings; often going to
work before daylight, and working after school as
late as nine or ten o'clock in the evening.

While I do not think that habits of work are
the worst things that can be learned by a boy,
yet there is such a thing as overwork; and the
more I did the more my uncle exacted.

I had found out, before being with my uncle
long, that his dominant passion was the acquisition
of money. During the summer I worked, as did
the others of the shop, on the farm, at planting,
hoeing, haying, and other work which, though
hard, I liked much better than shoemaking, for
which I had acquired the utmost distaste.

My aunt, during all the time that I stayed with
Deacon Alden, was very good to me. The poor
woman had no children of her own, and her heart
seemed to warm in sympathy toward me. Many a
time she comforted me; and more than once gave
me, from her scanty purse, money earned by stitch-
ing and binding shoes. For after doing the
housework for a large family, my uncle permitted

her to earn money in this manner for her own clothes.

The winter following I was not sent to school, as business was what my uncle called " too driving."

At that time my stint was the lasting and pegging of twelve pairs of men's shoes each day, often supplemented by cutting wood for the house, and milking the cow. Eighteen cents a pair was at that time considered a good price for making ; and our shop's crew " made and carried in " two sixty pair lots for each team, every five days.

At first I had tried to write to my mother as often as once a month ; but the cost of postage and paper, and the work of writing, not to mention the folding of letters, which, in those days before envelopes were in use, was a work of art, were to me almost insurmountable hindrances to correspondence, and I finally ceased to write home.

My mother had not made answer to a letter I wrote complaining that I had not been sent to school, and the letters I had received were filled with counsel to respect and obey my uncle.

Little occurred to break the monotony of my hard work during this time, except the passing of an occasional circus, which I was not allowed to attend ; or, " Musters," as military trainings of those days were called. Most of the men in our shop belonged to militia companies, and when there was no farm-work I was allowed to go.

The first muster I attended was for me a great

and never-to-be-forgotten event. I gazed almost breathlessly at the glittering pageant.

I never expected, however, to become so brilliant a member of society as one of those button-spangled creatures, a militia-man. I had, by extra work, saved a little money for this occasion; and this I spent at a mock auction, where things were going so cheap that I felt that it was ruinous not to invest.

Finding my money almost gone, in order to make it last the longer, and to have a final blow-out, I bought a bunch of fire-crackers, and a cinnamon cigar, at which I puffed, lighting my fire-crackers thereby, until not feeling well I reeled down the railroad track on my way home, occasionally halting to play " Niagara Falls," as Add termed it, for I was dreadfully sick, and felt that I should not live to get home. Uncle Richard was furious because I was too sick to do the evening "chores." By this experience at my first military muster I learned, if nothing else, to avoid the pernicious use of tobacco, which is an injurious habit for man or boy, and one which cannot but be severely condemned.

Soon after this event Add became possessed with a musical craze; he bought a brass instrument, and set the neighborhood wild while practising on it, back of the house and in the barn, mornings and evenings.

My uncle was paying Add five dollars a month

and board for his shop and farm work, and considered himself defrauded by the time given to the trombone; for that was the intricate instrument Add was struggling to master.

The result was, that as Add grew earnest in blowing that instrument, the disagreement with uncle Richard enlarged, until at last Add indignantly packed his kit, and moved to another town, where he got work, and declared that his musical study should not be interrupted.

William Reed also moved to a town nearer Boston, where he had bought out a blacksmithing business; for like many other New England mechanics he had "more than one string to his bow," and was a blacksmith by trade — shoemaking being simply a makeshift.

My work in the shop after this had become harder than ever before. I was very fond of reading; and Richard Alden considered this an offence, because it diverted my attention in another direction than that of his own business.

At this time the anti-slavery agitation was at its height. The speeches of Wilson, Banks, Sumner, and Burlingame and their opponents were exciting national attention; and I had become very much interested, and at times excited, by reading the occurrences of that period.

My uncle took no newspapers, but borrowed those of his neighbors. He was a pro-slavery Democrat in politics, and had but little sympathy

with the abolitionists, as he designated all who
differed from him.

One of our neighbors was the widow Mason,
with whose son I became quite intimate, and who
sometimes worked in the shoeshop. He loaned
me books, and was very well-read.

My uncle had sent me to borrow the *Boston Post*
of them one morning, and I was reading it while
slowly coming down the road. On arriving in
front of the house, where he had been watching
me, I found him in a great rage over what he
termed my loafing. I was so much interested,
however, that I read the concluding paragraph
of a speech before I handed the paper to him,
whereupon he struck me a blow with the cart-
whip which he held in his hand.

At this time I was over fourteen years old, and
large and athletic for my age. My sense of injustice and tyranny, long restrained, now broke
its bonds; and when he attempted to strike me
again, I wrested the whip from his hand, and stood
flushed with anger and defiance before him.

"That's the way yer show yer gratitude to a
man that keeps yer out of the poorhouse, is it?"
he exclaimed.

At this taunt, which was worse to my pride than
the blow, I angrily replied, "Where's the schooling
you was to give me? Where's my father's money
you took from him when he was dying?"

At this my uncle turned pale, actually staggered

as if struck, then went to the shop, and brought out a large sole-leather welt and a rope, and, furiously coming towards me, exclaimed, "I'll tie yer up and whip yer, yer dog, till yer take that back!" at the same time attempting to seize me. I reversed the whip, which I still held in my hand, struck his knuckles until he let me go, and then ran from the vicinity of the house.

I had many times thought of running away from home. I had, however, considered that any action of this kind would grieve my mother, who, I well enough knew, had care enough without any additional from me. I had been taught to respect my elders, and my conscience was not a little troubled at the thought of my assault on my uncle. Although in maturer age I cannot justify my attack on him, yet I certainly had some excuse for my conduct. It was, at least, not all the result of headstrong wickedness, as Richard Alden afterwards declared. I knew enough of my uncle's character to know that he would abuse me more than ever if I now submitted to him, and that in any case I should get a most terrible beating if I remained with him.

A blow has always angered and filled me with resentment; and now that I had once turned on my tyrant, there was no other course but to continue resistance, or run away from Richard Alden's control. I determined first, however, simply to go home to my mother's house.

CHAPTER III.

A RUNAWAY.

My experience in life has taught me that memory registers less of pain than of pleasure. That I cannot even now recall the scenes of which the foregoing chapter is a record, without a return of the feelings which I then suffered, shows the mental anguish I endured, and which prompted my determination to run away.

So long as Richard Alden was in the house I could not return for my clothing without a collision with some one within. I no longer feared my uncle, but simply wished to avoid him forever.

I did not, therefore, venture in the direction of the house until late that afternoon, when I saw him leave with his team, " to carry in shoes " to the manufactory at the Corners, as he often did in the evening, in order to save time. Then I went to the house, and confided all my griefs to my aunt, as if to my own mother. It comforted me greatly that she did not utter a word of blame. After she had fed me, and shed some sympathetic tears, I told her I could endure it no longer, and had made up my mind to go back to my mother.

Uttering no word of censure against her husband, she, in reply, pointed out to me that my mother would probably send me back again, and then it would be the worse for me; while if she did not send me back, it would be the worse for her; that uncle Alden would probably foreclose the mortgage on our farm, as he had often threatened to do.

But no argument could change my resolution; and an hour afterward I had reached the railroad, with my poor satchel, in which, besides a change of underclothes, there was a tin box with a lunch of meat and bread.

I had three dollars in my pocket, two of which my aunt had forced upon me from her own scanty earnings.

I walked that night some five miles to Waterbridge (a station on my way to Boston); looked up Addison, who was working there; was entertained with the music of his trombone, which seemed large for so small a boy; and slept with him that night, with the intention of walking to Boston the next day. Add disapproved of this walk, although he heartily approved of my running away.

"Better save your breath," said he, "to cool your porridge. Why, a walk to Boston will wear out your strength, and your clothes and shoes; and you'll need them all when you get there."

I could have hired out at shoemaking in Water-

bridge, where Add worked; but, not liking to be
so near my uncle, I determined to seek my fortune elsewhere.

I got up early that morning; for how could I do
otherwise, when Add was up at four o'clock to
practise in his bedroom on that trombone?   It
was fortunate for me that I did so.

I bought my ticket, and got on the first train
for Boston, and was just moving from the station,
when uncle Richard drove up furiously too late to
catch me.

The last seen of him, he was standing up in
his wagon, making frantic gestures as if to stop
the train.

Arriving in Boston, I at once inquired the way
to Pearl Street, having been told that there was
a large number of boot and shoe firms there.   It
soon appeared, however, that they were large deal-
ers, instead of shoe manufacturers; and after endeavoring all day to get work, I concluded to go
to Spindleville, supposing that William Reed lived
there.

That evening, believing myself on my way to
the station, I came to a long bridge — crossed it,
and stopped at a little building at the farther end,
where pies, cakes, and peanuts were sold.   The
" Little Red Bonnet," as I think it was called, was
kept by an old Scotchman, with so kindly a face
that I inquired of him the way to the station.   He
informed me that I had come the wrong way, and

must retrace my steps across the bridge, and then probably should not reach the station in season to take the last train for Spindleville.

My face must have expressed my anxiety; for he began to question me, and soon learned my story. He invited me into a little room back of his peanut stand, where there were two box-like beds, in one of which he told me I could sleep that night. I there learned, what my experience has since confirmed, that the poor are often more kindly and charitable in proportion to their means than richer people.

The next morning, after a breakfast of bread and toasted cheese, for which the kindly Scotch-man would accept no payment, I went on my way, and took the cars for Spindleville. The price of my tickets took all but ten cents of my remaining money.

On arriving at Spindleville, I began to inquire at every blacksmith-shop for William Reed. No one knew him; and my heart sank at the prospect when afternoon came, and no trace of him had been found in that city. I had spent the last of my money in crackers and cheese for my dinner, and my chances looked gloomy.

On my way to one of the large cotton-mills for employment, I saw a blacksmith-shop, where were a number of men at work. Entering, I once more inquired for William Reed. The boss, who was working at a forge, after hammering a while, put

his iron in the fire, and, with his arm on the huge
bellows, inquired, "What do you want of Reed?"

"To get work with him," I replied.

He looked at me keenly, and then said, "You
are in the wrong box, young feller. I know Reed;
his shop is in Lowell, not Spindleville." Then
after a while he said, as he drew a huge iron from
the fire, "Can you strike?" At his direction I
took up a sledge, and struck the iron with it, repeating the blows he lightly struck with a hammer.
He seemed pleased with the result, but said doubtfully, "Pretty good; but did you ever strike before?" I replied that I had not. "Well," he
said slowly, "you'll do nicely after a while; we
need another striker in this shop. You'll find it
hard work at first, but you seem a good strong
young fellow." It is needless to say that I joyfully closed with an offer of two dollars a week
and my board.

That night, after a good supper, I was given a
neat room, and went to my rest happy as a king at
the prospect of steady, well-paid employment, and
of learning a business more congenial to my tastes
than that of shoemaking.

My employer, Henry Grim, was about twenty-
five years of age, but lately married to the
daughter of his foreman, William Crandall, and
had just settled in business. He had been something of a traveller, though still a young man. He
told me that during the Kansas troubles he had

"Can you strike?"
— Page 24.

been in that State, and had previously been in several portions of the South. He was an intelligent, if not a well-read, man ; a good judge of human nature, and a keen observer of events, and I inferred from what he told me, rather fond of adventure.

My father had instilled into me a love of books ; and this love, if not equivalent to an education, sometimes results in obtaining one. Grim, seeing that I was fond of reading, allowed me, on coming to his house, to use his books ; and I was soon interested in Abbott's " Napoleon."

When Grim saw me thus engaged in reading, as he said, " as if hungry for it," he nodded approvingly, saying, " A boy is all right who has a liking for good books ! "

I served two years with Henry Grim, working in happy contentment.

To say that politics raged at this time would be putting it very mildly ; and Grim, finding my opinion similar to his own, often discussed the political situation with me. He was what his father-in-law called " a Black Republican." The only sneer I ever saw on Grim's face was when some one insinuated that he might be induced to vote for Breckinridge, one of the Democratic nominees for president in 1860.

Several times I went with him to listen to speeches by some of the noted speakers of that time, among them Wendell Phillips, Theodore

Parker, Henry Wilson, and N. P. Banks. The two last named were my favorite speakers; not only because they were conservative men, but because they had come up from the ranks of the working-people of Massachusetts, and represented their hardy common-sense.

"If I cared nothing for law," said Grim, after listening to Wendell Phillips, "I should be an abolitionist; but we must obey laws, or descend to anarchy or revolution. The abolitionists say slavery is wrong, and I agree with them; but not with their logic, when they propose to negative law in order to destroy slavery. I am a Republican, because they propose to restrict slavery to the States where it now exists by force of local enactments. It can't be wrong to keep slavery out of the States hereafter seeking admission to the Union."

The political campaign of 1860 was very exciting. One night Grim and myself had been to Boston to listen to Anson Burlingame. In reply to a threat made by some Southern man in case Abraham Lincoln was elected, "to hurl upon the North a million of armed men," Burlingame exclaimed, "A million of armed men! Let them come, with their spades and coffins lashed to their backs!"

On our way home, Grim said, "That Burlingame may see more of the spade and coffin business than he likes."

At another time we heard Jefferson Davis in the old "Cradle of Liberty," Faneuil Hall. He was introduced by Caleb Cushing; and during his speech, with clinched fist, Davis said, "If you don't stop this discussion of our affairs and your interference with slavery, we'll dissolve the Union!"

"Pretty plain talk, that," said Grim, when we had got on the returning train. "There must be fire where there's so much smoke. We'll have civil war sometime."

Afterwards when he repeated what Davis had said to Crandall, he replied, "Oh, that's political bluff!"

Grim was a member of the Sixth Regiment of State Militia, and I had often spoken to him of my desire to join it when I had become of proper age.

One day, in reply to something Grim had said about war, his father-in-law said, "Nonsense! men have learned better than to cut each other's throats when they don't agree; now I kinder believe with Burritt (I used to work with him) that this is an era of peace, and that probably we shall never have any more war."

Grim answered thoughtfully, "Well, human nature ought to be hammered into that shape, and maybe it will one of these days; but we sha'n't act like angels until we have less of the brute in us than at present. I kinder expect to see war yet;

just the same as I expect to shoot the first burglar that breaks into my house to steal, and then tries to murder me because I resent his attempt!"

During all this time I had been steadily learning my business, until I had advanced from striking, to the forge, and could do as good a piece of work, so Grim declared, as "any young feller in the business."

My wages were also advanced; and it was a happy day when I was able to send my poor mother fifty dollars, with the promise of a small sum thereafter each month. This I did through William Reed, whom I hunted up a few weeks after my arrival in Spindleville ; for it was deemed best not to let my mother know where I was at work.

Thus I worked on in that happy contentment that comes from heathful toil and congenial surroundings.

At last great events, in part to me unexpected, broke up the pleasant tranquillity of my life, and forced it into broader and stormier channels.

CHAPTER IV.

THE FIRST CALL TO ARMS.

THOSE were exciting times. Important national events followed fast after one another. The exasperating language and action of Southern fire-eaters and of Northern abolitionists, the secession of South Carolina, the talked-of plot to assassinate the new president on his way to the national capital, his arrival in Washington, and his patriotic, wise, and moderate inaugural address, — all followed in rapid succession.

"Yes, that's it exactly," said Grim, after reading the address. " Listen to this, Father Crandall : —

" ' In your hands and not in mine, my dissatisfied fellow-citizens, are the momentous issues of civil war. The government will not assail you. You can have no conflict without you yourselves being the aggressors. You have no oath registered in heaven to destroy the government, while I have a most solemn one to preserve, protect, and defend it. I am loath to close. We are not enemies, but friends. We must not be enemies. Though passion may have strained them, it must not break our bonds of affection. The mystic cord of memory, stretching from every battle-field and patriot grave, to every living heart and hearthstone all over this broad land, will yet swell the chorus of the Union, when touched, as they surely will be, by the better angels of our natures.'"

Crandall, who had listened thoughtfully, looked up with interest, and said, while Grim was folding the paper, "I'd like to read the whole of it." Then, after reading, he remarked, " It's good, practical common-sense ; no bluster in it. Kinder seems to me Abe Lincoln's got more sense than all the rest of you Black Republicans put together."

I was working at the forge one cold, crisp morning in March, 1861. Grim had been unusually thoughtful and silent that morning, although it is never common for men of his mould to talk at their work. We had just been hammering at a huge piece of welding ; and he stood at the anvil waiting for it to reheat, the great beads of sweat standing on his broad, thoughtful brow, his keen gray eyes non-focussed in thoughtful abstraction. Crandall was working near by, occasionally casting glances at Grim from under his shaggy, projecting eyebrows.

Just then a customer came in hurriedly with a job, which Grim turned over to his foreman, and then in a still more abstracted manner resumed work at the anvil. *Clink ! Clank ! Clink ! Clank !* How musically the iron rang out in answer to the hammers, and what a healthful odor came from the forge !

The iron was welded. Crandall came up and looked at the work with a critical eye as we removed our aprons preparatory to washing for dinner.

"It's a good job, Grim! But it is a wonder; for your wits have been wool-gathering all the morning! I've known you ever since you first came down here from New Hampshire to learn your trade, eleven years ago; and when I see you in one of them fits, I always expect some new move. It's a pity, too, for you've got the best business of any blacksmith in town. I expected to see you sober down, kinder contented-like, after yer married my daughter Mary. There ain't any wool in her wits!"

"Want ter buy this business?" Grim threw out the query in gruff tones, turning sharply on the speaker; then continuing, "I'm ready ter sell."

"See here, Grim!" exclaimed Crandall, "what does all this mean?" Then after a pause resumed, in answer to the other question, "No, I don't want ter buy; I've got a purty good head for work, but it isn't much for business. You're the man for that, Grim; and it's kinder a pity you can't stick to it."

"Listen to this," said Grim, taking a newspaper from the forge-shelf, "it's an order from Governor Andrew in this morning's *Journal*. Guess you ain't read it?" And Grim read an order, the substance of which was, that each commander of the militia, who were uniformed and armed with the

latest pattern of Springfield rifles, was to inspect
his company; and all enlisted men who, from dis-
ability, business, or other causes, did not wish to
respond to a call from the president to "protect
property and enforce the laws," should be discharged, and the ranks recruited to their maxi-
mum strength by those willing to comply with
this requirement.

"Hum! firebrands!"   With this ejaculation
Crandall turned away with something like a scowl
on his overhanging brow; then sharply adding,
"Them abolitionists!"

Grim folded his paper, washed, put on his coat;
and, as we walked along together, said, as if in
continuation of his thoughts, "Didn't you say
you would like to join the militia, Alden?"

"Yes," I responded; "but I ain't old enough."

"Hum! not seventeen? You look nineteen or
twenty." Then, after a pause, Grim continued,
"How old are you?"—"Sixteen, most seventeen."—"Pretty sizable feller. I guess you will
pass. What say? Will yer try it? I kinder
want you ter go if I do."

The result was, that when evening came I went
to the armory, and was enrolled; and I am not sure
when asked my age that I did not allow Grim to
answer for me.

After this I began drilling evenings, and soon
knew as much of the manual of arms and company movements as the majority of the men.

Not long after this, about the first of April, 1861, Grim sat reading his newspaper, while I was reading Abbott's " History of Napoleon." My imagination was all aglow with its rose-colored description of war, when a member of our company brought a letter for Grim. He read it, then looked across the table at his wife, and said, " Mary, the field and staff officers of the Sixth met at the American House in Lowell last evening, and tendered their services to the government. I suppose we are likely to be called out at any time. I think father Crandall will tend to the business if I'm gone a while."

The little woman turned her face to him ; and tears stood in her eyes as she lovingly looked at her stalwart husband, saying, " You know best, Henry. But I was in hopes you cared enough for me to want 'er stay at home."

Grim bit his lip, and a lump rose in his throat, as he said, " God knows I care for you, Mary ! But you wouldn't have me show the white feather, if my regiment should be called out, would you ? "

" No," said the young wife ; " I dun know as I should. Y' couldn't be a coward if y' should try, Henry."

" Well," said Grim musingly, as he put on his coat to go down to the armory, "perhaps it will all blow over ; kinder hope so." That night when we arrived there, and the order was read, all present were in favor of going whenever we should be called out.

" Consider yourselves ready, then," said Grim, looking at the young fellows gathered around him, " to respond to the tap of the drum. There's been talk enough. This means something besides talk. It may mean fighting ! "

On our way home Grim said, after a thoughtful silence, " This'll give them that hev talked a chance to back it up with courage and muscle, I guess. I'm sick of dilly-dallying. Speeches don't amount to a snap of my finger ! "

" You don't imagine," said Crandall, when something like this was said in the shop the next morning, " there'll be anything *but* talk ? "

" I dun know," said Grim, pausing in his work, with a far-away look of abstraction in his eyes. Then he began pounding furiously, as if he had the Southern Confederacy on the anvil, saying, " If them Southern brethren of our'n push us too fur, I ain't a-goin' to say it's best to back down, though ! "

The crisis came at last.

On the 13th of April, 1861, while on our way to the shop, our attention was arrested by a huge bulletin-board, on which, in large head-lines, was the following : —

WAR INAUGURATED BY THE

SOUTHERN CONFEDERACY!

FORT SUMTER ATTACKED AND TAKEN BY THE REBELS,

AFTER A TERRIBLE BOMBARDMENT ! ! !

MAJOR ANDERSON AND HIS WHOLE COMMAND

PRISONERS OF WAR ! !

We were too much excited to think of work. Crowds were gathered around the bulletin-boards; and when the newsboys began crying the Boston papers on the streets, there was intense excitement, and an eagerness to get the news prevailed.

The Carolinians had dared the first shot to "fire the Southern heart;" but they had also ignited the Northern heart (so slow to wrath) as a result of that unjustifiable bombardment of a national fortress.

The change from apathy to indignation was a noticeable feature of the hour. Men who for months had been bitterly opposed to the administration, turned squarely around, and were now bitter in their denunciation of the rebels and their attack on Fort Sumter.

As we went down the street on our way to the shop, we saw little groups of men on the sidewalk and in the doorways, gravely discussing the situation. The general sentiment seemed to be, "The Southerners have gone too far this time. We must punish them in some way, so they will respect the law."

When we reached the shop we found Crandall earnestly at work. Grim read the news to him as he stood at his anvil. As the full import of the news struck him, he stopped work, knit his brow thoughtfully, chewed solemnly at his quid of tobacco, then deliberately took off his leather apron, and, while washing his hands at the tub,

said, " Boys, I've always been in favor of giving
the South fair play, but they've gone too far this
time ! We must make them understand that they
can't fire on the American flag without getting
into trouble ! We must make them take a back
seat." He enlisted in the Sixth Militia that day,
and never put on his blacksmith apron again until
the Rebellion was ended.

A short time after this, while we were drilling
at the armory, we got the president's proclamation,
calling for seventy-five thousand men. Grim read
it aloud. How our hearts thrilled at its patriotic
tone I shall not forget if I live another fifty
years : —

"Whereas the laws of the United States are obstructed by a combination too powerful to be suppressed by ordinary judicial proceedings ; therefore,
I, Abraham Lincoln, by virtue of the power in me
vested by the Constitution and the law, have thought
it fit to call forth, and do call forth, the militia of
the several States of the Union, to the aggregate
number of seventy-five thousand, in order to suppress
said combination. I appeal to all loyal citizens, to
favor, facilitate, and to aid this effort to maintain the
honor, the integrity, and existence of our National
Union, and the perpetuity of popular government,
and to redress wrongs already too long endured."

This call to arms seemed to strike the keynote
of moderation and good sense which, amid all the
terrible discords of civil war, sounded strong and

clear above the tumult of rebellion against the Constitution and the law.

After reading it, Grim said, "That's an argument as well as a call for men."

"Yes," said Crandall; "it's calm and clear as a mill-pond, and strong as if double-bolted. It shows we are right; we are simply upholding the law, and mustn't back down!"

It was the 16th of April when this first call to arms was read, and we of the Sixth Regiment were expecting to be ordered out at any hour.

A little past four o'clock that afternoon (the 16th) we left the shop to go up town, when we encountered Crandall coming towards us, exclaiming excitedly as he reached us, "We're ordered out! Here's a despatch! I'm on my way to notify the captain and other officers!" Grim said to me, "Hold on a minute; I must go and tell my wife."

When he rejoined me we went to the armory together, unlocked the door, ran up the national flag, beat the long roll as well as we could, put on our uniforms, and were ready to march at five P. M. This roused the town, of course, and the people came flocking to the armory to learn what it meant.

We left town next morning on the eight o'clock train for Lowell, where we joined the other companies of the Sixth, making eight companies in all. We proceeded by rail to Boston, where we

arrived about noon. Here, on the 17th, we went
to the State House, and drew overcoats and got
our colors.

Three companies, one from Boston, two more
from Worcester and Stoneham, joined us, making
in all eleven companies, to which was added a
band. There were in all about seven hundred
men, commanded by Colonel E. T. Jones. (The
lieutenant-colonel was an old man, and did not
go with us.) Major Benj. F. Watson, editor of a
Douglass Democratic newspaper, took his place,
and was very popular with the boys.

We left Boston at seven o'clock that night,
with orders from Governor Andrew to report to
the War Department at Washington.

We went all the way by rail, and awoke the
citizens with our music on our arrival at New
York in the morning of the next day. Among
the members of the band I saw a young fellow
who, when the music had at one time ceased,
still industriously pumped hideous sounds from a
big trombone. It put me so much in mind of Add's
performance on that instrument, that I laughed.

"What," said Sergeant Grim, "is so funny,
Jack?" So I told him about Add, of his leaving his place on account of his trombone, and
also of the concert he had entertained me with
the morning I left him in Waterbridge. Grim
laughingly said, "We ought t' have him with us
to scare the rebs."

One-half of the regiment, including my company, went to the Astor House that morning, and the other half to the Metropolitan Hotel. We stacked arms in the lobby of the Astor, and there took breakfast; and after this, formed in line and marched down Broadway.

Great excitement prevailed in the city; banners were waving everywhere, and the crowd was so dense that we had to push our way through it.

On the morning of the 18th we arrived in Philadelphia, and left on the morning of the 19th for Baltimore.

CHAPTER V.

THE SIXTH IN BALTIMORE.

ABOUT an hour before our arrival in Baltimore, the captain of our company came into our car, saying he had just been to see the colonel, and then added, " The orders are, that in marching through Baltimore, every man is to keep his face square to the front, and take no notice of anything said to him."

" That means," said Sergeant Grim interrogatively, " that if they sass us, we are not to sass back ? "

" Exactly," said the captain, nodding and smiling; " as near that as anything. You are not to resent any kind of talk coming from citizens, no matter what they say, but march square to the front."

Ammunition, ten rounds to each man, was then distributed to us, our captain at the same time remarking that there would probably be no trouble, as the cars were to be drawn by horses across the city to the Camden-street Station.

On our arrival in Baltimore, we found a crowd of four hundred or five hundred people congregated at the railway station, many of them seeming only interested spectators of our arrival, mere lookers-on ; while others called us villains and abolitionists, and shook their fists at us. Horses were at once attached to the cars, containing seven companies, together with the field and staff officers ; and these were at once drawn to the station, across the city. The cars containing companies C, D, I, and L were left behind.

Sergeant Grim threw up the window, saying, "Le's have some air!"

The crowd had meanwhile continued steadily to gather ; and, with a gesture of contempt toward them, Grim said, "Them fellows are as chuck full of cussedness as they can hold!"

"The regimental band is in one of the back cars," said one of the men. "I wonder they don't play something lively."

I sat in the seat with Grim ; and, as the window was raised, I could hear as well as see what had now become a mob of men. Some of them shook their fists at us, calling us, "Yankee villains!" "white niggers!" and other vile names.

"See 'em," said Grim ; "they're itching to get hold of us. They'd skin us alive if they could. Them fellows feel wicked all through."

A villanous-looking bully here came up to the open window, uttered a fierce imprecation, glared at us angrily, and finally spat tobacco juice upon us.

Private Crandall, who had at this time come to our seat, angrily drew back to strike him, when Grim arrested his arm, saying, "'Gainst orders, father Crandall," and then shut the window.

In about twenty minutes orders came to leave the cars and fall into line. This we did while the howling mob was cursing and threatening us.

The officers held a hurried consultation. Captain Follansbee took command, wheeled the men into column of sections, the crowd all this time growing more and more excited and violent in their language and gestures.

"We're goin' to hev trouble here," said Crandall, his shaggy brows scowling down over his eyes, as he bit solemnly into a huge plug of tobacco.

We began our march, the crowd following with exasperating jeers, curses, and insults. As soon as the order was given, the same ruffian who had looked in at our windows threw himself squarely in front of our column, bearing a rebel flag attached to a rude pole, as if to stop its advance. I saw our men wrest it from him; and in the struggle for its possession it dropped to the ground, and was trampled as we passed over it.

The police all this while seemed to be idle spectators. One exception, however, occurred when one of them, who had been requested to show us (or lead) the way across the city, directed us by saying, "Keep the railroad-track," and was

"Threw himself squarely in front of our column bearing
a rebel flag."

— Page 42.

immediately knocked down with a stone thrown by some one in the mob.

On turning into Pratt Street, shortly after leaving the station, the mob began to throw bricks and stones, one of which struck me on the side of the head just as I was turning the corner. It staggered and confused me, so that if Crandall and Grim, who were by my side, had not held me up, I should have dropped in the street.

Grim said in an undertone, and with a sarcastic grin, " Sumthin' of a contrast to marchin' through New York, boys, them —— devils ! I wish the captain would give orders to fire!"

Still we marched with our faces square to the front. My heart was throbbing like drum-beats, and a lump constantly rose in my throat. The crowd soon became still more furious. Shouts, howls, pistol-shots, stones, and bricks were hurled at us from every side. I saw some of our men lying wounded in the street, with yellow-white faces and ugly blotches of blood on them, turned up to the sky.

At last, about a third of a mile from our starting-point, we came to a canal. The bridge across it had been torn up; its planks, together with barrels and boxes, were piled up on it in such a manner as for a time to stop our advance.

For some reason the mob did not fire on us here; and by stepping from one timber to another, and levelling the barricade as much as possible, we finally got across. The mob quickly followed us up again, firing quite rapidly, and howling like fiends.

" Ain't they wadin' in considerable deep?" said Crandall coolly, but with suppressed wrath.

" Look at them fellows up there in the third story of that block," said Crandall in a low but sharp tone. " Look!" I glanced upward, and saw three or four men with muskets pointing downward, as if to shoot.

Crandall brought up his Springfield rifle, when Grim seized his arm, saying, "Stop it! Wait for orders!" The men at the window fired. Two of our men dropped; and then the order came, " Fire at will! Fire!" Grim at this command brought his musket quickly to his face; and at its sharp report, one of the ruffians, with a crash that made my heart jump, tumbled mangled on the sidewalk. Then the men began firing rapidly, not at random, but coolly, at those who were most conspicuous in the assault on us.

At our first fire the crowd had fallen back; and as the smoke thinned we saw dead and wounded men occupying the space thus cleared. Then the furious mob closed in on us once more, howling and cursing with redoubled fury, exclaiming, " We've got graves dug for all of you Yanks!" " We'll manure the soil here with you, you white Yankee niggers!"　　" We'll learn y' to come down here!"

" Oh, shut up!" said Grim, with an imprecation; for he was now angry all through. A ruffian seized me by the collar at this time, and
would have pulled me from the ranks; but Crandall struck him with his club-like blacksmith fist,
and the ruffian, with the blood spurting from his
nose, fell to the pavement. A number of similar
attempts to club our men were made here. We,
in return, aimed, as a general thing, only on those
whom we saw shooting or clubbing our men.

The companies had followed the railroad-track
until the head of the column came to a switch.
At it we halted for a moment. We heard some
of the mob who were stationed here threatening
and cursing, apparently in an attempt to prevent
us from turning into a side street. I afterwards
learned that Captain Follansbee had been unde-
cided which way to go, until the threats of these
men to kill him if he turned down that way,
showed him that the right way to the station was
in that direction.

The mob still kept up their attack on us, with
pistols, muskets, stones, bricks, and lumps of coal
from a coal-yard near by; the crowd hooting, yelling, and calling us all the foul names they could
invent.

Our column still moved on, reached the cars,
got hurriedly on the train, and was soon moving
away.

I was not so fortunate as to reach either station

or train. Just as I saw our men at the head of the
column getting on the cars, I fell. I remember
thinking that my foot had tripped; then I was
dimly conscious of being dragged into an alleyway
or side street, and knew no more until I found
myself in bed in a strange place.

I was in the confused condition of one who
awakes after a profound slumber, unable to recognize time, surroundings, or that which had preceded his going to sleep.

"Where am I?" I inquired. "Where are the
boys?"

A girl about three years older than myself
stepped lightly to the bed, and, placing her cool
hand on my throbbing head, said, "You are
among friends, Union people, and father says
that you must lie still."

I tried to rise, saying, "But I must get away
with the regiment."

"You can't; they've been gone for hours. You
must lie perfectly still, or you will get the bandages off," and she coolly turned back the clothes
at the foot of the bed and proceeded to inspect
something there, which thing I soon found to
be connected with a terrible pain in one of my
legs.

"I'm awful thirsty!" I exclaimed. She gave
me a cooling drink and said, "Lie still." The
girl's manner was one of mingled assurance and
firmness, and I gazed at her in astonishment.

"What," I asked, "does it all mean? How did I come here?"

"You were wounded and brought in here by good Union people; my father's a Northern man; I am your nurse; you are my first case; and you must keep very quiet." This last was said with an air of great firmness; and, as I wonderingly watched her moving lightly around the room, I fell into a deep sleep.

I was awakened some hours after by a light rap at the door, and a moment afterward a gentleman walked into the room. I knew at once that he was a doctor, by that indefinable manner of cheerfulness and assurance that men of that profession have.

Addressing my nurse, he said, "How's your patient, May? Hum, — been asleep? That's good."

The doctor was a man of medium size, and quick in his motions. His distinguishing mark was a huge shock of sandy hair and whiskers, with hazel or almost black eyes. This contrast of his light bristly hair with his dark eyes gave him an almost ferocious look, that was, however, dispelled at once on hearing his voice, which, though deep, was very pleasantly modulated. His tones were those of a man who commanded but never assumed; who expected obedience, yet did not fume if it was not accorded him.

He came to my side, looked at me, addressed

a few words to the girl, unrolled the bandage from my leg, restored it, and then said, "Well, young man, how do you feel?"

"Rather bad, doctor; will you please tell me how I came here?"

"You came," said the doctor, with a grim smile, "feet first. You were brought here. A friend of yours was dodging around, trying to get to the depot. He said he was doing the best he knew how to mind his own business when he saw you shot down; dragged you out of the way; happened to hit on me for a doctor; some Union man told him I was from the North, I believe. We brought you here, and put you under boss May," smiling and nodding towards the girl.

"Who," I asked, "was this friend of mine?"

"One of your band; he had slipped on a pair of overalls, an old blouse and a soft hat, left his instrument in a shop, and was skulking around trying to reach the train when he saw you shot down."

"It's all a mystery to me," I said, "I don't know a soul in the band."

"I fear you've talked too much already," interrupted the girl, looking toward her father. "Rest after such a shock is the best thing for you. Your nervous shock, my father says, is worse, if anything, than your wounds."

After the doctor had left, I lay still looking at

the wall, and at the girl sitting by the window. The light had begun to fade away into twilight, with no sound in the house except the ticking of a clock in the hallway, when she said, " Here comes your friend." Soon I heard a step in the hall, and when she opened the door there appeared the ruddy, laughing face of Add.

I was never more surprised or glad to see any one. He soon told me the whole story.

" The band," said Add, " was in the rear car; of course we couldn't shoot anything but wind at them fellows. So we just got away the best we could. The mob had gone howling after you so we didn't have so much trouble in mindin' our own business as the rest of you did."

" What became of the rest of the band?"

"Skulking around the city somewhere; most of 'em have bought or borrowed citizen's clothes."

He told me he had tried to reach the car in "overalls" and a soft hat which he had bought of a Jew, and had then followed the regiment with the intention of getting aboard the train with them.

" I was just going to make my final rush for the cars," said Add, " when I recognized you, and in a moment more you were down. I know the very house you were shot from. You see they thought I was one of the mob. Then I got a feller to help me carry you. Then the doctor come along, and over in the drug-store they told me he was a Northern man; and then we had you brought in here. That's the whole business, without black-ball or burnishing," said Add, with one of his droll twinkling expressions, which might be called a wink.

"Lost my instrument, too ; softest and sweetest toned one in Boston ; makes me *so mad* that I could tear down their old rat-trap of a city ; plague me if I couldn't!"

When I remembered the tones of that trombone, so like a clap of thunder pumped through a coarse sieve, I laughed almost convulsively ; for Add's music was to my mind extremely ludicrous.

I finally said, "It must have been you, Add, whom I saw pumping that thing all alone down on Broadway the morning we left New York."

Add grinned, was a little provoked, but finally joined me in laughing as he said, "Some of them band fellers did call me 'lone thunder,' but you bet I can drown out the whole band with my trombone! Some of them chaps are so envious that they got mad after I joined, because they thought I'd use up all the wind in the band-room."

Add or the laughing did me good, and I could see that both the doctor and my nurse thought so ; for after that they encouraged him to visit me every day. I was quite touched by his devotion to me, for he said he was "goin' to stand by me until I was able to go on to Washington ; for," added he, " the Rebs have burned all the bridges 'tween here and Washington, and tain't no use ter try."

I learned from my doctor that one of the small arteries of my leg had been severed by the bullet, which had caused me to lose much blood; and though the bone had been slightly splintered, yet it was not broken; and there was some inflammation, but he hoped to have me around again in a few days.

One day, a week or two afterward, the doctor had been examining my wound, when Add responded to some teasing remark I had made, by saying, "Now, Jack Alden, you shut up or get up. You ain't so awful sick as you pretend." It was the first time my name had been mentioned, and the doctor turned around to Add, then to me with a questioning look, and said, "Is your name John Alden? and was your father's name the same?"

I replied that it was; and after some other answers to his questions it turned out that he and my father had been college chums.

The doctor was, as I have already intimated, a strong Union man. I learned that he was a widower, and that Mary was his only daughter, though he had a son older than she who was then living in the South.

I recovered strength rapidly; soon obtained a suit of citizen's clothes, and in a few weeks was able, with the doctor's aid, to be about, and thought of attempting to rejoin my regiment in Washington, if I could get there.

CHAPTER VI.

THE YANKEES HAVE COME.

AFTER the passage of the Sixth Massachusetts through the streets of Baltimore, railroad communications between Washington and the North were for a time cut off.

Maryland was in a ferment. Her legislature only awaited a favorable moment to proclaim its adherence to the Southern cause, and to raise the standard of Secession.

For the weeks during which I remained in Baltimore, rebel influences controlled the city. Though there were many loyal people, they were overawed by the noisy insurrectionists, and Union sentiments were not freely expressed.

The loyal but timid Governor of Maryland had even permitted an act of war, in the destruction of the railroad bridges communicating with the national capital. The authorities of Baltimore had collected arms and munitions of war, organized military companies to resist the passage of Union troops, seized the telegraph wires, forbidden the export of provisions, and in other ways usurped the functions of the Federal government

by regulating the departure of vessels. A Confederate recruiting-station had meanwhile been
opened, and was in successful and unmolested
operation.

Directly after these scenes of mob violence on
the 19th of April, General B. F. Butler, on his
way to Washington with the Eighth Massachusetts, finding his passage to the capital cut off in
that direction, had energetically opened, and held
open, a new route by way of Annapolis.

Wednesday, April the 27th, the Eighth Massachusetts and the Seventh New York (the latter
made up of the better element of that city)
started out from Annapolis on a twenty-mile
march, to open communications with Annapolis
Junction. The mechanics of the Eighth Massachusetts patched up a wrecked locomotive and
a few dilapidated passenger-cars, and, with these
for their supply, baggage, and passenger train,
advanced twenty miles to the Junction, relaying
the track (which had been destroyed by the insurgents) as they advanced. Maryland's prominent
men meanwhile protested against the passage of
troops across the State.

While this was taking place, gloom and uncertainty overhung the national capital. President Lincoln anxiously awaited the arrival of
the volunteers, which would insure its security.
The rebel sympathizers and plotters hoped that the
Confederates would advance from Virginia, and

seize Washington before the arrival of national troops. This uncertainty did not prevent eager politicians from besieging President Lincoln for office meanwhile; and he quaintly expressed the situation by saying, "I felt like the man who let lodgings in one end of his house while the other end was on fire."

At last, on the 22d of April, the Seventh New York arrived in Washington, bringing with it a spirit of enthusiastic loyalty which thenceforth abided at the national capital until the war ended.

So much is needful to be said, that the situation at this critical period of our national affairs may be the better understood by my young readers. My wound, although still unhealed, did not prevent my getting out into the streets, and I was fast becoming impatient to rejoin my regiment. Through the doctor, I had procured me a suit of citizen's clothes, that I might not be interfered with by officious rebel sympathizers.

On first going into the street, and listening to the conversation in the markets and shops, I had found that war was the all-absorbing topic of conversation. The sympathizers with rebellion were often out-spoken, though I soon discovered that there was also a deep undercurrent of Union sentiment, which, however, found very little open expression.

Among the mercantile classes there was dis-

satisfied grumbling about the loss of trade because
the city was cut off from communication with
regular routes; and this dissatisfaction in time
bore fruit in Union sentiment, when the control
of the city was assumed by the Union authorities.

I had several times, during my stay here, proposed to leave Dr. Milner's house, lest I might
compromise him among those of his friends who
were disunionists; but at each attempt to leave
he urged me so pressingly to remain, that I had
yielded, not unwillingly, to his wishes. Early in
our acquaintance I had told him of my previous
life, to which Miss May listened with evident
interest. When I mentioned my work at shoemaking, blacksmithing, and farming, she said in
a tone of surprise, I thought, " No one but negroes
and very common people work at such employment here."

" Well then, they must all be common people
up our way," I replied; "for most all work there.
My father was an educated man, and a gentleman;
and he thought every man should work at manual
labor a part of his time, for health as well as for
moral effect."

Dr. Milner laughed, and said, " Yes, Miss
May, I worked at one time as a carpenter, —
my father's business, — and in that way earned
money to assist in paying my way through college. You see," said the doctor, addressing me
half seriously, " May has been brought up in select

Baltimore society, and she can't understand how any one with pretence to good breeding can follow useful employment without lowering himself socially."

At this I expressed the natural surprise of a New England boy, by saying, "I have never thought my work to be degrading. I have been proud to earn a living."

"And it isn't degrading," said the doctor quietly. "It is the curse of slave-labor that it puts a bane on useful employment; and that is just the difference between the Northern and Southern standards of manhood. I suppose, however, Alden, you look forward finally to something different from blacksmithing?"

I replied that it had seemed possible to build up a business of my own, and employ other men in the work; that it was true I should like a profession, — would like to study law, and had already partly read "Blackstone's Commentaries on the English Law," and some other law-books; but I had first to think of earning a living, and helping my mother. My father was said to be well read in the law, and had two cousins who were quite eminent in the profession.

"Oh, yes," said the doctor, nodding, "the Rich brothers; they are both fine lawyers. How would you like to come into my office and study medicine?" And then after a pause he added, "If this trouble blows over."

I replied that while it would please me, it would be a great expense, and prevent me from assisting my mother.

About the 1st of May I had begun, with the aid of a crutch, to take long walks, sometimes with Add or May or her father. The doctor encouraged me to believe that I should be able to get around without a crutch or cane in two or three months more.

On one of my rambles with Miss May, I noticed a howitzer pointing out of a second-story window over the street which I remembered that my regiment had passed through on the 19th.

"What is that for?" I inquired, as I stood looking up to the window. A fine-looking young fellow, about nineteen years of age, here came up. May introduced him as Mr. George Raymond, and put to him the question I had innocently asked.

"Those cannon?" said Raymond, with a gesture toward the window. "Why, they are for defence. We intend to sweep these streets of any Yankee regiments that may attempt to pass through Baltimore in the future. We made a mistake in not doing it in the first place." At the same time he flashed a suspicious glance at me, and said, "Maryland will follow South Carolina and her sister States soon." Then turning to May, he said, "I heard this morning that your brother has joined the Washington Battery, and received a commission as first lieutenant. There will always be an opening in our army for educated men like him." There was in his manner of saying this an assurance of superiority; and I was pleased when May said, —

"Oh, I hope it isn't true! It can't be that brother Jimmy has taken such a step without consulting my father."

"Miss Milner," said Raymond with a look of surprise, "it can't be that *you* sympathize with those nigger-worshipping Yankees?"

May made no reply, when Raymond, with another glance of suspicion directly at me, said, "Which side are you on Mr. — Mr. Alden? Do you favor the North or South?"

I had not learned to conceal my political sentiments, — as indeed what Northern man or boy ever did? — and therefore instantly replied, —

"I am a Northern Union man, Mr. Raymond."

His face flushed with chagrin or anger; he gave a look at May that I did not understand, and then, without speaking to me again, he raised his hat to May and took his departure.

"He will make trouble for us, I fear," said May. "He belongs to one of the best families in Baltimore, and they own a large number of servants. He's a violent Secessionist; and I have heard it intimated that, though so young, he is to be colonel of the regiment they are recruiting here for the Confederate army."

On our return May told her father of our conversation with Raymond.

"I thought you were a great favorite with Raymond," said her father; then to me, in a half-joking manner, "You see, Raymond attempted or pretended to study medicine with me at one time; but I always thought he had more of an eye on May than on the profession."

Instead of replying to her father, Miss May said, "I'm afraid I have bad news for you, papa; and I don't know that I ought to worry you with it now, as it may not be true."

"Well, out with it! What's the matter?" said the doctor.

"Raymond says that brother Jimmy has accepted a commission in a Southern regiment."

"No," said the doctor; "I don't think Jimmy would take such a step without consulting me. But he may get into it as thousands of others will, thinking that the trouble will blow over without any fighting. Maybe that young lady he wrote you about has influenced him; but I don't believe it." Notwithstanding this statement, the doctor looked troubled.

I had a good opportunity while in the shops and on the streets to hear the talk of the people regarding the war; and it was instructive to observe the difference between the Northern and Southern points of view.

One day, while with the doctor, who was at a

market, I heard a young man say, " The Yankees shoot our people down, and then talk about peace."

" They'll find out, the cowardly Yanks, if they attempt to march through our city again! See how our people drove them out of Baltimore!"

" Without arms, too," added another.

" Not cowards," said a grave man about forty years of age; " I reckon it isn't any use to call them cowards. It took a right smart of courage to march through here the other day, without turning right or left, until they got orders to fire. It took pluck to hold their temper. No, sar! I believe the Yankees will fight, sar!"

I could not refrain from saying, " That's so, sir. I know them well enough to know that."

" What do you know about them? What's the matter with your leg?" Thus interrogated a rough-looking marketman, who continued, " You're a white-livered Yankee sympathizer, I believe; maybe a Yankee yourself."

" Maybe I am," I replied hotly; " but I don't allow any rough to dictate to me, though."

The doctor, overhearing the altercation, came up and took my arm. " He's all right," said the grave man; " Dr. Milner's son is in our service."

I learned afterward from the doctor, that the man who had spoken so temperately was the worst Secessionist in Baltimore; and, added the doctor, " He's all the more dangerous because he appears so reasonable."

Before this, the doctor had received a letter from his son, saying he had accepted a commission in the Washington Battery; for if he had not done so, public sentiment would have put a stigma upon him. That it was believed in the South, however, that there would be no war.

"Well," said the doctor meditatively, "it may all blow over soon."

A day or two after this the doctor came in, excitedly exclaiming, "Have you heard the news, Alden?"

"No; what is it?"

"This morning General Butler arrived at the Relay House (it's only eight or nine miles from here) with two thousand men. He has mounted artillery on the viaduct, and the Secessionists here are in a great ferment! He has completely invested the city on the north."

This was on the 5th of May. It was about the middle of the month before we heard much more of General Butler. The general opinion was that he would not dare show his head in Baltimore.

Early one morning, after a sharp thunder-storm, while I was sitting at the doctor's study window, I saw people running down street as if to a fire. The office window was nearly on a level with the street; and to some of the gamins who were running forward, I inquired, "What's up?" Without turning his head right or left, one of them yelled out, "The Yankees hev come to town!"

So it proved. Under cover of the storm of the morning, about a thousand men had been marched into the city, had taken possession of Federal Hill above the town, and had just sent down a detachment to disarm the Baltimore rebels. Their arms, consisting of pikes and muskets, were seized, piled on teams; and when I arrived on the ground, the police were using their clubs freely to protect the soldiers from the Secessionists, who were furious at what they were pleased to call "an outrage." Among the dissatisfied people on the street I saw George Raymond, with a fierce scowl on his face.

I went out with Add into the street to catch a glimpse of the Yankee regiment.

"Our people will never allow them to stay here!" exclaimed a man near me; "they'll shed their last drop of blood first." But, notwithstanding this; and similar assertions, all hostile demonstrations ended in bluster. I found to my surprise that the regiment was my own, the Sixth Massachusetts!

· I was heartily greeted by the officers and men of my regiment, and was soon shaking hands with Crandall and other acquaintances, some of whom I had supposed were killed in the riot.

I was glad enough to be once more with the boys, where, as Add said, "A feller could breathe and speak without looking over his shoulder, and where he could walk like a man, and not be skulking through the streets, fearing a row."

I left the doctor's house that day, put on my uniform (which had been renovated), and felt like a free man, if not like a soldier, once more.

Our camp on Federal Hill had a very pleasant outlook on the waters of the little bay which forms a harbor for Baltimore. I introduced my friend Add to Grim; and as we one morning sat brightening our buttons, in reply to some remark about the band, Grim smiled sarcastically, and said, " Well, a band is well enough for peace, but I notice the old regulars have only a fife and drum for music. You'd better join a regiment as a soldier, for actual service. If you have got any kind of gimp in you, you want to do somethin' more than blowin'! Blowin' 's well enough for peace; but when you come down to real blows, a musket is the thing for a man who wants to be of service to his country."

When I interviewed the captain, he told me that the governor had ordered all the wounded men home.

" But, Captain," I said, " I want to stay in Baltimore with the company."

"Soldiers," said he, "obey orders; they don't consult their personal wishes."

When I told Grim that I was to be sent to Massachusetts, he said, " Well, Jack, you've got a chance ter be a live hero. They're making a great fuss over wounded men at home, and you've got a big chance. I wouldn't mind goin' home with

a little wound — sort of a decoration, ye' see —
myself. You're all right for a commission, too,
if you ask it, in case this war keeps on."

I soon packed up, and hobbled down town to
say good-by to Dr. Milner and Miss May. I wore
my uniform, had taken unusual pains with my
hands and collar, and with what by courtesy was
supposed to be a mustache ; and as I was five feet
ten inches in height, muscular, broad-shouldered,
had very dark hair and eyes, I felt when I presented myself at Dr. Milner's to say good-by, that
I was looking very well.

The doctor was in his office ; and when told that
I had come to say good-by before going home,
he sent for Miss May, saying as she came in, —

"May, here's Alden as good as new. He's off
this afternoon for the blessed land of baked beans
and brown bread ! "

The sight of Miss May's refined face abated
somewhat my conceit in my own personal appearance. She was slight, light and graceful, and perfectly self-possessed, while I felt awkward and
self-conscious. When I stammered out my thanks
for her previous kindness, she replied, —

"Oh, that is nothing ! I'm fond of taking care
of sick people. Had I been a boy I should have
been a surgeon like my father. I was very much
interested in your case. I have nursed our servants when they have been sick, but never had a
real wound to care for before."

It must be confessed that my vanity was not a little piqued at this remark, since it seemed to indicate that she considered me in the light of a patient, rather than as a young man and an equal. This wound to my pride had the effect of changing my blushing confusion to coldness and self-possession, — qualities which were more natural to me than the reverse.

Dr. Milner, who was an acute observer, as I afterwards recognized, noticed the change; for he hastened to say, —

"May, as well as myself, is glad to have been of service to my old friend Alden's son. By the way, you look like your father this morning. He was as strong as an ox; always took my part in college when I got into a row, though he wouldn't hurt a fly on his own account. There wasn't any bully in college could back Jack Alden down."

At last I said good-by for the last time, and walked away, feeling blue and lonely. That day I took the train, and in the course of the next day was at my home in Centerboro' once more.

CHAPTER VII.

HOME AGAIN.

I PASSED through the streets of Centerboro' with conflicting emotions. There had been but few changes, though I had not seen my home for four years (and how much longer are the years of youth than those of middle life). I had grown to a man's stature in that time; all else seemed to have stood still. Hurrying through the village streets, I saw familiar faces; yet though there were many curious glances at my uniform, no one spoke to me or appeared to recognize me.

"The old Alden place," as our homestead was called, was a little outside the village; and I hastened forward until its familiar surroundings came in sight. The odor of apple blossoms and of ploughed land mingled with the scent of the monument-like balm-of-Gilead trees that fronted the house.

The house standing back from the road; its capacious front yard of greensward, on which the dandelions were plentifully sprinkled; the tillage land sloping back in graceful undulations to the river, glimpses of which could be seen as I approached, and which, remembrance told me, was grumbling impatiently at the rocky bed over which foamed its shallow waters, — all seemed but miniatures of what I had last seen. The buildings and distances seemed shrunken.

A sight of the old burial-ground, high upon the opposite bank of the river, its white monuments and slabs relieved by a background of dark pines, dampened with gloom my joyousness; for there my dear father (with other generations of Aldens of the old Pilgrim stock) was buried.

I hurried forward, opened the yard gate, went up the walk; and when the front door opened my mother came bustling out, and I was in her dear arms once more. A young lady, who also came out, I soon discovered to be my younger sister Sarah, who, after a few moments of curious surprise, exclaimed as she recognized me, —

" Why, it's Jack! but how big he's grown!"

I was soon seated in a favorite corner of our "front room," telling my mother and sisters, and my brother, who had come in from the farm, my experiences since I had left the old home.

My brother was much interested in what he called my adventures; and all were very indignant when I gave them for the first time my account of the treatment I had received from my uncle Richard, who had represented the situation in a totally different light.

That evening a number of our neighbors came

in to see me, and to hear of my experiences in the much-talked-of "battle" at Baltimore. I found their imaginations had depicted it as a much more bloody affair than it really was, and that in their hunger for sensations they did not appear to be satisfied with simple facts.

I afterwards found that some of my listeners had embellished my plain narrative with what they evidently considered needful incidents, until, like a rolling ball of snow, my story grew larger and larger as it advanced from its starting-point. It was not long before we heard that it had been reported that I had lost both of my legs, besides receiving numerous other wounds in divers parts of my body.

When curious visitors were told that my crutch was made in Baltimore, even that became an object of hungry curiosity.

The editor of the little village paper came to "Alden House" to see the terrible wounds of which he had heard; and I was almost ashamed to show him the insignificant gunshot wound which he insisted upon seeing, and which report had magnified beyond all truthful proportions.

When the *Centerboro' Gazette* came out, there was a half-column given to me. It said:—

"Our young and esteemed fellow-townsman, John Alden, who so gallantly conducted himself in the bloody passage through Baltimore on the 19th of

April, is now at his old home, where we had the pleasure of an interview with him. Though but a boy, we found him modest, manly, and stalwart, but still pale from the severe wound he received in the battle with the Baltimore rebels. He intends to remain at his home only a short time, as he is *en route* to report to the surgeon-general of the State. As it has been reported that he is in a dying condition, we are glad to say that, though his wound is a terrible one, caused by a bullet which passed through the leg, shattering the bone, yet he is on the road to recovery. He showed us a letter from Colonel Jones of his regiment, recommending him to the governor as a gallant and deserving soldier. He informs us that the re-entry of his regiment into Baltimore on the 14th of May — seizing the arms of the insurgents and fortifying Federal Hill, above that city, where their camps are now pitched — was a very gallant affair."

This was the first time I had ever figured in a newspaper; and its statements seemed so exaggerated, and conveyed so many false impressions, that I went at once to the village to correct it. The editor coolly informed me that it could not be corrected before the next issue, and that by that time it would be forgotten in other matters of interest.

I had been paid off before leaving Baltimore, and had some forty dollars, most of which I gave to my mother, to assist in paying taxes and necessary household expenses.

I learned from my brother that a considerable sum in interest had been added to the mortgage uncle Richard held, and that he evidently felt already secure in finally possessing the place, and was apparently only awaiting a favorable opportunity to do so. He thought if we could clear up the mortgage, we might sell the land skirting the street for house-lots, for a sum which would leave us free from debt, and at the same time not decrease greatly the value of the farm. A new shoe factory and shovel-works, in another part of the town, were bringing many new people to Centerboro', and the land was likely to become more and more valuable every year. I inquired of my mother about my father's cousin in Boston, Mr. Rich, and proposed to visit him when there, and get advice as to my father's estate.

My brother informed me that my uncle had come to Centerboro' several times, ostensibly to see how "the widow was getting on," but in reality to dictate how the woodland should be cut in order to preserve its value. That he had then suggested to my uncle that this portion of the land be sold to clear it of debt; but that my uncle Richard had threateningly exclaimed, "You'll lose the whole farm if you ain't careful! You want to improve the farm, and not let it all run down, as you are doing."

"I believe," said my brother, "that he thinks we are fools; and I believe he is a sharper, and not the good man that some people think him to be."

In my talk with brother Richard, I found that he was hard-headed, and, though not much of a talker, had determination, courage, and rare good sense.

"I wouldn't work a day on this farm," said he, "but that it is giving mother and the girls a home. I must look carefully before I act, for uncle Richard is waiting to take advantage of any mistakes I make. I hear he talks of coming here to start a shoe factory; but I believe he wants to watch his chance and gobble up the Alden place as a part of his profits."

I told him my suspicions that Richard Alden had never loaned my father the full amount of money for which he held a mortgage; that when he found the mortgage and its acknowledgment of value received in his hands, his greed was so great that he could not resist taking advantage of the circumstances, and that he had then made memoranda to account for all the money covered by the mortgage. I then told him of the effect of my last angry accusation. We agreed that when visiting Ivory Rich, I was to see if something could be done to get the farm out of the clutches of Richard Alden.

I was at home only a few days, and had a very pleasant time visiting acquaintances and school-mates, among whom were Dick Nickerson and Jed

Hoskins, both of whom had been at Fort Sumter during its bombardment and capture. I met them at Silas Eaton's. He, at that time, had begun to state his "idees," as he called them, "about the war." "It's my opinion," said Silas, "referring to the passage of the Sixth through Baltimore, "that yer cap'n was a fool, or he'd hev stopped and hev throwd up a barricade, and 'a' shot down them secesh fellers right and left. They'd kind 'a' got sick of interferin' with yer 'fore long, I guess."

"But," said I, " what would them fellows have been doing while we stacked arms and dug up the paving-stones for a barricade? We should have had to get over the distance somehow, and we were under orders besides."

" Seems ter me yer hain't got no sense, Alden. You could 'a' formed a holler square 'round yer workin' party, and stood 'em off a while, while yer barricaded," said Silas in his most querulous and dogmatic key.

I found a great many home critics who were dissatisfied with the work done in the field, yet who had never found time to go there in person to settle, by their intelligent direction and helpful work, its difficulties.

I remained at home but a short time, then took leave of my mother, sister, and brother, and reported one forenoon to the surgeon-general in Boston.

I was very tired upon reaching his office; and

"It's my opinion, that yer cap'in was a fool."
— Page 72.

as he was very deaf, I made myself the more so in trying to make him hear. The kind-hearted old surgeon-general, when he understood that I was a member of the Sixth Regiment, ordered refreshments, and treated me as if I was his own son. I told him that as my mother was a widow and poor, and as I was not able to do military duty, I should like my discharge, in order to get to work as soon as possible.

"A good son as well as a good soldier," bawled the old surgeon-general to a pleasant-appearing gentleman who had come in, and who proved to be Governor Andrew, the same who had pathetically ordered the Sixth Massachusetts dead "to be packed in ice, and tenderly sent forward."

That afternoon I went down on Court Street, looking up at the constellation of lawyers' signs, and soon found my cousin Rich's office.

Rapping at a door on which was a sign which read, "I. N. Rich, Attorney and Counsellor at Law ;" and on hearing a rough voice say, "Come in," I entered a musty-smelling office where sat a large man with his feet elevated on a desk, smoking a clay pipe, as if he were pressed for time to accomplish a stated task. Without removing his pipe or offering me a seat, he said presently, "Well, what is it?"

I looked the lawyer over, and took in his personality as follows: A large head covered with thick red hair; steel-blue penetrating eyes, which assumed at times an abstracted look; ruddy complexion, a massive jaw, a clean-shaved face, broad shoulders, and a long body.

When he understood who I was, he rose and gave me a chair; and I then discovered that he was six feet in his stockings. Once seated, he began to ask questions, as if cross-examining me, all the while with an abstracted look in his eyes.

When I had told him of my father's death, and what part my uncle Richard had taken in our affairs, he ejaculated hoarsely, " He's a pirate! "

My experience in the Sixth Massachusetts seemed to interest him; and our conference ended by his inviting me to go home with him when he came from court. " Got to go into court soon," he said; " be here at four o'clock, or you can stay here and read."

" You will want to shut up the office," I said.

" Naw; no one wants anything from a law-office! " he exclaimed. " We always leave the door open! Come around, or sit here and read." So I sat there and read the *Journal;* and, to my surprise, found there quoted what the Centerboro' paper had said regarding me.

I found my cousin Ivory Rich a different man in his home than in his office. Here he left behind that dictatorial, bullying, cross-examining self, and was the most simple and companionable man I ever knew. I have since met military men who had this same double manner, one for duty, another for friends when off duty.

During the evening I asked his advice about my mother's affairs, and plainly stated to him my suspicions that when my uncle got the mortgage in his hands, he had been too greedy ever to pay over to my mother the money that had been agreed upon between him and my father.

" Well, yes — very probably — you and I may have convictions founded upon our knowledge of character and circumstances; but that is not evidence. We can't get a judgment on that. We can scare him, perhaps. Let the matter rest with me. I'll see what I can do. I'll write a note, asking him to call on me, and see what he says. We'll scare him a little."

In the course of the conversation I said that as soon as I got employment I was promised my discharge, and asked him what I had better do.

" Well," said Ivory, with tones long drawn out on the well, " you can't go home and live on your mother, and you draw pay now, — let me see. There's a client of mine down on Washington Street, a ' patent rights ' man. He wants a clerk to take charge of his collection of rat-traps and corn-shellers, coffee-machines, washing-machines, and all sorts of traps that he calls an ' Industrial Museum.' He wants some one to write, and stand around and show people the place, and, if they get interested in a machine, to introduce them to his office, where he'll sell them a patent right. I'd as lief buy a house-lot in the moon; but the fools ain't all dead yet. I guess I can get you the place at ten dollars a week and board. What do you say?"

CHAPTER VIII.

A PATENT RIGHTS MAN.

THE next morning I was introduced to my future employer. On our way to his place, Ivory Rich said, " Blusterson is all right if his business goes right ; but he plans too big sometimes, and if he gets into a hard spot, some one will have to suffer, and it won't be Blusterson."

I replied, " You don't mean to say he'd " —

" Here we are," interrupted Ivory Rich ; " this is the place."

We had stopped before a large, flatiron-shaped building facing a triangle, called in Boston, by courtesy, a square.

Around the outside and at the second story of this edifice was stretched a canvas, on which was painted in large red and black letters, " The Great Industrial Museum."

We went up one flight of stairs, and entered an office, fitted up apparently as much for show as for use.

Here at a desk was seated a large, handsome man, carefully dressed, who rose and shook hands with Ivory Rich in a hail-fellow-well-met sort of fashion.

"This," said Rich, introducing me, "is young Alden of whom I have spoken to you."

"Take a seat, young man," said Blusterson; then bluffly added, "think you would like to come here and take charge of things?"

"I don't know," I said inquiringly, "exactly what the work is."

He replied, "You are to take charge of the rooms of the museum, show people around, and make yourself agreeable to ladies and every one else. That'll suit you, won't it?" and Blusterson, throwing back his head, looked smilingly down into my face, then added, "Lame, I see."

I explained to him that I had been wounded in the Baltimore Riot, at which he professed great interest, saying, "I've been a militia colonel myself, and strutted around gay as a peacock, with brass buttons and feathers. I've felt full of fight for months, but can't leave business now."

My pay was agreed upon, and was made larger than I proposed; because, as he said, "A man who has been in the battle of Baltimore will be an attraction to the exhibition."

Blusterson said this in a manner that made me feel that he did not himself believe this assertion, but was determined that I should. There was something in his manner that seemed to say, "I am determined to put every one on good terms with themselves, and consequently with me."

"How does your show go, Blusterson?" inquired Rich.

"The show? It hasn't begun yet; wait a week,
and I shall be as famous — well, more talked about
than any other man in the country."

"Do inventors seem interested?" asked my
cousin.

"Well, they are waiting for each other; when
they get to coming, they will come in a bunch,"
said Blusterson, throwing back his head, shaking
it, and compressing his lips, with an expression
half between swagger and smiling determination,
as if he wished to convince his listeners of
that of which he was only partly convinced himself; namely, that events generally went to suit
him.

After Rich had gone, Blusterson showed me
around what he called the "establishment," which
consisted of four stories of space. These rooms
had shafting overhead for running machinery,
not much of which, however, had arrived. There
were patent churns, washing-machines, corn-shellers, sewing-machines, and various other Yankee
patented articles.

I soon saw that Increase Blusterson had a mar-
vellous faculty for understanding and running machines. When once or twice during our rounds
his attention was called by an attendant to some
trouble in their running, he explained to the oper-
ator in an instant what the difficulty was, and in

some instances set machines running with his own hands.

" Ah ! here is something that will interest you," he said, stopping in front of a machine. " It's a pegging-machine." (I had told him that I had worked at shoemaking). " Here ! it goes in this way." Thereupon he adjusted the belt, and, after lucidly explaining its workings to me, caught up a shoe made ready to peg, and said, " See if *you* can use it;" and he stood patiently instructing me until I was able to use the machine to his satisfaction, and then said, —

" Show it up, Alden, to every shoe-man that comes in; and if any of them seem interested, bring them down and introduce them to me. I'll sell them a patent right, perhaps — if they've got the money."

There was something almost boyishly good-natured and winning in the large, handsome proprietor of the Industrial Museum; and though I was not long in discovering the counter fact, that he was one who would not be very considerate of any one's interests where they interfered with his own, that charm continued to hold its influence over me.

As he stood by my side, six feet and over in height; a ruddy, smiling, but determined face; a dome-shaped forehead, very broad at the base; massive jaws, well-rounded with flesh however; keen blue eyes, well set back under his overhanging brows, I could not help thinking that nature had cast this man in a very strong and unusual mould, and that here was one with great aggressive force and courage, naturally disposed to do business on a large scale, and who would break through extraordinary obstacles by brute force, if he could not invent a way to get around them without violence.

I had not been many months at the "Exhibition," as he called it, before there were signs that it was going to prove a failure. The receipts were small and the expenses large. Inventors did not send in their machines, and people did not come to the exhibition, notwithstanding lavish advertising.

The necessity of sending my mother money caused me to ask for my salary each week, and it was paid without hesitation; for Blusterson would not admit by word or look that this " business " was not a success.

At one time, when a patent clothes-pin was among the things exhibited, he said, " Show it up, Alden; such little things take. Perhaps I can sell the patent to some one."

" Do you think," I incredulously ejaculated, " that any one will buy that?"

" Buy it! " he exclaimed, throwing back his head, compressing his lips, and with a half-humorous smile, " Bless you, my boy! they'll cry for it."

After the first battle of Bull Run he came in
with a newspaper containing the news; and, as we
sat talking it over, he for the first time made a
half-acknowledgment that his exhibition might not
be a great success, by saying, " I'm afraid this war
will attract more attention than my museum will;
two big shows can't be run together, at least not
successfully. If I'd known this war was to be
so serious, I'd have had some new war machines.
But," he added, with a tone of satisfaction, " I
sold the patent of the Great Western Corn-sheller
yesterday ; got some money and some notes: money's sure, notes doubtful."

I had, meanwhile, become very expert in running the pegging-machine, and had suggested that
we get shoes from the manufactories. So every
once in a while a sixty-pair lot of brogans was
pegged, and sent to the factories free of cost.
This naturally attracted the manufacturers to see
the machine.

Now, among the qualities possessed by Increase
Blusterson, was his ability to throw a glamour
over the eyes of men, and make, as he expressed
it, "a handful of peanuts look to be a bushel."

In selling a patent right, he would begin by im-
pressing his customer with the importance of the
machine ; then deftly getting him to state how
many machines or articles governed by the patent
he thought could be sold among a thousand people, he would proceed thereon to figure out the

enormous number that could be sold in a given territory, and would end by saying, " Will you take this chance to make a fortune, sir?" Finally, he would end by getting all the money his customer would give, and take the rest in notes, even if the latter were contingent upon selling a definite number of machines.

After one of these transactions he would smilingly shake his head and say, with his half-humorous compression of lips, " Now I've got what *I* want, *he* must scramble around and get what *he* wants."

In showing up the pegging-machine, he always allowed me to run it, because, as he said, " Then I can say that any one can run it; and the fact is, you have got the hang of it so that you can beat the man who made it!" This statement was no mere compliment; for by practice I had become very expert in running it, and knew most of its weak and strong points.

I had just come in from some errand outside one day, when I heard a voice in the office which I at once recognized as my uncle Richard's.

" But," I heard him say, " can any one run it?"

" Run it!" Blusterson exclaimed, " why, sir, it almost runs itself! A mere twenty thousand dollars for the State is nothing for the patent, sir! Any of these boys can run that machine, sir." Then touching his bell, he summoned the porter, and said, " Where's Alden?"

On being called, I came into the office. Uncle
Richard recognized me, and with a cold glitter in
his eye, and a frosty sort of voice, ejaculated,
"Humph! it's you, is it?" Then, as if desirous,
on second thought, of making a good impression,
he came forward, shook hands, and said, "I'm
sorry you are lame; I heard all about it, Jack."
Then, in an undertone, "You mustn't hold any
grudge against me." Then again to Blusterson,
who was keenly observant of the scene, as if he
had caught a cue from it, said, "Let us go up
and look at the machine again."

When we were once more at the machine, and
a shoe was put on the jack ready for pegging,
Blusterson turned to me and said, "Here, Alden,
you show him." This I did by pegging three or
four pairs of shoes in an easy, careless way, which,
I could see by the glitter of Richard Alden's eyes,
very much impressed him. Blusterson saw it too;
for, as if desirous to close a bargain before this
impression wore off, he said carelessly, "Well, le's
go to the office; it's more comfortable there," and
led the way down. My uncle Richard stayed behind just long enough to cast a suspicious glance
at the machine, while he whispered to me, "There's
no trick about it, Jack, is there?" I answered,
"You see for yourself the machine pegs as well as
you or I can, and faster than twenty of us could.
I wouldn't pay much money, though."

After this, as I passed the office, I heard Blus-

terson say, " You see a boy can run it, and there's
no doubt there's a fortune in it! Now's your
chance to make a million dollars; or, if you want
to give your neighbors a chance to get rich with
you, I'll sell you the patent right for your county
for five thousand dollars."

Increase Blusterson and my uncle Richard were
closeted for several hours; and then the office-door
opened, and I heard the clinking of glasses. In a
short time I heard the patent-rights man's voice as
he said, " You might as well close the trade now,
and go to dinner with me." And then I knew
that my uncle Richard was in the web of Blusterson, as many had been before.

In a few moments they came out arm in arm.
I noticed that uncle had an uncertain glitter in
his eyes, and his head was thrown back in a
consequential, self-assertive manner, as he passed
out of the office to a hotel near by, where Increase
Blusterson took his visitors to dine after the
consummation of a bargain.

I did not see my uncle again at that time, and
only knew that the pegging-machine in the exhibition had been taken down and sent to him,
and a new one substituted. When I questioned
Blusterson, he replied, " Yes, I made a small sale.
It's only a small trade, mostly notes; but then,
the money is *all* gain."

My evenings at this time were mostly spent
at the armory, drilling recruits for the different

regiments forming at that time under the call
of the president; for I was considered quite pro-
ficient in drill.

I had by this time dispensed with my crutch,
and, though still lame, used only a cane. I was
treated with much respect by those entering the
army, because it was well known that I had seen
service, as it was then termed, at Baltimore. Afterwards an engagement in a street riot would not
have been designated as service.

In the course of the next six months the Industrial Museum, as an exhibition, was so complete a
failure, that even Blusterson said allegorically, —

" When I was a youngster up in Vermont, there
were two kinds of boys: one dug to the end of
the woodchuck's hole, and, if the woodchuck
wasn't in, stopped; and another kind who still
kept on digging, until they were way beyond the
hole ! "

I understood this simile better by after events
than I did at the time he used it.

One morning he came into the office dressed
with unusual care. I could not help thinking
that he looked the very picture of cheerful prosperity. He talked for a while about forming a
stock company to manufacture a new mowing-
machine, and then, putting into his capacious
pocket-book a number of promissory notes which
I had been writing by his direction, he sauntered
leisurely down State Street.

He came in late that afternoon, and taking from his pocket a great pile of bank-bills, asked me to count them. I announced the sum, which was over ten thousand dollars. These he put away carefully in his pockets, saying in a satisfied and confidential undertone, "There! I've got what I want; now let them note-shavers down street get what they want!"

Turning to me, he said, "Very likely I shall not be in to-morrow, for I've got some business out of town, and may be gone for a day or two. Stay in the office while I'm away, and answer questions."

Two weeks passed. Blusterson did not come; but there came a letter, saying that he had been called West on important business. He asked me to keep the office going, and enclosed a certified check for my three weeks' wages, and the pay of the porter and watchman. In some way I got the feeling that Increase Blusterson had skipped the country, and that this check was the last money I would get from him.

In a few days there came numerous duns for money due; for I had opened all letters, sending to him only those that contained money, or that related to real business.

Then came the sheriff, and the Industrial Museum was closed. But the creditors, in attempting to dispose of the property, found themselves checkmated by a business-man of Boston,

who held a bill of sale for all the property formerly belonging to Blusterson.

About this time there came another letter from
the absentee, saying, —

"I send you by express a package of notes of hand
from different persons, from which you will be able
to get money enough to make good your pay. I see
by the papers that the 'Industrial Museum' is closed,
and that they are after the undersigned with 'sharp
sticks.' Well, I am offered a commission in the
army; and if they want me, let them come to the
front with their prods.

　　　　　　　I am, dear sir,
　　　　　　　　　With great respect,
　　　　　　　　　　　INCREASE BLUSTERSON.

"P. S. — If you get more than enough from these
notes than will pay yourself and the men, you may
keep the balance. I don't want you to suffer any
loss; and with these you may get square with that
sharper, your uncle, in some way.

　　　　　　　　　　　　I. B."

I shuffled the notes over carelessly. They were
promissory notes of hand from patent-rights cus-
tomers of Increase Blusterson. Some of them
were conditional, and that, too, on conditions
which I knew would never give them maturity.
I threw them into my trunk without giving them
any more attention at that time.

One thing stood out more apparent than anything else, and that was that I was out of a place. I was in no great need of money, however, as I had some fifty dollars by me.

Blusterson's remark about going into the army I considered as merely a blind to throw me and others off the track of his real intentions.

CHAPTER IX.

I HAVE THE WAR FEVER.

AFTER the collapse of the "Industrial Museum," I returned to Centerboro', and after a time obtained employment, with small pay, as clerk in the village store.

I found that my uncle Richard had opened a shop there, and, with a large gang of workmen and the aid of his pegging-machines, was doing what the villagers called a "smashing business" in bottoming men's and boys' brogans.

The summer of 1862 was a period of great excitement in military affairs. McClellan had advanced with an army of over one hundred thousand men up the Peninsula, and had fought the battle of Fair Oaks; but while the people were waiting anxiously for him to capture Richmond and the Confederate army, there came news of the Seven Days' Fight, and the retreat of our army to Harrison's Landing.

The military spirit ran high, so far as talk was concerned. Men well off in worldly affairs were generally more enthusiastic in urging their friends to go than in going themselves. There were those who criticised me for not putting my military experience, as they called it, to account, by going to the front.

I heard fragments of sly talk, such as, "I guess Alden got 'nuff of it the fust time;" and that, too, by those who were able-bodied, and were not ashamed that they had not shown their martial spirit by going into the army in the hour of their country's peril.

My uncle Richard was one of those who talked loudly about the duty of able-bodied young men in the national crisis, but he never offered to go himself; and it was noticed later in the war, when there was talk of a draft of able-bodied men, that he complained of rheumatism and other ills, grievous, but never before known to keep him from working fourteen hours a day at profitable employments.

I was young and enthusiastic, as boys of eighteen often are; I was also not a little irritated by insinuations that my courage had oozed out with my first military experience.

My brother thought it was the duty of one of us to go; and, as he was the most needed at home, I naturally felt that I was that one. Still, I made no effort at that time to enlist again, although I had obtained my mother's and brother's consent.

My pay was small; and I was secretly chafing at the necessity that kept me at home (for I had really seen little but fair weather soldiering), when

an incident occurred that made me once more a
soldier.

I had been to Boston on some business connected with the store, when, going up Beach
Street from the station, I encountered my old
friend Grim. I had not seen him since leaving
the company at Baltimore, although I had heard
that after his discharge he had again gone to the
front in another regiment.

"Just the man I was thinking about," said
Grim, shaking my hand, and unconsciously crush-
ing it in his powerful grasp.

"Where," I inquired, "are you going?" Then
I noticed that his left hand was bandaged, and
that although sunburned he looked ill.

"I'm home for a while on a sort of furlough,"
said he. "Got a little swamp fever on the
Chickahominy, and a reb bullet at Malvern Hill."
Then looking me over he continued, "Going back
soon as I can get a few good men." Throwing
back his cape, and touching the captain's straps on
his shoulders, he looked at me with an inquiring
smile, as if to say, "Why are not you at the front,
wearing something of this kind?"

"Wasn't the Peninsula Campaign rather a
fizzle?" I inquired as we began to walk towards
Washington Street.

"Humph!" half laughed Grim. "Well, we
gave and took! The Rebel army is good stuff;
the kind you can't flatten out in one heat. But

you'd ought to seen us give it to 'em at Malvern Hill! 'Twould have done your soul good!"

"But," I said, "what made you get down to Harrison's Landing so quick the next day after you had whipped them at Malvern Hill?"

"Humph!" said Grim, knitting his brows after the old fashion of contemplating a piece of forge work that did not suit him; then after a moment, flashing out into a stern smile, he said, "I wasn't running the Army of the Potomac just then, Alden, or I'd have gone for them with the heaviest sledge I had. Easy work to criticise, but there are a good many things to take into consideration in handling an army; you've got to be near the work to see the difficulties. I find all I want to do in handling my company."

We walked along, jostled by the crowds of people on Washington Street, when Grim said, "I see you've got over your lameness all right, Alden." Then, after a moment's pause, he continued, "Why won't you come home with me? Wife will be glad to see you; living in Lowell now, you know."

"I've got my errands done, and am going up to see my cousin, Ivory Rich," said I, with a touch of pride at my relationship to a man so well known. "I'm going to his office now; you'd better come along with me, and perhaps I'll go home with you afterwards. Come along! He'll be glad to see you; he's heard me speak of you. You'll like him; he's your kind of a man, — no airs."

"All right," said Grim; and after a long silence, as he walked by my side with his long, swinging stride, he resumed, "Why don't you go back with me, and join our regiment?"

"Three years," said I suggestively, in answer, "is a good while to enlist for."

"Well, yes," said Grim slowly. "But then, there's the promise, 'unless sooner discharged.'" Then his face settled into a frown, as he said decidedly, "What's the use of beating around the bush? You know, or at least I know, that we are likely to have a long, bitter war! It's just begun; and every man who can has got to go to the front. We've got a big job on hand! I sometimes think we've bitten off more than we can chaw, in trying to lick the rebs. But I'm going to stay in it as long as it lasts, unless I'm sooner discharged — or shot down! Of course it looks discouraging; but that's all the more reason for going. We've got to settle down into this war like days' works. Every man who loves his country must fight for it."

Grim had unconsciously touched the right cord in my make-up, for I was strongly combative, as well as patriotic; and when he depicted the cause as doubtful, I was more drawn to enlisting than if he had pictured the situation in favorable colors. Besides this, Grim's unselfish patriotism and enthusiasm were contagious; and I felt a strong desire, like an invisible cord tugging at my heart-strings, impelling me to yield to his urging, although I put off saying "yes" at just that moment. "Grim," I said, "I thought when I lay with a hole in my leg at Baltimore, that I had got enough of fighting and ventilation to last me the rest of my life, but I shouldn't wonder if I went into the army again before the war ends; I'd like to!"

"See here, Alden, you had a nice time of it there in Baltimore!" said Grim. "Have you heard from the old doctor or his pretty daughter lately?"

I must have blushed, for my thoughts of entering the service and my patriotism were strangely mixed with the image of May Milner; and Grim, seeing my confusion, added, "When a man has once tasted the danger and excitement of army life, he longs to get back to it."

"Yes," I replied; "it's akin to fascination. Danger and fighting seem to appeal to a half-savage instinct that is latent in one."

"I don't know what it is," said Grim, with one of his half-laughs, "but I know most men and boys can't even see a dog-fight without wanting to take part on one side or t'other."

We had now reached the door of my cousin's law-office on Court Street, and, going in, found him engaged with a business-man, whom he introduced as Mr. Hewitt.

"Sit down; we are all through business. I haven't got to go into court for two hours yet," said my cousin. "Well, Alden, so the great Industrial Rat-trap has shut up since I saw you last, has it?"

"Yes," I replied; "it didn't succeed."

Rich laughed, and said, "Blusterson couldn't make it go, and so he went himself, hey? And they say that more than one old State Street rat got caught when the trap shut up."

Although I knew Blusterson's business methods were open to criticism, yet I did not like to have him made the subject of ridicule by the man who had induced me to enter his service, and so made no reply, but changed the subject by asking Mr. Rich as to the advisability of my going into the army again.

"See here," interrupted Ivory, "I'm not going to give you any advice about it, so don't ask *my* opinion! If you make up your mind to go, I'll do the best I can to get you a commission. I know Governor Andrew well enough to ask such a favor for a deserving young fellow who has seen service. My boy is going out in the ——th; and I don't suppose it will do any more good for me to try to persuade you not to go, than it has for me to argue with him."

"I don't think you would hinder him," said Grim shrewdly, "if you could."

Lawyer Rich made no direct answer, but said,

as he began to walk the floor, as Grim afterwards said, "like a lion in its cage," "To tell the truth, if it wasn't for my family and business I'd go myself." Then stepping in front of Grim, added emphatically, "Such men as you make me ashamed of my shallow patriotism! This country won't be worth living in if the rebs beat us in the war!"

Hewitt, who up to this time had been only a listener, here remarked sarcastically, "Rich, if you folks don't let the South alone, it's my opinion that the licking you have got so far will be a small circumstance to what ye'll git before ye are through! It's all politics, this war is, anyway."

Grim here turned towards the speaker sharply, and, with a smile on his face not unlike the expression of a bull-dog when preparing to bite, said, —

"See here! excuse me for speaking before I'm spoken to; but it seems to me that this war and politics have now got to be, as Daniel Webster said of liberty and union, 'one and inseparable.' Just as 'tis in my dog; I can't tread on his tail but that the war end of him, as you might call it, turns around and snarls and bites."

"That's it exactly," said Rich with an approving laugh. "They are like the Siamese twins they had on exhibition down here on Washington Street; you couldn't pinch one of them but the other one would holler."

"Well," said Hewitt, "I believe it's a good idea for people to attend to their own business, and let their neighbors' affairs alone. If you Black Republicans hadn't been stirring up the Southerners, — interfering with their niggers all the time, — you wouldn't have had this trouble. Now you've got Abe Lincoln and the abolitionists and a war on your hands all at the same time."

"See here, sir," said Grim, still preserving his bull-dog smile, " I guess you're one of the kind of men they call Copperheads! And it seems to me that we need to clear such men out of the country first. We think it's a bad plan in the army to leave an enemy sneaking in the rear while we are fighting at the front. Seems to me, any one with the sense of decency that a man ought to have, would take hold and help when his own people are in trouble, instead of acting as if he was glad, as you seem to be. Why don't you help the other side, if you sympathize with them ? "

" The abolitionists have dissolved the Union by their folly," said Hewitt; " and now " —

" Humph ! " growled Ivory Rich like a good-natured lion. " You are old enough to know better than to talk like that, Hewitt! I'm not going to have it in my office, either ! I'll throw you out of the window if you spit out such stuff here."

At this, Hewitt rushed out of the office, slamming the door after him.

" A good man in a way, but so full of secesh

poison, that I shouldn't be surprised if he bit himself some day, as some kinds of snakes are said to, and died of his own poison; he'll never dare to bite any one but himself, anyway," said Rich meditatively.

After Grim had given some interesting descriptions of fighting on the Peninsula, and as we were leaving the office, Ivory Rich said to me, —

"Oh! I saw that pirate of an uncle of yours; he came in here to get legal advice about some notes he don't want to pay. I guess he'll consent to your folks selling enough of your farm to pay off the mortgage he holds, although he wouldn't say so. Tell your brother to go ahead and sell it; I'll back him. Sha'n't cost him anything for my fees, either. I'll do that much for you."

That night I spent with Grim, talking very late; and it was agreed that I should return to Centerboro', and recruit as many of my acquaintances as possible for the regiment.

"Did I tell you," said Grim, while accompanying me to the station the next morning, "that the young fellow that blowed the trombone in the Sixth — what's his name? — is in my company?"

"I guess," I suggested, "that you mean Add Key!"

"Yes; that's his name," said Grim apologetically. "I ought to have remembered his name; he's one of my sergeants. He said he got enough of instrumental fighting at Baltimore, first time try-

ing ; said since he heard a mule concert down on
the Chickahominy, he'd lost all conceit for army
music, and wouldn't set up to beat it ; " and Grim
gave one of his low chuckles, which showed that
he appreciated the funny side of Add's character.

He afterwards added, in reply to a question I
asked him regarding Add, " Yes, he fights like
a day's work ; he's full of nonsense, but he's just
as full of fighting, and makes a pretty good non-
commissioned officer too."

On my arrival in Centerboro', my mother again
gave a reluctant consent to my enlistment. I did
not at once give up my place in the grocery, but
continued my duties for a while, as it brought me
in contact with many young men of the village,
whom I influenced to enter the service.

I had recruited about twenty men in four weeks,
when Grim came out to Centerboro' to see how I
was getting on.

He was much pleased with what I had done,
and showed me an order he had just received,
directing him to join the regiment with such recruits as were enlisted up to that time. " Looks
as if they expected some work this fall," said
Grim. " And I suppose you've got a stiff upper
lip for it."

CHAPTER X.

WITH THE ARMY IN THE FIELD.

WE arrived in Boston, and were sworn into the service of the United States on the 15th of August, 1862. As a reward for my recruiting services, and because I understood the drill, I was given the position of sergeant.

"A good substantial set of men, Alden," said Captain Grim with a glance of satisfaction, as the recruits one after another stepped up and signed the papers. "Who," he inquired, as a magnificent specimen of young manhood came forward, "is that man?"

"That," I replied, "is George Standish, a lineal descendant of Miles Standish. He is well educated. The recruits from Centerboro'," I said proudly, "are all educated. Notice the signatures."

"If that Standish fellow's looks don't belie him," said Captain Grim, "he'll make a first-class man. These recruits I've brought in from Spindleville are all sorts. Some Irish, some German, some English; pretty good stuff, though!"

Captain Grim's manner was more reserved towards these recruits than I liked; and his way of looking the men over and commenting on them, as if they were so much iron or steel to be worked up, grated on me. For the men, at least those who had been recruited at Centerboro', were most of them sons of well-to-do mechanics or farmers, or small manufacturers, and socially many were the superiors of Captain Grim.

"See that little fellow? I recruited him for a drummer; he's as chipper as you please, and as bright as a dollar!" And Grim pointed to a boy about ten years of age.

I was set to work at once drilling the men in their facings and the manual of arms and company evolutions.

The first day that I drilled them in the manual of arms, my captain was for a while a silent looker-on. I soon discovered, however, by the expression of his face, that there was something about my instructions that did not suit him. I therefore halted and dressed the men, and, saluting, said to him, " Have you any orders, sir? "

" Your work is good enough," he replied, " as far as it goes, Sergeant; but you must put more snap into it! Sort of start them out of their boots. This way!" And he took the musket from me, giving the command, " Shoulder arms! " This he brought out by giving a long-drawn intonation to the first or precautionary word, and to the last word, the command of execution, by sud-

denly forcing the breath from his lungs, and pro-
nouncing it as if it was spelled " harms ! "

" Seize the muskets," he cried, " as if you had
steel springs in you! Make them rattle!" And
suiting the action to the word, he gave the commands, and went through the drill with the men.
After thus drilling the squad for a while, he
turned them over to me, and I continued the
work, somewhat chagrined, since I believed I
knew how to drill.

The captain must have seen a reflection of my
feelings and thoughts in my face; for, after a
while, he said to me in an undertone, " The
men are taking it up in great shape. You understand the tactics first-rate, Alden. My criticism
is simply 'bout the style. Our colonel, you see,
is particular 'bout that; and it's better to begin
right, so as not to have to learn it all over."

In a few more days of drill I caught the
" style," as Grim called it, and succeeded in communicating it to the men. We were doing very
well; and after a week's work the captain said, as
I turned over the squad to him, " You've caught
it! That's the kind of snap you must put into
drill. The men have got snap enough now."

Some of the men overheard the remark; and,
although the compliment pleased them, they, from
that time, nicknamed the captain " Old Snap."

This was during the latter part of August, 1862,
when the newspapers were teeming with vague

hints of anticipated movements; among them, that General Pope was about to supersede McClellan, and close the war.

Not long after this, Captain Grim came into the barracks, where we were finishing the morning drill. At his request I halted and faced the men, when the captain said to them, " Men ! hold yourselves in readiness to move at any moment. Three days' cooked rations will be issued to you at once ; write or telegraph to your friends, if you wish to see them: there will be no passes given."

That day there was polishing of buttons and boots and straps. Before long, friends and relatives thronged the barracks to see us off, and to say good-by. Among those who came were my mother and sisters; and somehow my attempts to cheer them stuck in my throat as never before.

The mother of little Mike, the drummer, came to see him. She was a poor little woman ; and at parting she took him in her arms, and, turning to me, said, " Be good to me b'y, and may God and the saints be good to you!" Thus saying she turned her back on him resolutely, and went her way.

At last we embarked on the cars, and with a snort from the engine, and rattle of the cars, we were on our way to that unknown field, " the front."

When we arrived at Baltimore, and had crossed the city to the Camden-street Station, Captain

Grim told me that there would be a delay of several hours before we could get transportation, and added, " You can run up town and see your friends here, if you want to. Corporal Standish can take charge of the men of your squad."

This was doubly gratifying, from the fact that it gave me a chance to see my friends, and conveyed to me, for the first time, the information that my friend George Standish was to receive a billet as a corporal of the company.

As I approached familiar localities, I found my heart throbbing like drum-beats in anticipation of meeting the doctor and his fair daughter, whom I had heard from but once since leaving the city in 1861. When I came in sight of the house, its closed blinds and untenanted look seemed to say, " Not at home," and sent my expectations down to zero. I rang the bell, however, and, after waiting a while, impatiently knocked on the door with my fist.

At last an old servant came, and, opening the door a little way, finally recognized me, and invited me into the sitting-room, which was dark and lonely enough.

" Where's the doctor, Auntie? " I inquired.

" Dey's dun gone, honey. Dun'no whar. Dun gone out ob dat do' fur Washin'ton, an' dey toted a right smart o' saws and knives an' lint; dey wur in a desprit hurry. 'Pears like, 'twas plumb foolishness; but dey's gone."

From auntie's chaos of talk I finally learned that they had been gone three days, and that Miss May had gone with her father, and there was no certainty as to when they would return. "When the doctor war puttin' up dem things, Miss May, she war windin' little heaps o' cotton, and war talkin' larned words to her farder. But dey's gone, honey! Dey's gone, sho' nuff!" This she repeated deprecatingly, as if I suspected they were hidden somewhere in the house.

When I returned to the Baltimore and Ohio Station, I found Captain Grim, and the men as well, reading from newspapers, and much excited over the news that had just come that a heavy battle was being fought between the forces under Pope and the Rebel army, near Bull Run.

"What do you make of the news, Captain?" I inquired.

Captain Grim was coolly turning over his newspaper; and the only sign of excitement he showed was, that he worked his jaws on a quid of tobacco like a trip-hammer at a forge, as he still continued to turn the paper, re-scanning its columns as if to find an answer to my question.

"Well," he said finally, slowly folding up the sheet, "as near as I can make out, Pope is in the fight, and I guess several divisions of the Army of the Potomac have been moved from the Peninsula. The news is rather jumbled, but I feel pretty sure of it. I hope the rebs will catch it; but some way, from what I read, it don't look like it. Old Stonewall Jackson is too near Washington, gobbling up our trains. Kinder looks to me as if there'd be another skedaddle! It ain't any use to hammer a solid piece of iron with a lot of small hammers! Get 'em all together, and then strike! Well, maybe we'll get 'em, but it don't look like it, much."

In another hour a train was ready, and we were off for Washington, where we arrived that evening, and were marched to what was called "The Soldiers' Retreat." The only appropriateness we could see to this name was, that after lying on its hard floor, and partaking of its salt junk, we were not displeased to get an early order to retreat from it.

As soon as it became light enough we began marching, with the usual clatter of canteens, and the interference of the butts of our muskets with our haversacks, up Pennsylvania Avenue, through Georgetown, and then across the bridge into Virginia.

"Where are we going, Captain?" I inquired. "Is there a fight?"

The captain, with a surly smile, replied, "Guess we'll get enough of it, maybe. I got orders last night to rejoin our regiment somewhere on the road to Bull Run. They're at the front; and if we get there in time, we'll get into the fight. If we don't find the regiment, they'll put us in somewhere. My opinion is, from what I hear, that the army is skedaddling, though!"

Our knapsacks, and forty rounds of ammunition, and three days' rations, had become a terrible load to our men, who had never made a march before. As the sun arose, it grew suffocatingly hot, and the sweat ran down our faces and dropped upon the dusty Virginia road.

"Take it easy, men; and don't throw away anything you will be sorry for afterwards," commanded Grim, with a half-laugh, as the men began to throw away their coats and overcoats, extra boots, underclothes, and heavy keepsakes.

"You'll need," I said to one of the men, "some of that stuff you are throwing away."

"Let 'em alone," said Captain Grim. "Nothing like a good march to get men down to a common-sense outfit. They'll get more light on what they really need to-day than they would in a month's lying around in barracks!"

Later, we encountered some dusty soldiers coming in on the road from Alexandria. They were sunburned and grimy, and, as Corporal Standish said, "the only clean thing about them seemed to be their muskets." Those gleamed and flashed in the sunlight like silver. As they marched along the road with easy, swinging steps, and with arms at right shoulder shift, they saluted us with "Hallo, recruits! Stopped ter get yer paper collars washed, hey?" And with laughter and

"A party of stragglers with a wounded man."

-- Page 109.

talk in their ranks, they were off in a cloud of dust.

"Gracious!" exclaimed one of the Centerboro' men. "See them fellers get over the road! You can't see their heels for dirt. Who are they?"

"They are tough old vets from the Army of the Potomac," said Captain Grim to me, as if in answer to the inquiry.

I expressed some surprise and discouragement at seeing them march past our toiling and wearied men so easily.

"Oh!" said Grim, "you'll get down to it after a while; takes time to get your muscles up to such work."

And then I began to realize what I had not fully comprehended before, that we were raw recruits, and not as yet real soldiers.

While we were halting by the wayside, some New York volunteers passed us, who, without stopping, informed us that they had come up from Acquia Creek, where they had arrived the day before, and were on their way to the front.

In the afternoon we began to meet baggage-wagons, artillery, caissons, ambulances with wounded men, and other indications of the defeat of the army under Pope.

"Where are ye goin'?" inquired a party of stragglers, with a wounded man in the midst of them.

"Recruits," replied our captain; "we belong to

your corps, and are going to join our regiment somewhere at the front: seen 'em on the road, the —— th Massachusetts?"

"Cap'n," was the saucy reply, "you set right down side o' the road anywheres, same's the feller did for the keyhole to his door when he was out too late; they'll come along: the whole army's on the skedaddle!" And the skedaddler disappeared down the road in the dust.

The skies began to darken as we wearily went on, and the heat grew more and more suffocating as premature darkness enveloped us with the stifling atmosphere of an approaching tempest. The piled-up clouds, the rolling thunder, and the darkness, foretold the heavy torrents that soon began to fall, drenching our already sweat-dampened clothing.

The roads were soon converted into a compound that for sticky perversity exceeded anything that I had ever encountered. Out of this our feet were laboriously drawn, accompanied by a noise not unlike that which uncouth boys make when eating soup. When drawn out of the mud our feet resembled long, irregular loaves of raw sweetbread, yellow and nasty.

As darkness set in, and the rain still came down in torrents, we picked our way by the vivid flashes of lightning.

The roads, meanwhile, were more and more crowded by interminable files of baggage-wagons, mingled with batteries of artillery and infantry, marching in the other direction. These were met by a tide of stragglers and wounded men drifting from the front.

The shouts of teamsters, the orders of officers, mingling discordantly with peals of crashing thunder and the plaintive chorus of hungry mules, produced a tumult in the confusion of which it was difficult to hear or recognize our own men.

When we finally reached the village of Fairfax, we found with us only twenty of the fifty men with whom we left Washington that morning. Little Mike, our drummer, was among these; for he had stuck to us, as Captain Grim said, "as tenaciously as the mud."

At Fairfax everything seemed in direst confusion. Huge fires were burning in every quarter of the streets, and in gardens and barnyards. Around these in the drenching rain stood or reclined groups of men. By the light of the fires could be seen confused masses of ambulances, artillery, and baggage-wagons, mingled with which were men from every arm of the service, — the orange stripes of the engineer, the red of the artillery, the yellow of the cavalry, and blue of the infantry.

These men were breaking up fences, tearing down outbuildings, and unhinging doors to replenish fires or to start new ones.

Officers and men mingled, invading barns and

houses, making attempts to pitch their tents in the enclosures.

They were men, as we learned later, of different corps, — some neither sick nor wounded, — who, after the defeat of the army at Bull Run, had mingled with the escort of trains. These were among the stragglers and marauders, although most of this host were disposed to join their regiments at the first favorable opportunity.

Captain Grim established a guard of four men, under Corporal Standish, and by his advice we went to rest under the shelter of an outbuilding, with the mud, as one of our men said, "scrutching" up under our rubber blankets, which we spread on the ground, and with the rain still pouring.

In our soaked garments, we rolled ourselves in our wet blankets, and, with wet and mud-enveloped feet protruding, went to sleep, tired, hungry, and dazed.

I was awakened by the clatter of a drum near my head, and was brought to consider once more whether the bubble of military reputation was worth pursuing through so much mud. But nothing prevented us from boiling our coffee and munching our hard-tack with good appetite and satisfaction.

We learned, later in the day, that there had been a battle at Ox Hill during the night, in which our brave General Kearney had met his death.

As day dawned, army trains and stragglers moved in ceaseless procession towards Alexandria, while a large number of men around us started out inquiring for their regiments.

We, meanwhile, under Grim's direction, gathered most of our men together, counted noses, as Tobin, one of the Irish recruits, called it, and found that only ten were missing. We joined the extreme rear guard of the army, and before long found our regiment. Without much more ceremony we, with some veterans, were at once detailed for picket-duty, on a road where it was said the enemy was likely to come in at any moment.

The veterans of our regiment were worn out with marching and fighting, and most of them slept, while the recruits stood guard, expecting an enemy in every bush and behind every hill.

Before night we got orders to take up a retrograde movement, and joined the throng moving on all the roads towards Washington. The next day we got a newspaper that announced that the army was *safe* behind the defences of Washington.

Such was our introduction, from scenes of peace, to the tumult of war, and which is so impressed upon my memory, that it seems but an event of yesterday.

That day all our straggling recruits but one joined us, and I was calling the list of names, when some one slapped me familiarly on the

shoulder, exclaiming, "Geewhitaker! as sure as I
am a hornblower, if here ain't Jack Alden!"

It was a soldier, in faded, dirty, tattered uniform, and with a not-over-clean, sunburned face.
But for his voice I should not have recognized
him as Add.   Among the peculiarities of his
outfit was a small frying-pan lashed to his lean
knapsack.

He looked every inch a soldier, however, and I
was not a little ashamed when he noticed my
sergeant's chevrons.   Ashamed because I felt
that I was surrounded with brave and tried men,
who deserved more of their country than I did.

When I quizzed Add about his frying-pan, he
scowled and said, —

"Why, I'd rather lose my whole outfit than
that!   That's a whole kit in itself: a feller can
cook anything in it."

The next forenoon we heard great cheering
along the line of the army, and learned that it was
caused by the appearance of General McClellan,
who was said once more to have assumed command of the Army of the Potomac.

The veterans expressed great satisfaction at this
event, and, as Add said, "It gives the boys a
new backbone!   They don't take much stock in
Pope, anyway."

CHAPTER XI.

A RECRUIT ON THE MARCH.

THE next morning we went into camp on the high land near and south of the Potomac. The veteran members of our regiment passed the day in cooking, washing, cleaning their muskets, sleeping, and grumbling about Pope.

"Our old boys," said Add, "lay in a stock of sleep and do their grumbling at such times as these!"

The recruits, on their part, nursed their sore feet and the chafed spots which had accumulated plentifully on their persons since starting out, and cultivated the acquaintance of the elder members of the regiment.

The veterans expressed great satisfaction at once more being in the vicinity of Washington. Some thought they might get passes into the city, but were peremptorily refused by their officers.

I could see but little ground for the enthusiastic satisfaction expressed, for these veterans certainly showed signs of hard campaigning. Some were in tattered clothing, others destitute of shoes or stockings, and all wore threadbare and faded uniforms, while their clothing was infested by invaders that disgusted the recruits.

Some of them had reminders of the Peninsula Campaign in the shape of chills and fever; others were thin and pinched with diarrhœa or the swamp fever, from which they were scarcely convalescent, or which they had bravely withstood without abandoning duty. None of them had superfluous flesh on their bones, but most had muscles like whipcords, in compensation for this deficiency.

I made a remark, embodying something of these observations and reflections, to Add, who replied, "Well, yes, they are regular fighting and marching machines; and if they had not been, Pope would have got left worse than he did."

Contrasting with these ragged battalions of the Army of the Potomac, there came well-dressed, tinselled officers from Washington. Luxurious carriages filled with fashionably dressed men, and fair women with fresh, beautiful faces, rolled along the magnificent wood-skirted drives, near the camps. — if the collection of little dog-tents could be called such. Thus the squalor of "grim-visaged war" was contrasted with the luxuries and refinements of civil life.

Wood and water were plenty; and the veterans expressed satisfaction on that score, as well as at the opportunity afforded for rest, and a chance to buy pies and cakes and other goodies, and to cook strange messes in their half-canteens and tins.

Our rest proved, however, of but short duration; Uncle Sam had other uses for his children in blue than indulging them in even a moderately good time.

On the 4th of September the army, under their faded and bullet-scarred flags, marched into Maryland, once more to battle with the enemy who had crossed into that State.

The soldiers of our regiment, at the time of our coming, consisted of what might be called sifted men. The great sieve of war had winnowed away its chaff of weak, faint-hearted, or cowardly men, until by " natural selection " of campaigning, battle, and hardships, only the choicest of its members had remained. Most of them were beardless boys, many of my own age, some even younger, though all were toughened veterans. Fighting, hard fare, and wearisome marches, had left set lines on their young but weatherbeaten faces.

Over these men Captain Grim had gained a marked supremacy. His fitness for his position had been vindicated by the best of all tests, — service in the field. He had been proved brave and tenacious, but not foolhardy. He was cautious, yet bold when circumstances demanded it, and had gained the reputation among his men of never sending them to places of danger where he was not willing to lead.

Our first lieutenant, Elbridge Mason, was a young, beardless fellow, not over eighteen, but every inch a soldier. It was some time before I recognized in him my former school and shop acquaintance, the son of Widow Mason. The *personnel* of the rank and file was of the very best. All of these young men had a common-school, some of them an academic, education, and they were mostly the sons of thrifty mechanics or small manufacturers from the towns around Boston. Some of the more mature men had left good positions in civil life to serve in the ranks.

One of our sergeants, named Scott, had been a locomotive engineer. Another, Jack Hale, a tall, swarthy fellow, had been a school-teacher. Add, our fourth sergeant, was intelligent, and had a fair education " in streaks," as he said. He was reputed to be brave ; but one of our older privates remarked in my hearing, that he was rather too fond of skylarking and fun to exact obedience from the men, or to go higher in rank.

The orderly-sergeant of the company was my old friend Crandall, or, as he was familiarly known in the company, " Father Crandall." I soon discovered that the *sobriquet* was justly ac-quired, for he regarded the men of the company as his family, in whose welfare he was interested, and for whose acts he held himself responsible to his superiors. He was constant in his efforts for their comfort, and the quartermaster and commissary of the regiment had no desirable supplies of which he did not succeed in obtaining a share for the boys. Although he had not a very military appearance, he was a good disciplinarian, and his temper was as even as his will was inflexible. His ideas of duty were such, that while he made many allowances for tried and proved men, he would allow no flinching from actual duty. Among our new recruits who received billets was Standish. whom I have mentioned, and of whom the captain had formed a high opinion.

The *personnel* of the original officers and men was also very high. They were men who had enlisted from patriotic desires to save the Union, and not for the paltry pittance given them for pay. They were the best types of our Northern manhood, who, when called upon for dangerous or desperate duty, were actuated by pride and self-esteem to acquit themselves in an honorable and spirited manner.

I for the first time fully appreciated the honor attained by my captain in commanding such men; and by coming in contact with them, I learned that in point of knowledge and service, there were those then in the ranks who better deserved a sergeant's billet than myself.

After being corrected for two or three blunders made in drill, in a fit of humility I went to Captain Grim, and said, " Captain, I am barely seventeen, and can now see that I should not have accepted a sergeant's billet among so many men better educated and better qualified for the place. I want to resign, and step into the ranks, until I am better able to fill such a place."

The captain listened gravely and replied, "Sergeant Alden, I have thought of all you have said long ago; I, and not you, am the one to judge of your fitness. A good soldier obeys orders; defers to his superiors; when I see that you are not the right man for the place you hold, I'll reduce you without fear or favor. Lieutenant Mason is young, but he is one of our best officers."

I saw that he meant this, and felt the flattery, though I winced at the thought that he might reduce or punish me if found wanting or insubordinate.

I saluted, and was retiring, when the captain added, "Alden, every man must do his duty now, and more, for the country has never been in greater danger! Go to your quarters, and do the best you can." This was said with such a tone of dignity, that I retired with increased respect, and a sort of awe, for this New England mechanic who had once been my familiar acquaintance, and to whom the responsibilities of his position had seemed to give a stronger and graver manhood than years of citizen's life could do.

On the afternoon of the 8th of September we had pitched our little dog-tents by the roadside in Maryland. We had marched not over seven miles

"See here, you raw recruits! Beef taller's good for them
sore heels."

— Page 121.

a day since starting out from the Potomac, but my person had become just so many square inches of ache, and my feet were blistered and in a condition of excruciating soreness. I kept my hurts to myself, however, trusting that in time I should become accustomed to marching. Other raw recruits of the company complained as I should have done but for my pride.

"Do well 'nuff fer you," whined a little Irish boy named Tobin, from Centerboro'; "you've been there before! Jist look at the blisters on the heels and toes of me! Now, fer the love o' the saints, how am I ever to march with the same? An' the ole byes all the time saying, 'It's delightful to march in Maryland!' Sure, I'm rolling in a profusion of such delights; I'll give mine to some distitute feller that needs 'em!"

"You are as old and tough as I am," I replied, as I kicked off my boots and proceeded, for emphasis and illustration, to wash my raw heels and blistered toes. "It won't do to let those old vets have the laugh or joke on us; just grin and bear it like a man, and don't whine, Tobin."

"Well," said Add, who, unperceived, had come up with a broad grin, "they are just perfect sorrors to yer, ain't they, Alden? See here," he added, "you raw recruits! Beef taller's good for them sore heels, and put some on't on the counter of the shoes, to limber 'em up. They'll come 'round, them feet will, in a few days. An' you young squealer," addressing Tobin, " I guess I know something 'bout sore toes! I've got the worst set o' corns in the whole regiment, — achers of 'em. You can squeal if you want to, Tobin, but I guess you won't get much sympathy. 'Tain't manly to coddle any one in the army. We have to get as hard as flint. If you want sympathy, bear everything, and say nothin', like a man; then the old vets will respect yer! Then when yer can't stand it any longer, straggle — that's respectable; squealing ain't."

" Say nothing," said Tobin; " we ain't going to let them vets hear us squeak." Add gave me a complimentary nod, and continued, " The boys say, Alden, that you wanted to give up your place as sergeant; said you thought some of the vets deserved it more than you did."

I looked up angrily, for my interview with Captain Grim had hurt my pride, by giving me an even smaller opinion of myself than I had before.

" Oh," said Add, " you needn't look at me in that way! The boys like yer all the better for not thinking too much of yourself."

" I haven't said I didn't think well of myself," I replied stiffly.

" Well, ye'r foolish to try and throw a sergeant's billet over yer shoulder. I'd take any place, short of commander of the army; even a brigadier-general's place, with an ambulance to ride in and to carry good things. Don't throw *anything* over yer shoulder, I say. The captain said he'd break yer if yer deserved it, and he will. Captain Grim? Why, he's an old fighting cock! Yer ought to seen him at Glendale. He booted one of them young rebs that got among the battery we was supporting. Give him an awful kick, and yelled out as he kicked, 'Go home,' as if he was too small and young for his powder."

"I suppose," I inquired, "the rebels fight well?"

"I ain't laid up nothin' 'gainst them on that head," said Add, laughing. As he moved off he added to Tobin, "Well, grease up your shoes, and don't squeal, whatever you do."

As we advanced into Maryland, reorganization of the army went on, and, as some one has said, "all the faster because of our slow marches."

We had halted on the afternoon of the 13th of September, I think it was, and had gone into camp a few miles from Frederick City. The country through which we had marched showed every evidence of thrift and prosperity. Well-dressed women, clean children, and polite men had greeted us at almost every farmhouse and hamlet along the route. The number of black laborers excited my surprise. The Union flag was displayed on buildings, and Union sentiments were generally expressed by the people, with the occasional exception of a sullen old planter whose sons were in the Rebel army.

The delight of the veterans with Maryland was enthusiastic. They never foraged if they had money to buy chickens and sweet potatoes. The people sold willingly, but in many instances would not accept payment. The grist-mills were running even on Sundays, to provide flour for the unexpectedly large call on their stock. In the houses along the route sick Union soldiers were tenderly cared for by the hospitable people.

Here, while awaiting orders for another march, it may be well to see what was taking place on a larger field than the front of our own regiment.

After the battle of Bull Run, Lee had transferred the theatre of war from the front of Washington into Maryland. The harvests of the fertile valley of the Shenandoah had fallen into his hands, and his army had pressed confidently forward, with high hopes of conquest of the free State, singing as they advanced, —

> "The despot's heel is on thy shore,
> Maryland, my Maryland."

It was not Lee's intention, however, to make a direct move on Washington, but, after establishing his communications with Richmond by way of the Shenandoah Valley, to make a feint of moving against Pennsylvania, lead McClellan from his base of supplies, and then, after a decisive battle, seize Washington or Baltimore, or perhaps both.

He also hoped to recruit his ranks with enthusiastic young Marylanders, and for this purpose issued a proclamation, calling on her people " to throw off the foreign yoke and assume the sovereignty of the State."

He opened an office for recruiting in Frederick City.

The counties of Western Maryland were either decidedly Union in sentiment, or, at best, only lukewarm in their disloyalty. They did not in any case respond to Lee's call; whether they did not wish to be redeemed from plenty and receive the blessings of squalor, rags, and destitution represented by the Confederates who swarmed her soil, I do not know.

But the results did not, it was said, " pan out " largely for the Confederates; for they lost more soldiers by desertion than they gained by recruiting.

Real war, it must be confessed, seldom attracts; it is the tinsel of fresh uniforms and pomp of martial music — things but seldom known in genuine war — that draw young men to enlistment offices; and therefore Marylanders were no exception to a general rule in humanity, even if hostile to the Union.

The Union army had meanwhile moved slowly into Maryland. The uncertainty of the enemy's intention made it necessary to march cautiously, and to advance in such order as to keep Wash-

ington and Baltimore covered, and at the same
time to dispose the troops so as to be able to con-
centrate and follow quickly, should Lee take the
direction of Pennsylvania; or to defend Washington, if the movement into Maryland proved simply a trick to draw our forces from the defence of
the national capital.

Our army was therefore so disposed as to form
the circumference of a circle, described from the
centre of Washington, with a radius of twenty
miles, and with an extension of about twenty-
five miles from right to left.

Up to the time of our going into camp, as I have
mentioned in the foregoing narrative, our progress
had been slow, although, had it been faster, Heaven
knows the recruits would not have been able to
keep up.

I was caring for my blistered feet, or, as Add
expressed it, "putting myself on a war footing,"
when a colored boy, who had come, as he said,
"All de way from Fredrick," solicited me to buy
peach-pies. I at once recognized him as one of
the house-servants belonging to the Raymonds of
Baltimore, who had sometimes come to Dr. Milner's on errands when I was a wounded guest
at his house.

"Halloo, Sam! where did you come from, and
where's your master?" I exclaimed.

He did not at first recognize me, or pretended
not to; but after a while he exclaimed, "Golly! I

believe youse de Yankee soldier dat war dar at Massa Milner's. I 'clar', sar, I didn't know yer!"

"Where's your master?" I inquired again; for as he was Raymond's body-servant, I suspected his master or some of the Raymonds could not be far off.

Sam answered evasively, "Can't keep de run of de quality folks dese times."

Something in Sam's manner, however, told me that he not only knew where his master was, but that he was near by.

In the afternoon, near a farmhouse where a regiment of our brigade had stacked their muskets, I saw a young fellow come up with a bundle of newspapers, and rushed with others to buy one.

As I paid for my paper, I noticed that the man who sold them had the hands of one unaccustomed to work, although his clothing was that of a laborer. A soft felt hat was pulled down over his face. While watching him I saw him make a gesture of command towards Sam, who at once disappeared in the crowd. As I turned around to call out, the newsman too was gone. I jumped at once to the conclusion that the man in disguise was George Raymond, whom I had met in Baltimore at Doctor Milner's.

"What," was the query in my mind, "is this young and aristocratic man doing in disguise within the lines of the Union army?"

In the morning we continued our march, but I saw no more of master or servant at that time.

We were now hurried forward much more decisively than formerly; and the vets said McClellan had got his plans well settled for the campaign, and was about to execute them.

CHAPTER XII.

ON THE VERGE OF BATTLE.

On the 12th of September our advance had driven the Confederates from Frederick City, where, as we afterwards learned, they had met with but a cold reception.

When we marched into the town, the people exhibited every manifestation of pleasure. Women wearing decorations of red, white, and blue, came out on the sidewalk, and greeted us with enthusiasm.

"Thank God!" exclaimed one old lady, when referring to the Confederate army, "them dirty thieves and sneaks have gone!"

"We are right glad," said another, "to see the Union soldiers here."

"When the Confederates were here," said a citizen of Frederick, "all these shops that are now open were closed, and most of the houses had their shutters up."

Many other expressions of the kind showed that at least these people of Maryland had not responded to Lee's proclamation, which called upon them to "throw off the foreign yoke," as

the rule of the Federal government was designated.

"Just see," exclaimed Add, "the colors and
the pretty girls!" We looked up, and saw at the
windows of a house a dozen or more young ladies
wearing miniature flags; and stretched across the
street was displayed the national banner.

"Isn't it fine!" he exclaimed. "These folks
seem human."

I didn't see anything in these demonstrations
to make a fuss over, and said so.

"Well, my boy," said Sergeant Crandall, "that's
because you don't see the contrast between these
people and the people in Virginia, who acted as if
our soldiers were dirt under their feet! We ain't
accustomed to decent treatment by the people
where we're soldiering, and it seems kinder nice
to us."

"The Confederate soldiers who were recruiting
here," said a citizen, "sang that 'the despot's
heel was on our shore, my Maryland;' but when
them fellers tried to pull me into their recruiting-
office, I told them I thought the Confederate rule
here was worse than any Yankee yoke *we'd* had.
I heard their officer say they were losing more
men by desertion in Maryland than they were
gaining by recruiting."

We stacked arms on one of the side streets of
this quaint but hospitable town. On the window-
sills of the houses the people set out a profusion

of cakes, pies, bread, honey, and other eatables, such as had not gladdened the sight of our veterans for many a month.

Daintily dressed women, with their needlework in their hands, chatted pleasantly with us, while the air was full of the merry clack of children's voices, in strong contrast to the bronzed faces, flashing arms and equipments, of our warlike ranks.

While sitting on a doorstep, talking to a nice-looking matron, telling her about the Yankee country I came from, and, I fear, unconsciously drawing an unfavorable contrast to her own town, I noticed a young fellow lounging near. He was standing with his back to the house, with his soft hat pulled down over his eyes, apparently listening to my talk and that of others, and keenly observant of all that was passing around him. I should have thought nothing of it, had I not recognized something familiar in his manner. Afterwards his eyes met mine with a flash of recognition, and I saw that it was George Raymond, whom I have mentioned before.

He evidently saw that I knew him; for, removing his hat, he made a gesture, as I thought, half in defiance and half in salutation, and disappeared.

"What's the matter, Alden?" said Captain Grim, who stood near by. "What," he continued, as I did not at once reply, "do you see so strange?

Why, your eyes are sticking out of your head as if you had seen your grandmother's ghost!"

"I saw," I replied, "a young fellow I knew in Baltimore — at Dr. Milner's. He has just dodged around that corner. He's an awful rebel too."

"Shouldn't wonder," said Captain Grim in his gruff way, "if there was a lot more hanging around here. Better be here than with Lee's army, though."

"Maybe he is a spy," I suggested. "What's he doing here, when he belongs in Baltimore?"

"Shouldn't borrow any rebs," said Sergeant Crandall, biting off a huge piece from a hunk of natural-leaf tobacco. "We kinder think we'll have enough of 'em, my boy, without the multiplication-table; lots of things show that a fight is brewing."

"What," I asked, "are they? I don't see any: I haven't heard a gun fired anywhere around here."

"Well, that only shows ye are green, my boy! Three days' rations, sixty rounds of cartridges, officers' horses and red-tape slingers sent to the rear, with the orders we've had to be ready to march at a moment's notice, means that we are on the heels of the Rebel army, and are going fur 'em, and that a fight is expected at any minute. That's the way we read it, ain't it, Captain?"

Captain Grim nodded, and gruffly grunted out, "The signs are in the air, true as yer live!"

In the evening we went into camp near the town; and, after boiling our coffee and cooking our rations, men all over the camp began to button together the oblong pieces of cotton cloth, one of which was carried by each man; then two crotched sticks about four feet long were driven firmly in the ground, and, with a ridge-pole adjusted, the cloth was stretched across them for a tent.

Then, under the stars of a beautiful September night, while the distant murmurs of merriment in the town came to our ears, like echoes from our far-away homes, taps sounded, silence succeeded in camp, and we slept the sleep of young and tired boys.

It seemed to me that I was scarcely asleep before I was awakened by the rattle of drums, and the piercing notes of the fife, sounding the reveille. The roll was called by candlelight, and at break of day we were on the march.

That my young readers may know what was taking place on a wider field than mere individual observations can give, it is needful to glance at the operations of the Union and Confederate armies, approaching each other in Maryland.

As I have said elsewhere, it was not General Lee's plan, after establishing his communications by way of the Shenandoah Valley, to make a direct attack upon Washington, but to so manœuvre as to lead McClellan from the base of his supplies, and to uncover the national capital.

While carrying out this plan, Lee had not thought it necessary to go out of his way to capture or drive away a force of twelve thousand men who garrisoned at Harper's Ferry, — as his crossing above had rendered its occupation useless.

Although early in the campaign McClellan had requested that these men should join him by the easiest practicable route, Halleck had insisted that they should remain in this turned and worse-than-useless position. The whole campaign, which we are in part describing, pivots around this fact.

Imagine the astonishment of the rebel commander at learning, after his advance to Frederick City, that this garrison was still in his rear. He at once determined to capture the place, its twelve thousand defenders, and its munitions of war.

With this in view, he at once directed Jackson to move across the Potomac by way of Williamsport, to ascend from the rear and attack the garrison, while McLaws was to seize Maryland Heights, and a force under Walker crossed the river and seized the heights of London.

The advance for this purpose began on the 10th of September. The Confederate forces were in the positions assigned on the night of the 12th.

The Union defenders, like rats in a huge bowl, and with the cat's paws on the edge thereof, were inevitably doomed to be captured.

The Union Army had, meanwhile, as seen by our previous description, arrived at Frederick City. Here there fell into the hands of McClellan, Lee's official order, which fully disclosed in detail the movement for the capture of Harper's Ferry, and to carry out which, Lee had divided his forces in the face of his enemy. Here was an opportunity seldom offered to a general, — the full disclosure of his enemy's plans.

To avail himself of this division of the enemy, McClellan directed Franklin, with his corps, to march at daybreak on the 13th, and capture Crampton's Pass.

It has since been shown that had he ordered the march to be made on the evening previous, the Rebel army would have been cut in twain, and defeated in detail.

In war, time is often of superior importance, above even men and means. Stonewall Jackson illustrated his conception of its importance, when, in this emergency, leaving General Hill to receive the surrender of Harper's Ferry, on the night of the 15th he marched his corps fifteen miles, and joined Lee's army at Sharpsburg.

Meanwhile, Franklin had, after a sharp fight, driven away the rebel defenders of Crampton's Pass; and if he had debouched at once in rear of Maryland Heights, it is doubtful if McLaws could have escaped.

Such was the situation when, on the morning of

the 14th of September, we hurried forward, and
found the Union army crowding all the roads in
pursuit of Lee.

As we marched four abreast, mounted orderlies
and aids, with official envelopes in their belts,
hurried back and forth by the side of our marching columns.

The cavalry, the eyes of an army, were scouting
ahead, sending back reports as fast as they learned
of the presence of the enemy.

At a place where two roads came together, we
encountered another body of troops; and, as is
customary, when it was learned that they had orders to reach this junction first, we marched into
a field, and rested in place, waiting until this force
had passed.

Here a grizzly-looking individual, who was
seated on a snake fence, remarked, " You'll come
back right soon, I reckon, with our folks after
yer."

The roads were narrow, and not of the best,
and occasionally were encumbered with wrecked
wagons or broken artillery wheels.

The increasing haste of aids and orderlies,
meanwhile, showed. even to the uninitiated, that
orders were coming thick and fast to hurry up the
troops, and that the enemy was not far away.

That night we halted and stacked arms in an
open field, and lay down to rest with thoughts of
the impending battle.

The next day we crossed the range of the Cololtian Mountains, and descended its slopes into the beautiful Middletown Valley.

When marching down the western slope, we looked out upon the landscape, spread in peaceful beauty below and around us. Looking towards the north, we could see the roads dotted with white spots; these were our trains. Dark columns of men, fringed with flashing steel, were seen on all the roads, right and left, winding along the hillsides, pouring over the ridges, and descending by all the roads, furrowing, as it were, the landscape with dark columns of our army.

A mile or less from us the column had broken, and formed for battle in the fields.

The flash of sunlight on burnished steel was seen; and moving columns and the hurry of steeds made the scene one of unusual fascination.

As we neared the opposite mountain range, we heard the thunder of artillery, and saw the smoke of battle on the hills.

It was the sound of a conflict, in which the Union troops were attempting to wrest the passage through the Blue Ridge known as Turner's Gap from the possession of the enemy.

Later in the day we were marched up the hill from which there came the sound of conflict; and to my relief, instead of being sent against the enemy direct, we went into a field, and were ordered to lie down.

I said to Add, after we had lain there a while,
" What is all this about?   We don't seem to
be doing much except lying on our bellies, with
noise all around us, and a humming of shot and
shell whizzing over our heads!"

I had scarcely spoken these words when I heard
a long-continued yell of *hi-hi-hi-i-i-i-i-i*, and bursting through the thicket in front of us came a
body of men.

" Fire!" came the order from our colonel, and
then a wreath of smoke.

With heavy, saddened heart I saw the poor
wounded Southern boys fall before this deadly
fire, abandoned by their comrades, who had run
back into the woods again.

The sight was sickening; and, although they
were our country's enemies, I would have given
a year's pay to have been able to help comfort
them.

Before sundown the heavy boom of cannon
and the crackle of musketry among the hills had
ceased.

We then went forward to where we had seen
the poor wounded fellows fall. They were piti-
fully calling for water, as wounded men always
do. There were a dozen or more dead, and two-
score at least of poor wounded fellows clad in
butternut and gray. I, for one, helped and comforted them, and was very sad at heart. Their
faces were pinched and their persons thin, — made

so, no doubt, by forced marches and short rations; and I thought regretfully of the anger I had felt when I fired at those poor boys.

Our men gave the wounded every care possible under the circumstances, — shared with them their food and drink, and tried to ease their pain by cheerful words; but before morning four had died.

The next morning we did the best we could for them, but by seven o'clock were following once more our columns, which filled the mountain-passes.

At dawn intelligence came to us that Lee had withdrawn into the valley of the Antietam, and we were soon in hot pursuit.

The country was a beautiful one, and on every side were seen fields of grain ready for the reaper, orchards and meadows, cattle grazing in the fields; while comfortable farmhouses and barns showed that abundance was common to the country.

CHAPTER XIII.

BATTLE OF ANTIETAM.

On Monday morning our column approached a line of low hills, and turned off on the road to the left of them. After marching a short distance over this road, which ran parallel to the line of hills, we were halted for a rest.

Soon after we halted, prompted by that curiosity which is the Yankee birthright, I went with a few comrades to the top of the ridge, little knowing, however, that I was about to look out on what was destined shortly to become one of the world's great battle-fields. Below us, winding in its crooked course, and partly hidden by a deep fringe of foliage, ran a narrow river, the Antietam. On the left, across this creek or river, was a little village; with fields in front, enclosed by stone walls; as beautiful an undulating landscape as the eye could desire to rest upon.

In the green fields herds of cattle were grazing; orchards and yellow harvests, and here and there comfortable farmhouses, some on eminences, others half hidden by vines and shade-trees, gave variety to the peaceful valley.

A road ran from the village, almost parallel with the general course of the river, which here runs nearly north and south. Other roads forked from this pike, and ran towards the river.

"What village can that be?" I inquired, consulting my pocket map. "Is it Hagerstown?"

"It's Sharpsburg," replied one of my comrades, who was familiar with this part of the country. "Hagerstown must be twenty miles north of us; that road running north from the village is the Hagerstown pike. You could see the Potomac from here if it wasn't for the wooded hills."

Several stone bridges crossed the stream on our front, while the landscape was closed in on our right and left by wooded ridges.

As we stood here a group of officers came to the ridge, not far from us, viewing the country with their field-glasses.

"Just see that!" Captain Grim (who was standing by my side) pointed to little white puffs of smoke which arose from the road near the town. Before I could inquire its import, shells hoarsely whistled over the heads of the group of officers I have mentioned.

"Hear that, my boy!" exclaimed Crandall, as shot after shot was fired; "that means, just as plain as if 't was said in English, 'We rebs are here! And if you think you can drive us out, try it!'"

Just then, as if in response to the challenge, a

light battery, six horses to a gun, came galloping, with a whirl and clatter of haste, to the top of the hill, wheeled into position, and one after another of the guns opened fire with a furious rapidity and precision of aim that astonished me.

As the group of officers went down the hill, I heard one of them say, "The enemy is in force on both sides of that road."

"There don't seem to be much harm done," I said, "except the big noise they're making; no one is hurt."

"See here," said Add, who was one of our party, "'t ain't meant for fun or fireworks, you bet!"

"No," said Captain Grim, looking off across the river with his glass; "it's a defiance, rather than anything else; but it looks to me as though they were putting on a bold face to cover some deficiency: likely their whole force ain't up yet, and they want to stand us off a while. What's the use of firing when they don't touch us, or we them, did you say? Why, every one of them bronze pieces is asking a question; and they have got an answer. Question is, 'Where are you, Johnny Reb?' We've developed their position, and I guess from their fire that they are in force, and probably on both sides of that road. They mean to receive battle there. Boys, we'd better get back to the regiment! We are likely to attack, or at least go for 'em, just as soon as we can get ready.

We shall have some mighty sharp work before long, anyway."

The enemy's position was admirably chosen, their lines being drawn across an angle, formed by the junction of the Potomac with the Antietam River, which here runs nearly south, and obliquely towards the Potomac; and as the Potomac at this point forms, by a series of curves, a sort of horse-shoe bend in their rear, they were enabled to rest both flanks on that stream, while the Antietam protected their front. A line of abrupt hills, rising from the river, forming a half-circle, with the convexity in front, enabled their artillery to sweep the level land from right to left before them, and make it cost dearly in life to cross the bridges near the town.

On the afternoon of our arrival we were brought to our feet by cheering, which came nearer and nearer. It was for McClellan, who was riding down our lines, and was receiving an enthusiastic welcome from his devoted soldiers. As he came by us on his magnificent black horse, which out-sped the horses of his staff, we too threw up our hats, and cheered enthusiastically until we were hoarse. We could hear the cheering as he passed, sounding along the line until it seemed but an echo in the distance.

That night we slept on our arms.

Tuesday morning dawned hot and breathless. All that day we waited, expectant, but not anx-

ious, for the fight to begin. When we went to the
top of the hill, the Confederate gunners showed
us more attentions than seemed good for us, and
we speedily got down again, with the angry sput-
tering and hoarse screeching of shell over us. The
artillery was very noisy, and most of that day the
very hills seemed to shake with its explosions.

"Guess we ain't goin' to have much fightin', at
this rate," said one of the recruits, who was just
learning to grumble. Orderly-Sergeant Crandall,
who was cooking his supper, looked up and said,
with a smile of disdain at such shallowness, —

"Humph! you'll soon see enough of that business, so you won't hanker for it a'terwards, or
I'm much mistaken in signs!"

It was near sundown when Add exclaimed,
"There they go! Hear that!" And from across
the river there came the long roar of musketry,
showing that the battle had actually begun.

This is what was taking place. Hooker's corps,
with Mansfield's in reserve, had crossed Antietam Creek at an unguarded ford near Pye's Mills,
above us. His advance, under Meade, had, at
about sundown, encountered the enemy under
Hood, and driven him back. And then with a
sharp skirmish ended the fight for the night.

Let us now turn and see the field of action from
a more general standpoint than individual sight
can give.

The Confederate general, although in no con-

dition for the aggressive, had made careful preparation to receive an attack.

To guard the turnpike which we had observed
from the ridge (running north and south beyond
the town and across the Potomac), he had placed
two brigades under Hood, with Jackson near, as
reserve. Longstreet's corps was on the right of
the road, from Sharpsburg to Boonsboro', with
D. H. Hill's corps on the left.

Three of the stone bridges nearest the town,
crossing the Antietam on his front, were so well
guarded as to prevent a front attack by our army.

The plan of battle formed meanwhile by the
Union commander was simple and comprehen-
sive. It was to throw his right wing across the
river, and attack with Hooker's corps, supported
by those of Mansfield and Sumner. When this
manœuvre should have withdrawn attention from
his centre and left, the bridges were to be forced,
and the enemy there posted to be driven back.
Hooker's attack was in furtherance of this plan,
and the firing we had heard in the evening was
from this corps, engaging the Confederate left.

Shortly after this I saw our colonel in conversation with Captain Grim; afterwards Orderly
Crandall came to us, and said gravely, "Be ready
to move at any time. boys. It's likely to rain ; so
keep your muskets dry."

In the morning I was awakened from a dreamless sleep by hearing the call, " Turn out ! Turn

out there!" I sprang to my feet, and, amid the drizzling rain of the early morning, was soon engaged with my comrades in preparation for what might be before us.

We boiled coffee, refilled our canteens and haversacks, and growled about the weather.

I wondered how I should acquit myself in the impending fight; for, to tell the truth, I didn't feel very brave.

At seven o'clock we heard the first volley of musketry across the river, to which was soon joined the steady *boom, boom, boom*, of artillery, showing that the battle had begun.

As we got the order to march, half an hour later, the clouds cleared, and the sun came out, giving promise of fair weather. The colonel, a thick-set, grave, resolute-looking man, rode down our front, accompanied by a white-haired officer.

"That's General Sumner," said Add, "and he's a good one too."

"What have you got your frying-pan lashed to your back for, Add?" I asked.

"Carry it for luck," was the reply. "Maybe I'll be lucky enough to have a chance to fry something, you know!"

We crossed the river by a lower ford; and, as we halted, General McClellan again rode down our lines, and was again received by his soldiers with wonderful enthusiasm. The veterans threw up their caps, and cheered again and again. Their enthusiasm for him resulted, I believe, from their faith that he would not needlessly throw away lives.

" That," I heard Lieutenant Mason say, " will put life into them. A man can't cheer like that, and consistently turn his back on the rebs afterward. May God prosper the cause!"

As our young lieutenant said this, I could not help admiring his straight, athletic, although youthful, form. There were grave lines of manly resolution on his face, but not the first sign of a beard. He was a mere boy, yet had already gained a character for steadiness and bravery. He was the very impersonation of young Christian manhood; and one could not know him long without being impressed, as I was, that his courage was born of fear of God.

The order, " Forward!" came, and we moved on towards the discordant sounds of battle.

While our column is moving forward, let us for a brief moment explain what was taking place on our front, where could be heard the long volleys of musketry and the rapid firing of artillery.

Hooker had attempted to carry the Hagerstown road and the wood west of it. This was the aim, also, of the succession of desperate attacks that followed. So long as the Confederates held this wood, they were ambushed in a position to deliver a flanking fire on our troops as they advanced on the cleared land on the right of it.

After an hour's bloody bushwhacking, Hooker drove the enemy from a large cornfield near the turnpike. Here the fight, furious from the beginning, became awful. The lines of battle, swaying back and forth, had strewn the cornfield with a harvest of dead, whose blood reddened the blades of corn. The hostile lines had literally torn each other in pieces.

Hooker had thrown forward Meade in advance, to seize the Hagerstown road. The enemy's line, staggered and overthrown, was falling back, when the reserve division, under Stonewall Jackson, re-enforced by Hood's two brigades, rushed yelling from the wood, and hurled back Meade's columns, broken and bleeding. Such was the situation as we advanced.

It is the unknown quantity in danger that terrifies. As we moved forward towards the battle sounds, the cannon roaring louder and louder, and the musketry crackling fiercer and fiercer, like hemlock twigs in the flames, I found myself in a tremor of nervousness, which I could not wholly suppress. I had no desire to die a hero's death. There were too many heroes, and the prospect of being overlooked was not pleasing to one's egotism.

"How do you like it as far as you've gone?" Add asked this in an undertone, as if he surmised my thoughts, as one of our new men, pale and gasping with fright, fell out of line, and was forced back again by the file-closers.

"I hope I shall be able to do my duty!" I said this angrily, from the fact that I had my doubts, and yet was afraid of being thought a coward.

"I know," said Add, "'bout how you feel, I guess. But you don't fight any part of this fight, though, until you get there; don't bother 'bout anything till it comes!"

We marched at the sharp run called a double-quick, for a mile or more, then entered a grove almost clear of underbrush, where numerous dead and wounded men still lay on the ground.

Here, too, were faint-hearted men who had left the battle-ranks under pretence of taking care of the wounded.

"These men," I heard Captain Grim sarcastically remark, "are too thunderin' tender."

"Shows that old Joe Hooker," said another, "has had a hard pull for it."

One of the would-be-thought Good Samaritans, in answer to an uncomplimentary remark, angrily shouted in reply, "Laugh! but you'll come to the rear pretty soon, like a whipped dog with his tail between his legs! You'll get your stomach full out there before you know it!"

We had halted for a few moments to re-form our line, for every impediment of tree or rock breaks up a regular formation in an advance like this.

While this halt was made, the order was given that no one was to leave the ranks, not even to attend to our wounded.

The evidences of the fight seen in this wood, coupled with this command, were significant.

The dead and wounded of the enemy, as well as our own, encumbered the ground at almost every step. Some of the wounded were propped against trees, others were helping one another, and in some instances had bound up their wounds with blades of corn.

The fierce fight that raged here must have been appalling. Some of the wounded signalled us for help, which we could not give. My heart sickened; its pulsations were like a muffled drum.

We finally reached open ground, where the enemy's unseen artillery struck our ranks. Bullets hissed from foes in ambush as we ran on, and were finally halted, and drawn up in line parallel to the Hagerstown pike.

Between us and this road was a field of high, thick Indian corn. A fence was taken down while we were re-forming, and again on we went, still under fire from the enemy, passing over the dead and wounded who dotted the field.

Few men besides ours were in sight. It looked as if this affair was exclusively our own.

As we passed into the wood on the other side of the road, we were, for a short time, out of range of the enemy's fire. After marching a while, we encountered them again, while we were moved by the right oblique, to close an interval between us and another regiment. At this time we had reached a slight rise in the ground, and began to drive the enemy steadily before us.

It was at this time that a dramatic incident occurred. While the enemy were attempting to rally their men around a flag, not over fifteen yards from us, a volley was poured into them from our muskets. In the smoke of it, I saw one of our men run forward to the rebel color-bearer, who stood wounded and deserted by his comrades, wrest the flag from his hands, and, with the standard-bearer for a prisoner, quickly join our ranks with the flag, amid the cheers of our boys. It was George Standish.

The enemy had now fallen back to the cover of an orchard, a wheat-field, haystacks, and farm-buildings. From these they delivered a slow but deadly fire. The fight now became more and more furious, as the hostile lines, not forty feet apart, cheered, yelled, and fought like demons.

A section of Confederate artillery, stationed on a knoll about six hundred yards from us, was meanwhile delivering a destructive fire of canister. Twice we drove their cannoneers from their guns by converging our fire upon them, but the brave fellows returned again.

To add to the terrible destruction in our ranks, one of our own regiments had stupidly begun to fire at the enemy through our line, killing scores of our men.

We now got the order to advance. The enemy's fire was deadly as we breasted it.

The colonel, on foot, raged at seeing that his regiment had melted away before the fire of friend and foe. Captain Grim was smiling his dangerous, bull-dog smile, — giving his orders so they were heard distinctly above the uproar. His clear, cold tones calmed and reassured his men.

The ground was meanwhile covered with our poor boys, wounded and dead; for the order forbidding the carrying of wounded men to the rear was obeyed to the letter.

Suddenly the uproar increased. Worse had come! The enemy had been heavily re-enforced. It was a terrible moment. An awful fire of musketry from flank, front, and rear struck our ranks like a cyclone of death.

In a moment there were on the ground more of dead and wounded than living men; our ranks were crushed. Shouts of rage and despair were heard. Encouraging cries came from our wounded comrades, who exclaimed, " Stick to 'em! Don't mind us! Fight it out!"

Out of five hundred and eighty muskets carried into the fight by our regiment, only two hundred and thirty-four now remained.

Still we do not give it up. We face to the rear, deliver fire, and then sullenly retire, fighting as we fall back. Then all is hastened and precipitated. Our ranks dissolve like a thaw, yet we do not entirely lose the order of our line, but fall back, step by step, until under the protection of our artillery, not four hundred yards distant from the scene of our fierce conflict. Here the enemy converge their artillery upon our position, until we fall back once more to support a battery still farther in the rear.

While these batteries flame and thunder over us, we await, expecting to hear the order for another advance. But the fight is substantially over, and the order does not come.

Among the wounded who had come away with us from the scene of the morning's fight, was little Mike, the drummer, who said proudly, " I fighted 'em like the rest of ye's."

Captain Grim was wounded in the right arm, while Lieutenant Mason had two slight flesh-wounds. In opening my clothes to look for my wound, I found only a vivid welt across my chest, caused by the graze of a bullet. There were six of the Centerboro' boys among the killed and wounded.

My heart was sore, yet grateful; sore for my comrades, sleeping on the field, never more to be awakened; grateful, that by some mysterious chance, where it seemed none could escape from the maelstrom of death, I had passed unhurt, and had done my duty, so that no one but myself really knew the fears that had beset me. I was, however, in a tumult of doubt. I questioned again and again my courage, and was not satisfied even when Captain Grim complimented me on my good conduct in this, my first battle.

" I had my eye on you," said Grim. " Scared? Of course you were; I was myself."

Add had escaped unhurt, but bewailed the loss of his frying-pan. It had been struck and shattered by bullets, so that nothing but the handle dangled at his back when, as he said, he " took an account of stock."

"I think," said he, " I heard you ask, just as we were going into the fight, what I carried it for? Now you see I carried it for luck; it was my life-preserver."

It may seem to my readers who have never seen a battle, a very curious statement when I say that we did not know at that time whether we had been defeated or had won a victory. The combinations of a battle-field are so immense, that an individual sees but little. It is only after a fight that the many incidents of soldiers' experiences, told around the campfire, or reported by officers, give something like a complete account of all that has happened.

It was months afterwards that we learned that the Confederate brigades had worked around under cover of the woods, on our flank and rear, and had wrought such destruction in our ranks, that our division had lost 2,255 men. The effort to flank us, we also learned some days after the fight, had been checked by Barlow, who quickly changed front, and enfiladed the enemy's advancing line.

General Burnside, on the extreme left, did not attack until the battle was over on the right; and hence the Confederates had brought nearly all their forces from their right into the fight against us. When Burnside's men did cross Antietam bridge, near the town, on the left, and had pierced the enemy's line in the full tide of successful battle, General A. P. Hill, who had marched from Harper's Ferry, — seventeen miles in seven hours, — re-enforced the broken Confederate line, and drove Burnside back to the protection of the river bluff, with a loss of 2,202 men. This substantially ended the battle of Antietam.

CHAPTER XIV.

AFTER THE BATTLE.

As the sun went down the sounds of battle died away along the Antietam. Darkness threw its pitying shadows over the field, concealing the ensanguined work of man against man. Rest had come to those who had fought, and unstrung nerves and the despondency of reflection followed the fierce excitement of conflict. Pitying thoughts of wounded comrades, and even of foes, still lying on the field, prompted us to make an effort for their relief.

"Who," asked Sergeant Crandall, "will come with me to look after our poor boys out there?"

There was no lack of response, although the men were tired with the day's contest. More volunteered than it was safe or advisable to take on such an errand. I was among those selected to go.

"Take your blankets," said Sergeant Crandall, "and cut poles to wind them on for stretchers. Fill your canteens; the wounded always want water the first thing. No, you needn't take your muskets, or at least not more than one or two of you. The rebs won't interfere if they understand what we are up to; more likely we shall meet some of them on the same errand."

"Men who have been fighting each other don't feel very bitter," said Add, more seriously than was his wont. "But we are likely to meet with some of the cowardly, prowling thieves who strip the dead and go through their pockets; there ain't anything human about them."

"Maybe," said Crandall reflectively, putting an army revolver in his pocket. "Here, Add Key, you oughter be goin' too, — talk's if you was!"

"Want me to go?" said Add. "Well, I ain't hankerin' for it! I'll go, though!"

The starlight was bright as our party, equipped for the task of rescuing and comforting wounded men, made its way cautiously up the Hagerstown pike, and then stealthily through the cornfield, where some of the terrible encounters of the previous day had taken place. Occasionally, as we advanced, listening to every sound, we heard the cry of a wounded horse, or the groans of wounded men. We found several of our comrades on the outskirts of the west wood, and sent them back to the ambulance, which was expected to follow us on the road.

Peering into the shadows cast by rocks or bushes, pausing and listening, we cautiously advanced. Here were groups of dead which we passed without pause, except where we thought there might be some of our own company; then we turned up their faces to the starlight for recognition.

At one place near the pike was a group of Confederate dead around the wheels of a broken limber-box. We were about to pass on when we heard a smothered groan.

"Some one," whispered Crandall, as he proceeded to examine the group, "is alive here! This is him! Where ye hurt, old feller?"

"Water!" feebly gasped the wounded man.

I held the head of the poor fellow, and put my canteen to his lips.

"Here! you give him a little of this commissary with the water; it may revive him. Be careful, now! Ye want to know where he's hurt before ye fool around moving him much, or you'll do him more harm than good."

I didn't approve of the use of liquors, but I gave the wounded man some whiskey mixed with water from Crandall's cup. He uttered a deep sigh, and once more called for water. I gave him another drink, propped up his head with a blanket, and was about to leave him, when he faintly said, "Oh, please don't leave me here to die!"

"We are Yanks!" said I. "Shall we take you to our surgeon, and let him see to you? Where are you wounded?"

"My side! Oh, don't," he groaned, "leave me here!"

"Give him another sip o' that ere brandy," ordered Sergeant Crandall, "and put your blanket under him, and get him down to the road. Don't jolt him. Better wind a strip of this blanket around that wounded place."

A blanket was quickly put under the wounded man, poles were fixed to it for carrying, and Standish and I carried him down to the road without accident, and were fortunate in getting him into an ambulance at once.

We returned, and, cautiously advancing through the west wood, soon came to the scene of the morning's desperate conflict, which had so terribly thinned our ranks.

"The reb picket," whispered Crandall, "is just out there ahead; be careful now!"

Here we found more of our wounded men than we had thought possible, as well as several wounded Confederates, to whom we gave drink as to our own men. One of the Confederates said sorrowfully in a hoarse whisper, "Our folks have been here, and didn't offer to help me!"

In several instances we found our dead stripped of their outer clothing. As we advanced towards the open land, two or three shots came from the Confederate pickets, which were close at hand, in the edge of the wood. We sent a score of our men to the road, and even rescued some that were in the edge of the clearing. The pickets, probably aware of the nature of our mission, did not fire upon us again.

One of the wounded told me that a Confederate had been among them, giving them water, and at the same time had rifled the pockets of the dead.

All through the war I found the Confederates sharp plunderers. A battle won often meant to the poor fellows, food, Yankee watches, books, jackknives, and overcoats; while the Yanks, on the other hand, did not consider a dead Confederate worth attention for such a purpose. One can scarcely blame destitute men for thus compensating themselves for their services, as plunder was often the most valuable of anything they received.

It was about twelve o'clock at night when we again reached the hill where our regiment was encamped; and I was then too tired to think of the saddening scenes narrated, or for any thought or feeling other than a desire to rest. My sleep was dreamless, and so profound that when I was awakened it seemed to me I had but just closed my eyes the moment before.

It is because of this ability to sleep and quickly recuperate, if for no other, that boys often make the best soldiers. They can rest when older men are too tired and nerve-strained to do so. As Add put it, " A good soldier should be able to put in licks at eating and sleeping every time he gets a chance."

The men were soon astir all over camp, getting their breakfast of hardtack, pork, and coffee. Add on this occasion growled and complained of the

loss of his fry-pan, as if it were the principal loss
of the battle. "I might 'a' made a son-of-a-gun
if I'd had it. 'What's that?' Why, hardtack
soaked in water and fried with a little molasses
on 'em."

After breakfast was over the veterans lit their
brier-wood pipes, and began to smoke as if they
had a contract for it, drawing contentment from
the pipes, as Tobin said, "at the rate of forty yards
a minute."

" We may's well get in a good smoke before the
racket begins," said Crandall. " You can't seem
ter sense your smoke when you are in a fight.
The Cap feels pretty sore 'cause our reserves
across the river ain't hurried up; says we shall
need 'em ter drive the rebs into the Potomac;
believes we can do it too."

" Looked as if we should be drove into Tophet
yisterday about this time," growled an old vet
with provoking incredulity; "talk about drivin'
them!"

" Well, yes," said Crandall, scowling and pok-
ing the fire reflectively and slowly. " You see,
that place we got inter yesterday was a key-pint
of this battle-field, and the rebs knew it, and got
in some of their best work to back us out."

" Kicked us out, I guess yer mean," said Add
half seriously. " I don't believe in them keys. I
never see a plaguy mean, hard spot since I've been
in the army but what there was a key layin' round

near 'nough ter get men killed as fast 's they got there! Yesterday while fumblin' around for the key of this field we got licked; and, by jiminy! them rebs sp'iled the best little fry-pan in the army, and — killed a good many of our boys, too!"

"Well, boys, it ain't any use for us to growl or feel sore," said a voice back of us. I turned, and found Captain Grim, rather pale from his hurt, who had come up and was standing behind us. He had his wounded arm bandaged and in a sling. "We did our work like men," he continued, "and it wasn't our fault we didn't whip the rebs. My own opinion is, if we had had two or three regiments on our flanks to protect them, we shouldn't have got into the scrape, and would 'a' ben able to have given them as good as they sent. I heard some of our big officers say that General Sumner's an old cavalry officer, an' can't git fixed ideas out of his head; an' one of 'em is that infantry can get in a tight place, and cut its way out like cavalry. Oh, that arm," he said, smiling, seeing me glance toward the wounded member; "I suppose I shall have to wash and dress it like a baby for some-time. It's pretty comfortable now, though."

I listened respectfully to our wounded captain; but Crandall was heard to growl, "Well, we did cut out — them that weren't cut down."

Captain Grim then turned to me and said, "The Centerboro' boys all did well. Stuck to it, and obeyed orders like old soldiers, and I am proud of my men."

I winced, and replied, "I guess I was pretty well frightened; but I hope I didn't show it, Captain!"

The captain smiled, and said, "There wasn't a man of us who did his duty any better or more coolly. You only make the same confession that a good many others would make if they told the truth."

In answer to my inquiry as to how the battle had gone on the right, he informed me that Burnside's attack was not made early enough, and then it took his corps four or five hours to cross the bridge opposite the town; and when he had advanced he understood that he had neglected to protect his left flank, and had been attacked there by a Confederate force, and compelled to fall back.

It is now known that the attacking column of Confederates which decided the battle under Burnside on our left, was A. P. Hill's division, which had just come up from Harper's Ferry, having made a march of seventeen miles that afternoon. Thus it was that twice that day at Antietam a Federal division was broken for want of protection to its flanks, — once under Sumner, and again under Burnside.

There was some firing on our front, but not active battle, all the morning; and at last we heard that a truce to bury the dead had been agreed upon. It is now known that Lee used the time so gained to make preparations for his retreat across the Potomac.

That day we, with others, went out on the field to bury the dead and care for the wounded; and sorrowful indeed were the sights that met our eyes. The private soldier, concentrating his attention to the small focus of individual action, does not, during a battle, see the terrible whole which is presented to his sight when afterwards passing over the field. In the cornfield where Hooker had attacked and receded, the sight was dreadful. Friend and foe lay side by side, and reddened the blades of corn with their blood.

On the left, in a sunken road which had been enfiladed by a Union battery while crowded by Confederates, the dead lay in masses, piled across each other as they had fallen. On the same road men were found suspended on the board fence, where they had been shot while attempting to get over.

In another place, where the Confederates had made a desperate stand, they lay as regularly as if they had fallen on dress parade.

Almost every wall and fence was lined with a windrow of the dead. All over the field were broken caissons, crushed wheels, muskets, bayonets, dead horses, and men; some in groups, others lying singly, scattered in dreadful confusion.

Around one broken limber-box I counted twelve dead Confederate artillery men, who stood faithfully to their work, till shot down in the performance of their duty.

Captain Grim had thought it best to put himself under a surgeon at a hospital in our rear, and late that afternoon I accompanied him.

" 'T ain't much of a hospital," explained Captain Grim ; "nothing but a barn and house, with a few out-buildings. I'm in the barn ; got one of the horse-stalls : and a nice shakedown of fresh hay don't go bad for a bed, I tell you ! "

" I don't suppose you will remain there long," I said, " will you? "

" Well, I'll let them tinker on the arm while we are here ; but I expect to go when the company does. They want to send me to Frederick City, but I guess I won't go."

On arriving at the hospital, I found a hundred wounded — Confederates as well as Federals — in the house and farm-buildings.

On the barn floor men were laid, some twenty in number, in two rows, next to the stalls. The barn floor was the choice place of all the accommodations for the wounded, as there they had not only shelter, but plenty of fresh air.

" I've noticed," said Grim, " all during my army experience, that wounded men recover faster in the open air than in a house, barn, or tent, which shows that pure air is a prime thing to hasten recovery from wounds. So I've split the difference, and we keep the doors wide open."

After visiting the barn, my attention was called to the rough amputating-tables, where the surgeons, with their sleeves rolled up to the shoulders, were engaged in amputating arms and legs, and in other surgical duties.

Each surgeon was attended by several assistants. Squads of men were also at work caring for the wounded as they came from the surgeon's hands.

" It looks cruel and bloody, although it is really a work of mercy," said Grim. Then, with his bull-dog smile, he added, " They thought of taking my arm off, but concluded to let it be."

The most desperate cases were being carried to a table just at one side of the one I was viewing; and to this Grim turned, saying, —

" Here's the boss. They'd 'a' cut my arm off but for him."

The surgeon mentioned was carefully drawing together the bones of an arm (from which he had removed the shattered pieces) with a silver wire. " A case of resection," I heard him say to his attendant. " I think he'll be able to use his arm by and by nearly as well as if the whole bone were there." I at once recognized the voice as that of my old friend Dr. Milner. I spoke to him; and he recognized me at once, saying, " Well, Jack, at my old business, you see!" Then, after a moment,

as another subject for amputation was brought to
his table, he said, "You'll find May in the house
there; go in and see her. She's got her hands
full. She'll be glad to see you. We came over
here from Frederick only yesterday. She was one
of my helpers for a while, but had too much
sympathy for the men under the knife to be
first-class."

I turned to the house, and stood at the open
door of a large room, unobserved, for a while, looking at Miss May as she softly moved about like
a ministering angel among our poor fellows. To
all, as she gave them attention, she gave hopeful
smiles, which, as it seemed to me, filled the room
with sunshine and with a spiritual atmosphere,
brighter than sunshine itself.

I had expected to see her worn with her dreadful work; but when I caught a glimpse of her face
it was serene and healthful, but it also had a new
beauty which seemed to come from within, as light
is seen through a transparency.

"Miss Milner!" As I called she turned; and, on
recognizing me, her face lit up with a lovely smile,
and she extended her hands in welcome. She had
grown mature, and was more beautiful than ever;
but talked, after her first greeting, as she went
from patient to patient, in her old sunny, familiar
way.

The poor wounded fellows followed her with
their eyes as she went about the room, as if the

very sight helped them to bear their pain; and one young Confederate said, looking towards her, " It seems to me, Yank, that she's an angel!"

I spoke to him about his wound, and was not long in discovering that he was the same wounded officer that we had brought in on the evening of the battle. I had a friendly talk with him; and he said, " I'm a Virginian, sar. Proud of it, sar!" And then with an air of patronage, said, " I won't forget you."

During my conversation with Miss May I learned that she and her father had been at Fairfax, and afterward at Frederick City, attending to the wounded.

" Miss May," I ventured to say, " it is very kind and good of you to attend to these poor fellows; but is it quite the proper place for a young lady like you?"

She turned her flashing eyes on me, and said sharply, " I don't care whether it is proper or not!" Then added more softly, " It is merciful, and work that an angel might do among suffering men. I don't think of myself. If I did I couldn't do this. But where will I ever have a chance to do so much good again?"

There was around her such an atmosphere of purity, and in her face shone an iridescent light as if of heaven itself, that I could only stammer out an excuse for my question.

" God bless ye, mim!" said a wounded Irish

soldier; "yer eyes is all the light we want in this room!"

May laughed, and said teasingly, "But you wanted to light your pipe just now, Mike; and my eyes would have been a poor substitute for the matches I gave you."

"Whin ye's near enough to light me pipe by the eyes of ye," said Mike, "shure, I can do without smoking."

I stayed for an hour, and then, God forgive me, was almost jealous of the attentions she lavished on those poor boys, yet still blessing her in my heart for her goodness to my unfortunate comrades.

I was bidding her good-day when the doctor came in; and then remembering about meeting Raymond, I said, "By the way, Doctor, I saw your friend Raymond at Frederick City."

"Ah!" ejaculated the doctor, glancing significantly at May. "What was he doing there?"

"Selling newspapers," I replied; "and he was dressed in an old suit, and had on a slouch hat drawn down over his eyes. He was either dead broke or disguised. Looks to me as if he was acting the part of a rebel spy."

The doctor smiled and looked towards Miss May, who, I thought, seemed confused. Neither made any reply, but turned the conversation; and by that I inferred that they had seen him, or had known of his being in Frederick City.

" What is it," I queried to myself, " that they know about him?"   It is not possible that either the doctor or Miss May is disloyal?   No ; that is impossible!"   And so I dismissed the matter from my further consideration as I bade them good-day.

CHAPTER XV.

THE UNEXPECTED.

The day after the battle, McClellan, although urged by his corps commanders to attack the enemy at once, granted Lee a truce for the day, in which to bury his dead. It was generally expected by men of all ranks that on the morning of the 18th of September the battle would be renewed.

The day, however, was spent in burying the dead, bringing up re-enforcements, and making preparations for the expected battle.

When the morning of another beautiful day dawned, we were aroused at an early hour, and ate our breakfasts with the confident expectation of at once attacking the Confederates.

"Spect we shall go for them Johnnies, an' finish 'em up, or be finished up by 'em, pretty soon," said Corporal Osgood, in the growling tone characteristic of an old soldier. "I wish Captain Grim was with us!"

"The first lieutenant," I remarked, "is in command, I suppose!"

"Ye-e-s!" said Osgood, shutting one eye as

if to tighten some invisible screw of thought
thereby, puffing at his pipe contemplatively, and
speaking between whiffs. "He's young, — got
grit enough. Lacks judgment, perhaps; makes
men toe the mark, though: he'd stand up and
be shot down's if that's what he's made for — and
plague take it! he expects everybody else to do
it, and like to do it, too! Well, yes, he is good.
Pious, did yer say? Well, I guess! Pray the
harness right off a mule. I heard him prayin' fer
me once, after one of my swearin' fits; kinder
made me 'shamed. What's up?" he exclaimed
excitedly, jumping to his feet, and standing with
pipe in hand. "What's that cheerin' for?"

From the direction of Sharpsburg there came
cheers, at first faintly borne on the air, but growing louder and louder every moment.

"Humph!" said Add; "guess it's McClellan
riding along the lines!"

"No 't ain't," said Osgood. "It comes from too
many directions. Do you hear that?"

A little later we learned that the Rebel army
had retreated from Sharpsburg across the Potomac
during the night, and that it was the reception
of this news that caused the cheering that we had
heard.

"Can't see anything to cheer at," said Crandall
grimly. "The rebs have given us the slip, an'
they must have been kinder used up or they
wouldn't have been in such a hurry. The fact

that they've got away shows that we had ought to have been after them before this."

It is now known that Lee's army was at this time in very bad shape, and that it was only because of good luck and good fighting, and our general's blunders, that he had held his lines intact on the 17th of September. He had, in his campaign against Pope, lost thirty thousand of the seventy thousand men that made up his army when he left Richmond, and was so badly crippled by the battle just fought, that he used the truce granted by McClellan to make preparations for retreat.

It is now apparent, that, had he been pushed on the 18th with all the resources at our command, he must have been beaten, and possibly annihilated.

Tactically Antietam was a drawn battle; but to an invader a drawn battle is itself a defeat. It compelled Lee to abandon the invasion, and gather and recuperate his shattered army in Virginia. He had started out on this campaign with high aspirations, and had been compelled to turn back, his hopes and plans defeated, — driven from Maryland.

Fault has been found with McClellan for not urging the fight on the 18th of September. He formed his judgment on what he then knew, and not on what he learned afterwards; and in this violated no received principles of war.

It is claimed by the Confederates, that they

fought the battle with less than forty thousand
men; yet on the 20th of the October following
they had 67,808 men on the rolls of the army.
The Richmond *Examiner* of September 20th credits
Lee with sixty thousand on the field of Antietam.

Lee's army no doubt lost largely, as he claims,
by desertion; but probably not a larger propor-
tionate number than did the Federals. It is
doubtful if our army had over sixty thousand
men present for duty on that field. They attacked the Confederates in a strong, defensive
position selected by Lee himself, considering
which, this does not show a large disproportion
in the forces engaged; especially when we consider that the Fifth and Sixth Corps, numbering
in all nearly thirty thousand men, were but little
used.

That morning I, with Add, went over the field
where the battle had raged, and saw its heart-
sickening work. Squads of Union men were
burying the dead. Where the names of these
were known, the graves were rudely marked with
headboards, mostly made from cracker-boxes.
Hundreds of Confederates lay on the field still
unburied. It is officially claimed that over two
thousand of them were buried by Union troops.

In the woods by the Hagerstown pike they lay
singly or in groups among the ledges and by the
fences where they had fought.

The people of Sharpsburg who remained there

seemed glad to see the Union soldiers, and exhibited their joy by bringing out their hidden stores of cake and pies for our entertainment. They seemed to have no tender remembrances of their Confederate guests.

Said one woman, " Thank God, them thieves have gone! They ate up everything I had in my house."

" Where," I inquired, " were you? "

" Down in my cellar," she said, with tears of vexation in her eyes; "and that was the meanest thing about it! They advised me to go down there, 'cause they said it was the safest place in the house; and then they ate up all my victuals, and carried off everything in the house, even my best dress."

" Marm," said Add respectfully, but with a humorous twinkle in his eyes, " my experience is, that when a soldier is hungry his conscience don't work, — grub gets the best of it; and then they ain't particular, neither, where their grub comes from, so long as they git it. But as for dresses, — well, I guess that was an afterthought of them Johnnies."

The woman showed us a part of her dwelling where shell had exploded during the action, while her fence had in it marks of bullets, evidently fired by Union troops. The limbs and twigs of an apple orchard had been trimmed of their leaves.

In one of the churches there were a number of desperately wounded Confederates. It was the part of mercy as well as good sense to leave such behind, since their removal would have endangered their lives, while proper medical attention, which they were sure to receive from our surgeons, would save many of them.

The wounded were in a pitiable condition, having received only casual attention from any one since the previous evening. Add and I brought them water, and gave them all the food we had in our haversacks.

One of these wounded men was a young Confederate artillery officer, not over twenty years of age. I gave him water, and was turning away, when he said, —

"Now will you please get me something to eat? I'm hungry." His look and appeal were so straightforward and frank, that I replied, "I'll try."

So I went to a house near by, and bought some bread, eggs and milk and butter, and returned to the poor fellow. After eating, and drinking some milk, he said, "That's right good, and I feel better already." ·

"It will give you fever," I said, "to eat too heartily."

He smiled, and replied, "I am posted in such matters; my father is a surgeon. I needed this food, and feel that now I shall get around all right. Our surgeon," he said with a smile, "thought I wouldn't need anything long. I am going to make a live of it, though, if I *have* got a bullet right through me."

There was something very attractive and manly about the fellow, and I somehow felt that I had known him a much longer time than a few moments. Getting some hay from a neighboring barn to make him a more comfortable bed, and filling my canteen for him, I gave it to him, trusting to luck to find another on the battle-field.

As I turned to leave, he said, pointing to my name •printed in ink on the canteen strap, "Is that your name?"

"Yes," I replied.

"Well, I shall know you if I ever meet you again, John Alden." Then extending his hand, he said, "Thank you. It's all I've got to give, so I owe you something."

On my return I passed down a road on the east of the town, and thence across lots to the Hagerstown road. Just before I reached it my attention was attracted by the whinny of a horse. It was a wounded mare which had been fastened by a long halter to a broken artillery ammunition box. The poor creature had eaten the grass close to the ground for a radius of six or seven feet. Her look was almost human in its pitiful, pleading expression, which said as plain as speech could say, "Can't you help me?"

"Shoot the poor thing," said Add, "and put her out of her misery!" But, as we did not have our muskets with us, this could not be done. I untied her, however, and slowly led her to a pool near by, where she drank as if she had been without water for a long time.

There were two ugly wounds in her left shoulder and in her leg; but, although she limped badly, I thought the bone had not been broken. As there was good grass near the pool, I turned her loose, and she at once began to feed. As I turned to leave, the creature whinnied and came hobbling towards me, as if to follow. There was such an appealing look in her eyes, that I returned, petted and talked to her, and examined more minutely her wounds. One was a bullet-wound, and, although clotted with blood, I could see that the bullet had passed through the lower part of the leg.

The other was ragged and ugly, and was evidently the work of a piece of shell. I was now loath to leave her, and said to Add, "I'll get her up to camp or to the hospital!"

Add laughed, and said, "Well, you've got a nightmare; but I won't wait till night for you," and started on. Meanwhile I led the little mare slowly along to the pike, and then up the road, until I came to the house and barn where Dr. Milner was. This took more than an hour.

I found both the doctor and Miss May busy

" The creature whinnied and came hobbling towards me."
— Page 178.

with their patients. After the usual greeting, I heard a voice from the corner of the room, as if some one was trying to attract my attention, and presently May said, " Here's a man who knows you by your voice. He says you helped him off the field in the night."

The wounded man proved to be the Confederate officer we had found near the broken caisson, and had brought in the night after the battle. He was doing well, and seemed very grateful for the help he had received from " you uns, Yanks," as he called us.

After telling Dr. Milner and Miss May about the wounded Confederates I had seen at the church in Sharpsburg, and specially mentioning the young officer to whom I had given my canteen in the church, I asked them to visit the poor fellows.

" Humph ! " said the doctor. " There are lots of country doctors and citizens fooling around here, and if they don't manage to kill those fellows down in Sharpsburg before I get there I'll do what I can for them."

After this conversation I ventured to make known my principal errand, which was to get Miss May interested in the horse. So I told her the incident rather more in detail than I have given it here.

I must have told the story well ; for the phlegmatic doctor looked interested, and tears filled

Miss May's eyes. I concluded by saying, " Come out and see her; she is a beautiful little creature." They both followed me to the barn. Dr. Milner carefully examined the wounds of the horse, and finally said, " Pretty bad wounds, but she'll come around as good as new after a while, if they are dressed properly. What say, May? Will you take care of her? "

May, who had been petting and admiring her, said, " Yes; oh, yes! And how good of you, Alden, to bring her here ! "

" You see, Jack, all is fish that comes to our net," said the doctor teasingly. " If one wants to recommend himself to May, he must get half killed, or find something as a substitute."

Miss May had already begun with basin and sponge to dress the mare's wounds; and the intelligent creature seemed to understand, and to appreciate her kindness.

I now remembered that I had not met Captain Grim; but as I was inquiring of the doctor for him he came up.

" You want to keep pretty still, and not hurt that arm, Captain," said the doctor, rather crossly, I thought. " Your wound will be all right in two or three months."

" Months, Doctor ! " exclaimed Grim. " What's the matter with my doing duty now? "

" Humph ! " ejaculated the surgeon; " you are as uneasy as a stump-tailed bull in fly-time, and if you ain't careful you'll have trouble. Let me see."

The doctor unrolled the bandages, and exclaimed crossly, "Just as I expected, inflamed and irritated! Haste makes waste, Captain. You'll lose that arm if you are not more easy with it; then 't will take a year to cure you, and cost a limb besides."

The captain listened with his bull-dog smile, and said, "Well, I suppose I am under orders, and I mustn't waste Uncle Sam's property; kinder guess I *had* better go a little slower."

"You are to go to Frederick City Hospital from here," said Dr. Milner. "I know the head surgeon there, and will speak a good word for you."

When I returned to the yard, Miss May was just completing her work for the horse, with beautiful solicitude, by winding a bandage around the foreleg.

"She has been made a great pet of by some one," said May.

Before leaving I once more commended the wounded officer at Sharpsburg to her care, and said, "My pass has almost expired, and I must report for duty once more." I went to the horse and petted her affectionately, and said to Miss May, "Take good care of the little beast."

I shook hands with May, and was moving away, when the intelligent creature whinnied, as if to say, "Don't leave me."

"I declare, I'm jealous," said May. "She has fallen in love with you." And I knew by the tender look in Miss May's eyes that the little mare would lack no care.

I returned to the regiment, and gave Lieutenant Mason a message from Captain Grim. Later I met Sergeant Crandall, who seemed, by the expression on his face, to have unusual worry on his mind.

"Look here: Jack," he called out, — "Sergeant, I should have said, — I've been looking for you."

"Well, here I am!" I exclaimed nervously, for I was alarmed. "What is it?"

"Well, see here, I've been recommended by the colonel as second lieutenant, plague it! I should make a purty kinder of a sorter looking second lieutenant, shouldn't I?" he said, almost pathetically. "I make a tolerable good orderly-sergeant, but what a thundering fool I'd look in a second lieutenant's uniform! I'm goin' to ask Captain Grim to send in your name instead of mine, if you're willin'."

"Me!" I exclaimed; "I have all I can do to fill the place of second sergeant, and I mistrust that I only rattle around in it as it is."

"Well, now you've hit it, my boy! It takes a thunderin' sight more brains to fill a second sergeant's place than it does a second lieutenant's. Besides, you'd make a good appearance among the officers, and I should be as awkward as a cow in a schoolhouse learning g'ography! Orderly-sergeant's place is good 'nough for me! I don't want promotion backwards."

His distress was so real, that to gratify him, and because I believed the application would never amount to anything, I assented to his appeal, and for the time thought no more of it.

On the 22d we marched away from Antietam through Sharpsburg.

I had been too busy for any chance to seek either Doctor Milner or his daughter again, and should not have seen them at all but for unexpectedly meeting them in Sharpsburg as we were marching through. We made a brief halt near the Lutheran church, where I visited the Confederate wounded. Hearing my name called, I turned towards the sidewalk, and saw both the doctor and his daughter.

"I've got some news for you," said May. "The boy you helped in the church is my brother Jim!"

"Yes," chimed in the doctor; "I believe you saved his life."

"Forward — march!" came the order, and there was no further opportunity for conversation, much as I wished it.

CHAPTER XVI.

CAMPAIGNING IN VIRGINIA.

WE were sorry to bid adieu to the loyal and hospitable people of Sharpsburg. More especially did I regret leaving in the midst of so interesting an interview. But no one can become a good soldier until he has learned unquestioning obedience; and he becomes valuable as such, just in proportion as he studies to comprehend and obey, in letter and spirit, the orders of his superiors. He seldom knows of the plans or purposes of such orders, except such as are apparent on the face of them : he makes shrewd guesses, that is all.

As Captain Grim once sarcastically said, when I had inquired of him the purpose of an order, " The general hasn't called on me to explain his plans ; a man is a better soldier, officer, or citizen, who learns to execute the orders he receives without trying to fix them over because he don't comprehend them."

Leaving Sharpsburg, we marched down the east bank of the Potomac ; climbed the narrow, crooked roads that wind around the foot of the mountains ; passed under Maryland Heights; across the bridge built on the abutments of the ruined railroad bridge; then on through the weather-stained town of Harper's Ferry to Bolivar Heights, where we encamped.

Here we entered upon a much-needed season of recuperation, rest, and enjoyment. We swapped our coffee, tea, hardtack, and other provisions, for eggs, poultry, and milk. We also made delicious corncakes·by grating corn from the cob on graters made by punching holes through tin plates and half-canteens. The hominy obtained in this manner seemed the sweetest I had ever eaten.

While food was plenty with the army, the veteran members of the regiment were not well provided with shoes and necessary clothing. Their uniforms were faded and ragged; and generally they had no changes of underclothing, a thing essential in checking the encroachments of certain unpleasant invaders.

The autumn air was soft and beautiful with sunshine. The people on the Maryland side, especially in Pleasant Valley, were hospitable and friendly. They sold provisions willingly, and often gave to the soldiers without pay.

The reader may not understand, unless I explain, that when a soldier has no real duties, his imagination and legs both gravitate towards something good to eat. After obtaining it, he cooks it in unheard-of combinations in the attempt to produce a sensation for his palate. It was while on one of these "raids," as Add termed them, in pursuit of the almost unattainable luxury of something new and strange, that we found ourselves on Maryland Heights.

We forgot even our appetites in the unexpectedly beautiful view which spread out before us. At our feet, weather-beaten and gray from war's neglect, was Harper's Ferry, with the surrounding hills frowning down upon it. The waters of the Shenandoah meet the broader Potomac around the promontory where the little town is built, and then, as if joyful at their union, flow on towards the ocean, flashing and gleaming in the sunlight.

Looking towards the north-west, we saw the Union encampments dotting with white the vast furrow, two miles from edge to edge, known as Pleasant Valley. Mingled with the white tents were cosey farmhouses, brick mills, barns, and shocks of yellow grain and corn, green fields, dark woods, mottled orchards, and a stream gleaming like a silver thread through the lowlands. Over all this hung a veil-like haze of blue, softening the outlines of this beautiful picture framed in by hills rock-ribbed with age. I found myself unconsciously repeating, as I stood there, Whittier's beautiful verses, —

> "Yet calm and patient Nature keeps
>   Her ancient promise well,
> Though o'er her bloom and greenness sweeps
>   The battle breath of hell.

Still in the cannon's pause we hear
Her sweet thanksgiving psalm ;
Too near to God for doubt or fear,
She shares the eternal calm."

Here on the extreme apex of the Blue Ridge, two thousand feet above the level of the sea, we found a station of the signal corps. It was an open tent; and on it was posted a warning not to ask questions or touch the instruments, which showed, as Add said, that a good many New England Yankees had been there before us.

The man of the signal corps was talking with an invisible station far away on the southern hills. The talking was carried on with flags. A flag with large black figures on a white background is waved so many times to the right, so many to the left; and then a different one takes its place, and rises and falls in turn. By these combinations in flags, messages of from one to three words a minute are signalled. This is one of the methods by which armies communicate with each other. The stations are often twenty miles, or more, apart.

A few evenings after this, while we were on dress parade, Captain Grim's promotion as major of the regiment was read in general orders. Great satisfaction was expressed by most of the members of our regiment at this deserved promotion, although our company was loath to lose him as its captain. Our corps commander was also changed; and it was rumored that we were to have new brigade and division commanders. The former was to be an officer from a Western regiment, whose name we could not learn.

I was introduced to this officer sooner than official etiquette demanded, because of a scrape Add got into while on one of his favorite "raids."

Near our quarters was a fine residence, surrounded by shade-trees, with an attractive row of beehives between the house and the servants' quarters.

I knew well enough by casual remarks, and by the way Add looked at those beehives, that his mouth was made up for some honey. Now, in my experience in the army, it had always seemed that when a soldier desired anything which belonged to a peaceful person, he began by endeavoring to get his conscience in harmony with his inclinations. The usual method was to declare the possessor an "old Secesh." Having thus satisfied his conscience, he proceeded to take that which his heart craved.

But I could never get over the prejudice, in war or peace, that when a person takes anything that does not belong to him, he is a thief, "living on the enemy," "foraging," or any other term invented to cover the theft, to the contrary notwithstanding. So when Add proposed that I should join him in stealing a beehive, I refused.

"That old Secesh has got more venom in him

than a rattlesnake," said Add; "I'll bet he's out with his shotgun playing guerilla half the time nights. I went there to try and buy some honey this morning; said he hadn't got any. Said our general had engaged his quarters there; that was to scare me, yer see!"

Soon after I saw Add, accompanied by Tobin, go in a matter-of-course, businesslike way towards the beehives, throw a poncho over one of them, and move at double-quick away with it. Just as they got well started, a bee crawled up Tobin's sleeve and stung him. He dropped the hive as quickly as if he had been touched with a red-hot iron; the hive capsized on the ground, and the bees came out to make inquiries.

Add threw himself on the ground, and they mostly passed over him; but the duck-legged Tobin ran, with the angry bees striking at all parts of his person. Waving his arms like a windmill, he struck at the assaulting bees. Before him was a duck-pond. This pond had a green scum on its surface, was about five feet deep, and had an indescribable sediment at its bottom.

To get out of the way of the bees, Tobin threw himself into this pond and swam; finding the bees still stinging him, he dived!

This was not all; the uproar had drawn the owner and the servants from the house; and Add and Tobin were caught in the act, and identified by the marks put upon them by the bees. Add had escaped with very light punishment, having only been stung on his nose and under one eye.

The old gentleman who owned the hives made a complaint, however, to the new general of our brigade, who, unknown to us, had arrived that morning, and taken up his quarters there.

The general sent a file of men to arrest the culprits, and to my chagrin I was included in the summons; for, although innocent of everything except seeing the fracas, I was near, and was supposed to be an accomplice.

We were all marched under guard to the house. On the way I angrily complained to Add for bringing me into what I called a "dirty scrape." Tobin was dripping with the filth of the goose-pond, and was far from savory, while his face was one swollen mass of bee-stings.

"'T is too bad, I swan!" drawled Add. "Here's Tobin ain't fit to go into high society, like briga-diers; besides, I can't take my oath as ter who he is, he looks and smells so unnatural. 'T would take that whole row o' plaguy beehives to sweeten him!"

By this time Tobin had got near enough to Add to rub some of the filth off on him, saying in mock sympathy, "Sergeant, how's yer eye?"

On the back veranda sat the general, smoking, and making himself comfortable with liquid re-freshments. The guard saluted; so did we. The general returned the salute, and with his hand waved the guard back, and said in strangely familiar tones, which I at once recognized, —

"What's this I hear? Stealing from this good man? Tut, tut! bad business! Non-commissioned officers, two of you! What have you got to say for yourselves?"

He threw back his head, swaying it from right to left, and with a humorous compression of the lips continued "What shall I do with you, gentlemen, when you break all the Ten Commandments, and would break more than ten if you could? Whew!" he exclaimed, ordering Tobin to get farther to the rear; then turning to me, he asked, "What is your name, Sergeant?"

"John Alden, sir," I replied.

In a flash he recognized me, rose to his feet, and shook hands with me in his old expansive fashion; for the new general was Blusterson of the Industrial Museum.

He turned to the old gentleman, and exclaimed, "Why, I know this young gentleman and all his relations, sir! He is honor and honesty itself! I know all his family! Here, I'll do myself the honor to be responsible for him, and pay for the honey, sir!" And with this he waved the old gentleman off the veranda. Then turning to me, he said, "Alden, my boy, glad to see you!" Then to Tobin and Add, who were standing in open-mouthed astonishment, he exclaimed, "Not guilty! But don't you do it again! You owe it to the

friendly interest of Sergeant Alden that you are
not punished. Go to your quarters!"

When they had gone the general invited me to
be seated; and at his request I told him the whole
story of the raid on the beehives. He laughed
heartily (for he had a keen sense of humor), de-
claring it was worth a ten-dollar bill. The only
mention of the Industrial Museum was when I
spoke of the notes that he had sent me. When I
explained the trouble with my uncle Richard, and
asked him to make the notes payable to my order,
he at once promised to do so. Soon after this I
wrote to my brother, asking him to send them to
me by mail.

" Why is it," he asked, " that you have not received a commission before this?"

" I've been recommended as second lieutenant of
my company, General," I replied; " but am afraid
I am not qualified."

" Qualified!" exclaimed the general. " We've
got to take a load on our shoulders first, and then
learn to carry it. Dive in, and trust to luck about
coming out! I'll indorse that recommendation
for your promotion, only I'll make it first lieutenant instead of second."

" Lieutenant Mason," I said, " holds that position in the company, General."

" Mason; let me see," said General Blusterson,
taking a memorandum book from his pocket, and
consulting it. " He's been recommended for ad-

vancement. Is he a friend of yours? Well, we'll have him commissioned as captain, to make room for you."

By this time some of the general's staff had come up; and to them he introduced me as Lieutenant Alden, adding, "He hasn't got his uniform yet." Among these was a regular army second lieutenant named King; one of those young fellows with a waxed mustache, and a conceited air which is so distasteful to men who pride themselves on merit, and not appearances.

As I turned to go to my quarters, somewhat dazed by the occurrences of the morning, the general, as he returned my respectful salute. said, "Come again, Lieutenant. Shall be pleased to see you when I am not officially engaged."

I walked from the veranda, where I had expected arrest, but had received, if not promotion, the promise of it.

There was also a conflict between my liking for Blusterson and my moral disapproval of him. The strong magnetism in his personality controlled me in an undefinable way, as is often the case where the character of the magnet is at variance with our sense of propriety.

Of one thing I had no doubt, that Blusterson would keep his word, and would recommend me for promotion. Was I fit for the place? I queried of myself.

Before I had reached my quarters I had determined to accept the commission if it came to me; and in this determination I was influenced by thoughts of how I should appear in the eyes of Dr. Milner and, — never mind who.

A week afterwards, to the astonishment of my comrades, my name was read in general orders as first lieutenant, while Lieutenant Mason received promotion in the same order as captain of the company.

In a few days I had my uniform; and thenceforth military etiquette obliged me to keep up an official reserve between myself and my old acquaintances in the ranks. A second lieutenant for our company, named Sinclair, was sent to join us. He had seen a little service as private in an artillery regiment stationed near Washington, but, like many of his class, had shown no capacity for his position. For a time he made himself very familiar with the non-commissioned officers and men, but soon exemplified the old adage that "familiarity breeds contempt." It was discovered that he was addicted to drink; and at one time, when reported sick, there was sly talk that he was drunk in his quarters.

General Blusterson proved himself a very able administrative officer, and was spoken of generally in the army as a brave man.

We remained in this delightful locality until November without incident of special note, except a visit from President Lincoln. He was dressed

in a black suit, and his tall form loomed above
the heads of the officers surrounding him. His
face had a worn look, which was almost pathetic
in its sorrowfulness, as if care had long been his
constant companion. When he rode down our
lines his feet seemed almost to dangle to the
ground; and his person, when contrasted with the
brilliantly uniformed men around him, seemed
very homely and plain.

By the last of October the army began to move
forward. Most of the troops crossed the Potomac
at Berlin, five miles below Harper's Ferry; but we
passed up the Shenandoah Valley, and through the
Blue Ridge at Snicker's Gap.

McClellan had at first contemplated pushing
his advance against Lee directly up the Shenandoah Valley. He feared, however, that should
he move east of the Blue Ridge, the enemy, finding the way clear, would again cross into Maryland. At this time, however, high water in the
Potomac had removed this danger, and left the
army free to operate on the east side of the Blue
Ridge. By the 2d of November he crossed, and
advanced due south. These movements were skil-
fully concealed from the enemy by guarding the
passes of the Blue Ridge, and threatening to issue
through them. Lee was thereby compelled to
retain Jackson in the valley.

On the 7th, while on the march, a severe snow-
storm set in, and that night we shivered with cold

under our blankets. We reached Warrenton (the point of concentration for all the corps) about the 9th of November, and went into camp.

Lee had meanwhile sent half his army forward to Culpeper to oppose McClellan's advance in that direction, while the other half was still west of the Blue Ridge.

McClellan now contemplated moving obliquely westward, and interposing his army between the Confederate divisions. Before he could thus interpose, he was removed from command of the army he had fashioned into a mighty host, and which under him had received its first baptism of battle.

The general appointed by President Lincoln to take command in place of McClellan was Ambrose E. Burnside. We were in camp near Warrenton when the change occurred; and it was amid the profound sorrow of his soldiers that McClellan took leave of them.

We remained here for some ten days, during which our new commander consolidated the six corps of the army into three grand divisions of two corps each, and endeavored to gather the reins of control into his hands.

He abandoned the McClellan plan of operation, where he might have advantageously attacked the divided enemy by a few miles' march, and, turning back, marched to another field, where the Confederates were compelled to run and find him.

Burnside paralleled by this move the conduct of General Dumourier in Holland, when in 1793, to use the language of Jomini, " He foolishly abandoned pursuit of the allies to transfer the theatre from the centre to the extreme left of the general field."

On the 15th we marched forward rapidly from Warrenton, until on the 17th of November we reached Falmouth, opposite Fredericksburg, and went into camp in the pine woods, a mile from the Rappahannock River.

CHAPTER XVII.

ON THE RAPPAHANNOCK.

Our march to the Rappahannock was uneventful to me except in one particular. Our baggage-master found a colored boy, about seventeen years of age, asleep in one of his wagons, and, by giving the poor fellow an unmerciful beating, had endeavored to make him understand that the wagon was not, as he expressed it, "meant for nigger lodgings." The boy was as black as soot, and almost as broad as long. His meek submission to the beating had moderated even the rage of the baggage-master, and I soon persuaded him to let the boy off without further punishment.

"What," I inquired of him, "were you doing in the wagon?"

"I'se jist run away from ole massa Johnsing, back dar at Charleston, an' I toted 'long wid you alls; an', boss, it was right smart cold, and I got into de wagon an' go ter sleep 'fore I knows it!"

"What is your name?"

"I'se massa Johnsing's nigger — if he done git me, I reckon; ain't got nudder name!" And he rolled his eyes with a solemn grimace, until the whites of them only were visible.

"Didn't your master," asked the teamster, "use you well, you lampblack ball?"

"Yes, sar! Gib me a heap more to eat than I got since. I toted wid de Yanks all de way fro' Charleston, sar!"

"Wouldn't you have done better," I asked, "to have stayed at home?"

"Golly, boss! I'se run away to freedom!"

He was very stupid, but not stupid enough to be devoid of human instincts. He preferred freedom with the hardest of fare, to slavery with ease and comfort.

On the march he must have kept pretty good run of me; for at night I found him snuggled outside my quarters, in an old horse-blanket, fast asleep.

He attached himself to my fortunes with the tenacity of a sticking-plaster; and it proved as useless to remonstrate with him as it would have been to have scolded my shadow for following me.

He either really had no name other than that he had given me, or for politic reasons refused to give it.

Add, who seemed to see a great deal that was amusing in the solemn black-ball of a fellow, nick-named him Rolly-Pooly; and so, for the lack of a better name, we called him Rolly. He could brush a coat, black boots, and get chickens and other "fixin's" in the most barren localities, and where other foragers reported that there were none. But he developed one very inconvenient trait: he seldom bought anything that I asked him to buy, but bought anything that he fancied, and never returned any money intrusted to him. His reply when asked what he gave for any article would be, " Golly! I dun forgot!" Or he would simply roll his eyes solemnly, until nothing but the whites could be seen, and remain silent.

About the 17th of November the corps arrived on the line of the Rappahannock, and went into camp opposite Fredericksburg, in the woods back of the Lacy House, where General Sumner, then commanding the Right Grand Division, had taken up his quarters. There was ascertained to be a garrison of unknown strength in the city opposite; and we expected that General Burnside would order these divisions, as soon as it was possible, to cross the river.

General Blusterson had said to General Sumner, " Give me some axes, and five or six New England regiments, and I'll put a bridge across the river in twenty-four hours."

It is presumed that Yankee craft (as there were at that time twenty New England regiments in General Sumner's command) was not lacking for such a purpose, and that under a man like General Blusterson a bridge might easily and rapidly have been built.

The reasons that have been given by writers for not crossing the river at that time are that the bridge equipments had not arrived; but this could not have been the real reason, for by the 27th of November there were the materials for two boat-bridges, two hundred and forty feet in length, lying near us, in charge of the New York Volunteer Engineers.

The failure to make a crossing sooner was, in my opinion, owing to the indecision of General Burnside. While here the army received a large mail; but the letter from my brother, containing the notes I had expected, was not among those I received.

About this time Major Grim joined us. He looked quite well, but his wound was not entirely healed. He told me he had been in a Washington hospital, of which Dr. Milner was in charge; that Mrs. Grim had come to Washington, and was still there, assisting Miss Milner in the hospital work.

"That there son of Dr. Milner's," said Grim, "has given them lots of trouble."

"I thought," said I, "he was a very nice fellow!"

"Oh, 'tain't that!" explained the major. "He's a first-rate man; but his wound cured up too quick, and then he was declared exchanged, and insisted upon going back South again, although both his father and his sister wanted him to stay

North until the war is over. He seemed to feel
mighty bad to go; but said it wasn't a matter of
preference, but honor and duty compelled him to
show up in Richmond again. So he's gone back;
and you see what kind of a rebel sardine he is! I
respect him more than I do that other fellow,
though, that's hanging 'round the hospital."

"Who," I asked, "do you mean?"

"Why, that black-eyed fellow you saw at Frederick City! You thought he was a spy. Needn't
worry about that Raymond fellow; he'll stick to
the Union lines as long as Miss Milner does."

Seeing the dubious look on my face, he added, "I
thought that would put a bee in your bonnet, Alden.
She keeps him out of the rebel lines, though."

Our regiment was put on picket-duty opposite
the city, where the narrow river flowed between
the sentinels of the two armies. The Rebel sentinels here wore the Federal uniforms, and at first
we thought them our men.

"I say, Yank!" shouted one of them, who had
put on a Union overcoat which he took from the
man he had just relieved; "if you alls won't shoot
we alls, we alls won't shoot at you alls!"

"All right!" was the response from our picket.
"Fair play now, Johnnie!"

"There's a dog-gonned lot of you alls over
there! Where ye from?"

"We," shouted back Add, "are the 574th Massachusetts! Where are you from?"

"Mississippi," was the response. "We alls are Barksdale men. We knew there was a powerful lot of Yanks, but didn't know thar was so many from Massachusetts."

This informal truce was faithfully kept, not only by us, but by all who succeeded us on the picket-lines on both sides.

"What," shouted one of them, "are ye down hyer fer, anyway?"

"Well," replied Add, who enjoyed the novelty of these impromptu interviews, "we are jest goin' to keep you rebs shivering 'round here till you freeze to death!"

"I'll 'low 'tis mighty cold," rejoined the Confederate. "You'un Yanks have brought yer blamed Yankee weather with yer; but ain't it 'bout time we uns got in our crap o' fitin' fer the season?"

"Look here, Johnnie! this is the kind of weather we have summers up where we come from. We don't mind it."

There was a laugh heard at these sallies, and then a pause, as if this was a knock-down; but one of them finally shouted, "When you'un Yanks come over here, we'll make it so hot fer ye that yer won't need any overcoats forever!"

"And them Johnnies," said Add afterwards, "kept their promise as literally as they did the truce."

An exchange of coffee for tobacco, and hardtack for pones of cornbread, then began, by means of boards rigged up with sails, rudders, and centre-boards, which were sailed from shore to shore. The parties to these exchanges vied with each other in generosity, and the best kind of feeling seemed to prevail.

It was through this means that, when I was off duty one day, there came an open letter addressed to me, which was brought to my quarters. On reading it I found it was from Captain James Milner, and contained a few grateful words to me personally, and a letter to Dr. Milner, which the captain requested me to forward to his father.

This was about the 28th or 29th of November, and was the first intimation we had that Long-street's corps had arrived at that point. We knew that Captain Milner's regiment was of that corps.

Shortly after this, conversations and exchange of courtesies were stopped by officers on the other side.

Every day there were new indications of an impending battle. Among these were, that the streets of Fredericksburg began to be filled with vehicles of all kinds and patterns loaded with the household goods of the people who were moving out to avoid the dangers of battle. The Heights back of the city each day grew blacker with men, engaged in constructing earthworks and mounting artillery.

It seemed strange to more than mere under-officers and privates, that if an attack was contemplated by our general, so much time was given the Confederates for preparations. It has since been learned that Longstreet's corps of Lee's army did not arrive at this point until the 27th of November, and "Stonewall" did not arrive until a day or two previous to the battle.

Opposite to us the shores of the Rappahannock rose abruptly from the river for twenty feet or more, and then gradually ascended to the centre of the city. About a half a mile back of the city were Marye's Heights, skirted at the base by sunken roads. On the Heights were other roads.

On the north or Federal side of the river were Stafford Heights, rising abruptly, and completely commanding the city and intermediate plains. On these Heights were planted one hundred and forty-seven guns; and on these General Burnside depended for preventing the enemy from stopping the construction of bridges for crossing the river.

General Blusterson proposed detailing me as his aid, if Major Grim was willing and could spare me.

"What," asked the major familiarly, "is the matter with that Captain King who is already on your staff?"

"He! He really thinks he is what his name represents. Yes, he's a West Point man; but the conceit on him is an inch thick. He is one of

those literary fellows, and writes verses at every
girl that he gets sight of. He likes to poke sticks
at other people, but don't like the sticks to be
sharpened for him."

The general made up a face, as if some of the
qualities of the person he mentioned had run across
his grain.

Major Grim showed him that because of wounds,
sickness, and furloughs we were short of officers
in the company; and the general agreed with him
that I had better remain with the regiment.

"The general is a good friend of yours," said
Major Grim; "but an aid stands no great chance
of promotion, and just as good or a better chance
to be killed. If I know anything about men, the
old general is a fighter. Any one can see that he
hasn't a cowardly hair on him."

For more than a month we lay before Fredericksburg, the enemy gathering like swarms of ants on
the opposite hills, without a movement being made
by our army to cross the river. It was, as Add
said to me, "as if Burnside was saying to the
enemy, 'I'm giving you plenty of time to fortify
and get ready for us before I surprise you!'"

It grew more and more evident, however, that
we were soon to cross the river in the face of all
this preparation to receive us.

About the 9th of December there was held a
council of corps and brigade commanders, in which
want of confidence in Burnside was expressed.

What officers know, the rank and file usually know; and old soldiers in the ranks are often quicker to see a peril than their superiors.

Although there was a general want of confidence, yet the army was in the mood, as Major Grim said, " To obey orders, if they broke owners."

On the 10th of December General Blusterson came on duty dressed with unusual care. His boots shone, and his buttons had an extra lustre, as if, as Major Grim said, "he was unwilling to be found dead with a dirty shirt on." His manner was as cheerful and happy as when on a former occasion he discounted his notes on State Street, and left Boston.

Added to these indications of a crisis, came the order to issue to all the men sixty rounds of cartridges and three days' rations.

On the evening of the same day I saw the bridge train moving towards the river, which ran, dark and silent, between the hostile armies, giving no hint of the terrible scenes about to be enacted.

That night, on the heights opposite Fredericksburg, I could see a semicircle of the enemy's camp-fires shining through the gathering fog and gloom, like the red glare of danger-signals.

In the darkness of the morning, on the 11th of December, the report of two cannon reverberated with peculiar distinctness. They were the signals of the enemy for concentration, and showed that they had discovered the attempt that was being

made to throw a bridge across the river opposite
the town.

We soon formed in ranks and marched to the
river, where a dark fog, like a funeral shroud,
hung over the plains. An unfinished bridge swung
in the current. The pontoniers were attempting
to finish it. As fast as they advanced with balks
or with chess for covering them, they were shot
down, and fell clattering on the bridge with the
boards or timber, or fell into the river, and were
borne away by the swift but silent current. The
boat parties were shot down in a similar manner.

At last the guns on Stafford Heights opened
on the Mississippi riflemen sheltered in the cellars
and buildings of the town. The uproar was terrible; the discharge of artillery and the crash of
bombs made a great noise, but did not dislodge
the rebel sharpshooters.

Add said it put him in mind of the time when
Uncle Richard's bull attacked a beehive. The
bull roared and pawed the earth, but it didn't hurt
the bees any. The bombardment of a place is
more noisy than effective, and is seldom resorted
to unless real means are lacking.

There were several hours of this impotent uproar,
during which clouds of smoke arose from burning
buildings; and yet the hornet-like sharpshooters
of the enemy stuck undauntedly to their work.

About eleven o'clock the fog cleared, and some-
one at headquarters also had an illumination —
of common-sense.

The scows on which the bridge was to be constructed were filled, pushed off from the shore, and rowed undauntedly into the raining fire. The river was not over two hundred yards wide, but we saw man after man drop his oar and fall dead from his seat before the shore was reached. The passage was won with comparatively small loss.

Thus by a little common-sense and pluck was accomplished by one Michigan and two Massachusetts regiments, what a commander, who threw into Fredericksburg seventy tons of iron, had failed to accomplish.

The bridge was finished by two o'clock, and the crossing of men and munitions began. All hopes of a surprise, however, were at an end.

Three miles down the river, meanwhile, Franklin's Grand Division, numbering nearly one-half of our army, had crossed on two bridges constructed by the regular engineers, with but little loss, although its young and gallant engineer officer, Captain Richard Cross, was mortally wounded while directing his men.

The next day was entirely consumed in crossing and in reconnoitring the enemy, and in driving out the Confederates who had barricaded the upper streets of the city with boxes and barrels filled with soil.

Such were the opening scenes in a battle on which the sun on the morrow went down in blood.

CHAPTER XVIII.

THE BATTLE OPENS.

OUR brigade crossed to the city, and about sundown went into position on one of the upper streets, near where the Confederates had erected the barricades before mentioned.

They opened on us a sharp fire of musketry; but fortunately wounded only one member of our company, my old friend Add, who was slightly hurt by a bullet.

Our second lieutenant had reported sick on the morning of the battle, and had, I heard, no appetite for fighting.

"Hadn't ye better," asked the irrepressible Add, while binding up his wound, "send a flag o' truce over to them fellers, and explain that there ain't no need of all this fuss and parade they are makin' on our account? Tell 'em we only dropped over sort of informally, and ain't one of them regiments of brigadiers, we ain't, and are only entitled to one salute, anyway."

We took our company into the houses to make reply to the Confederate sharpshooting. The men had opened a tremendous fire of musketry, when

Captain Mason said to them, "Take aim! and fire slow, men!"

"That's it!" drawled Major Grim approvingly. " In battle our men fire too fast, and take too little aim. Then they all get out of ammunition, and want to fall back. The rebs lay low, and return fire slowly, and our boys get an idea that there must be a lot of rebs, because there is always some of them alive to return fire after such a racket. Some of the new men shut their eyes when they fire ; they are more likely to make a hole in the sky than in a reb."

After dark we found the Confederates had withdrawn from their barricade. The regiment was ordered from the houses, and stacked arms in the gutter, spreading their blankets on the sidewalk for the night.

The following day (the 12th of December) was consumed by our army in crossing the different corps of Sumner's command, and in reconnoitring the positions of the enemy. The streets of the ancient town were crowded with artillery and infantry, but an ominous silence reigned on the heights above us.

"The rebs," said some one, "are holding on to their ammunition; guess they're short!"

"That ain't it," said Jack Hale gravely. "I rather guess they don't want to discourage us from making an attack on them."

"They know," said a veteran, "that bombard-

ments mean more noise than hurts, and that we'll
soon get where they can hurt us some!"

We lay down on the sidewalk; and although
I was kept awake for some time by the cold, and
by the coughing of some men from a new regiment near us, I soon fell asleep. Before long I
was awakened by a tremendous racket that was
going on in a house opposite.

In spite of orders to the contrary, some of our
men had occupied the dwellings around us, making free with everything they found there.

"Let's go over and see what's going on," said
Captain Mason; "they may set the house on
fire."

Through the open door we entered into a broad
hall, and then into a large room that opened out
of it. A fire was roaring in the big, open fireplace, lighting up a grotesque scene of revelry.
A few men were cooking at the fire, but others
were singing and dancing, while at a grand piano
sat Add, playing with no unskilful touch, and
calling the changes of the dance. Seated on the
piano was little Mike, drumming an accompani-
ment to the music with his heels, while Tobin was
sawing away on a fiddle with but two strings.
Another man was tooting discordantly on an old-
fashioned hunting-horn.

Some of the dancers were dressed in cast-off
female wearing-apparel, such as hoop-skirts and
poke bonnets, which had been found in the house.

The centre around which all the extravagant changes revolved was Rolly-Pooly, who, with glistening teeth, rolling eyes, and distinguished gravity, was dancing in an extravagant manner. Every inch of him, from the wool on his head to the toes of his ragged boots, was keeping time to the music.

The captain smiled, for he was by no means a solemn person, and appreciated the grotesque scene as much as I did.

Some one touched my shoulder; I turned, and found it was General Blusterson. As if in response to an unspoken query he saw on my face, he said, " Let them alone ! " Then with his half-humorous smile and shake of his head, he said, with an undercurrent of pathos in his tones, " Let them get all the fun out of it possible. They'll have some tough work to do to-morrow, and they'll fight none the worse for this."

To this the young captain replied, as if speaking to himself, " ' Eat, drink, and be merry, for to-morrow we die.' "

" Well, yes ! " said the general shortly. " That's a motto good enough for a soldier, captain, and it's pretty near the keynote of life, anyway."

" Yes," said Mason thoughtfully; "and it's all the more reason, General, that while enjoying God's good things we should be reverent, even when most joyful, so that at any time we may be ready for our marching orders ! "

" We don't do as we wish in life," said the general still more sharply; "we do as we can! We are crowded into life, and kicked out of it again, without saying, ' By your leave, sir.' I believe in getting the best of it in the fight, and in keeping out of the mud, and in fighting with all my powers to keep out of a hole!"

I could see that the general was not only answering Captain Mason, but was excusing his life to his inner consciousness; and I thought as I rolled myself up in my blanket on the sidewalk again, " There are two men, both brave, but actuated by different motives.

"One says, ' Let us enjoy life, and fight when we must to preserve ourselves,' and he relies on himself alone. The other says, ' Let us do our whole duty, conscientiously and reverently. Death is near, but God is pitiful; let us trust him.' " The mists were gathering, and a damp, chill fog enveloped the city as I fell asleep.

I still heard, as if in my dreams, the sounds of laughter and music, as though there was no such thing as impending battle.

The morning sun dispelled the cloud of fog that enshrouded the city, and revealed dark lines of men, marching to their positions in readiness for battle.

While these hosts are marshalling, let us take a general glance over the field, in order that we may more clearly understand the significance of the incidents that came under my own observation, and which I shall try to depict here.

On the south or Fredericksburg side of the Rappahannock, running parallel with the river, there is a well-defined crest of hills. The battle-field may be generally described as a broken plain, stretching back from the southern banks of the stream. This plain is six hundred yards wide at the town, in front of Marye's Heights, and two miles wide at Franklin's position, otherwise known as Hamilton's Crossing. Marye's Heights and Hamilton's Crossing were the positions attacked by our army, and where the fighting took place.

Franklin's Left Grand Division, consisting of about fifty thousand men, had, as we have said elsewhere, crossed the stream with little opposition.

General Franklin had received instructions, by an order from Burnside, to send one division to seize the Heights in his front near Hamilton Crossing (where his army was confronted by that tough and resolute fighter, Stonewall Jackson); to keep it well supported by at least a division, with its line of retreat well open; and to hold the rest of his command in position for a rapid movement down the old Richmond Road. The Heights, covered with leafless oaks and dark pines, were occupied by the Confederates. In front of them was the railroad, and beyond that the woods.

Between nine and ten in the morning the fog cleared away, and revealed to the Confederates

Franklin's Grand Division, formed on the plain
against a background of light snow; and at ten
o'clock the flashing arms of Meade's division advancing to an attack.

As they advanced, the Confederates opened on
them with artillery, which tore gaps in their ranks
like the ploughshares of death. The lines closed
up, and advanced like a storm-cloud rifted by the
wind. The first of our brigade penetrated the
woods, swept aside from right to left like a cur-
tain the Confederates in their front; captured
many prisoners and battle-flags, and wedged itself
between two Confederate brigades of A. P. Hill's
division.

It was a gallant attack; but unsupported by a
fresh attacking force, it was shattered by its own
impetus, and went to pieces under a fire from the
enemy's front and both flanks, and fell back, pursued by the yelling Confederates.

Its five thousand men had attempted the work
of forty thousand, and failed. This attack had
been well supported by Reynolds's corps, which,
all told, lost four thousand men; while Meade lost
forty per cent of his whole command. Briefly
told, this was the battle on our left.

CHAPTER XIX.

THE ATTACK ON MARYE'S HEIGHTS.

WHILE the scenes narrated in the foregoing chapter were passing, Sumner's Right Grand Division was ordered to attack the formidable heights back of Fredericksburg. French's division was at noon ordered forward from the town, followed and supported by Hancock's division, and that to be followed by Howard's.

I was in the upper part of one of the houses, looking out at French's division, which was advancing by the plank and telegraph roads. It crossed the canal, and deployed in column of attack with brigade front, under cover of a rise in the ground.

From its first move on the roads mentioned, the Confederate artillery had opened from the semicircle of heights a terrible fire, tearing the ranks, which closed up again without perceptible influence on its advance.

Suddenly, at double-quick, in dark masses, it burst upon the plain with the impetuosity of a thunderbolt!

" That's grand! Magnificent! It makes a

man's heart come right up in his throat!" exclaimed Major Grim, whom I found standing by my side.

No sooner had the division left the cover of the embankment where it formed, than a converging storm of grape, canister, shot, and shell burst upon its front, tearing through its ranks. This did not check its hurricane-like advance. But the worst had not come. When it reached within a few hundred yards of the embankment wall at the foot of Marye's Heights, a blaze of red musket-fire sprang from the Confederates concealed in the sunken road, followed by volley after volley, and sheet after sheet of flame. The ground was covered with dead and wounded, and the attacking column was enveloped in the white sulphur-smoke.

"They break! Terrible!" cried Grim. "I never saw anything like that!"

"Major," said an orderly who had come upstairs, "the general's compliments, and says fall in your regiment at once!"

"I kinder think," said Grim with his dogged smile, "that it's our turn next. Come, Alden; I feel gloomy enough this morning. If I was a fool I should say I had a presentiment."

The company was already formed on the sidewalk; and as the general rode down our ranks, with an attempt at a buttonhole bouquet in the breast of his uniform, and with his boots polished and every button glistening, I heard Add re-mark, —

"The general looks as happy as a clam at high water."

"Then," I said, "we are going in soon. He wouldn't look so unusually happy if there wasn't something requiring nerve, — a crisis at hand."

So it proved. Blusterson reined in his horse, and said in distinct tones, but without raising his voice, "We are going for them chaps up there, men, with sharp sticks. We will show them all how to do it! I'm going with you, and will do all I can for you."

The order came. The division moved forward, the click of canteens against muskets our only music.

The men were silent, sullen, and dogged. There was no shrinking from the work, although they had no confidence in the attack. There was not a man in the ranks that day that did not know the hopelessness of the task, yet they did all that men could do.

As our brigade marched up the road, shell and shot, grape and canister, swept its lines, and left behind it, as its ranks steadily closed up, the dead and dying; but no man flinched. There was no cheering as we formed under the protection of an embankment, and then, at double-quick, with the impetuosity of a storm, burst upon the plain, and dashed like a dark wave on Marye's fatal Heights !

The general was on foot, with drawn sword, in the rear of his brigade, shouting, encouraging, and steadying the men.

There was an uproar of explosions beneath our feet; our ranks were torn and bleeding; and, as the men fell wounded or dead, its front shrunk at every step.

Amidst the *inferno* of sounds, a nervous impatience which I had at first felt gave place to a cool indifference.

Little things caught my attention in the line. I noticed that Sergeant Standish's hat was wrong side before, and felt an impulse to straighten it. I saw men drop their muskets and, with appealing looks, go down. I heard men shriek and fall, and yet did not realize that it meant peril to myself.

I noticed a bloody spot on Sergeant Key's hand where a bullet had struck it.

Meanwhile, in less time than it takes to read these lines, the brigade had reached to within musket-shot of the Heights. And then volley after volley burst from the sunken road, and a sheet of flame seemed to envelop the head of the column. We were within a hundred yards of the rebel position, and our column had melted away to a few straggling but desperate men.

The dead and dying were all around us; and a noise of humming bullets, like the din of a cotton-mill, passed over us, seemingly in sheets, and then our men scattered like chaff before the wind.

The strength of the enemy's position surpassed human bravery. In fifteen immortal moments our conflict was decided.

Some fled, and took refuge in the cluster of houses standing at the fork of the street below; while a good part of our line, with myself, had found partial shelter from the destructive musket-fire by lying down behind a rise in the ground a few rods in advance of an isolated square brick house, not far from Marye's Heights.

Here we were sheltered from the musketry, but not from the artillery of the foe.

I now seemed to realize for the first time how terrible the encounter had been. The wounded and dead thickly covered the ground just in front of us.

"See there!" And Add, who had crept up to my side, pointed before him.

One wounded man, prostrate on his face, was endeavoring to drag himself toward us by clutching the tufts of grass; another, lying on his back, was trying to push himself along by thrusting his heels into the yielding ground. Another painfully rolled over towards us once or twice, and was stopped by a sharpshooter's bullet. All over the field on our front was spread a writhing mass of our brave wounded men, grovelling in the mud, their blue overcoats making the waxen pallor of their faces still more ghastly. An army of human wrecks was around us.

It was not long before we heard the advance of another column, and we thought, as they charged, how hopeless the attempt was.

Six times that day the Union troops were hurled upon the Heights, and as many times were broken like waves on a rocky coast, and receded. The death-girdled Heights were impregnable to human assault. The last charge was made about dark. It was Humphrey's division, who came on cheering, passed over us, trampling on the wounded in our ranks; and then went to pieces before the deadly fire of the Confederates, like those who had preceded them.

A few torn and blackened remnants of the division that had charged the Heights meanwhile, prostrate on their bellies, still held the little ridge of earth before Marye's Heights. They could not advance, and would not retreat.

At once after taking my position behind the ridge, Add told me that Captain Mason and Jack Hale were both wounded. I crept to the captain, and found him with a bullet wound in the lungs. All that had protected him from immediate death had been a metallic case which contained his mother's picture, and from which the bullet glanced upward, but not without inflicting a terrible wound.

As I was crawling humbly along to reach Mason, I heard the voice of the general exclaiming, "Get down there, men! Lie down! If

"Get down there, men! Lie down!"

— Page 222.

there's enough of you who want to get shot to make it worth while, I'll lead you up there, and pull the Johnnies out of their hole!"

Looking up, I saw the general seated on the ground, looking very pale, but intent on keeping the men from needlessly exposing themselves.

"What's the matter, General?" I asked; "you look pale."

"That you, Alden? Glad to see you are all right! The rascals have spoiled one of my new boots; bullet through my leg; only just a scratch, though. The men down there are going to charge, I see! We'll get 'em yet!"

I persuaded the general to lie on his stomach like the rest of us; but the position seemed to dishearten him more than his wound.

It illustrates how sharp the firing was at this time, that in taking off my canteen to give Mason a drink, I had lifted myself a little from the ground, when a bullet cut the canteen strap, while another hit the hilt of my sword, and, glancing, wounded a man near me.

It was a wonder that General Blusterson had not been killed in keeping an upright position so long. Later, I was grieved to learn that our brave major was among the missing.

Almost every moment some one was hurt by the enemy's shell or canister. But in contrast with the greater peril we had encountered, the position seemed like one of tolerable safety.

The interval between the charge and sunset seemed days instead of hours. So much does a man measure his life by sensations, rather than by moments!

At last the great disk of the sun, reddened as if by reflection from that terrible field, sank slowly down, and merciful darkness came to succor the wounded and to protect the living.

Was our major among the wounded men on that dreadful field?

I silently prayed that he might rather be among the dead.

Darkness soon put a stop to hostile sounds, save shell firing, which occasionally came from the Heights, trailing bright lines across the black sky. From the cluster of dead and wounded men, there came crawling painfully, or hobbling on muskets, reversed for crutches, the wounded to our lines. Among these was Sergeant Crandall. He could give no intelligence of our brave major.

Crandall and little Mike were sent to the town with General Blusterson and Captain Mason.

I was now the ranking officer of the company, which was, however, now no great command. Many of our men were wounded or dead; others had taken refuge in a cluster of houses near the fork of the road; while still others had retreated to a ravine some two hundred yards in our rear.

There were members of different regiments mixed with us, — the most daring of those living of the six columns that had charged those fatal heights that day. They could not advance, and were too brave to retreat. Hungry, covered with mud, benumbed with cold, we lay prostrate on our faces before the enemy. The night grew intensely cold. Our garments froze to the ground. As fast as the men died, their bodies were piled up as a barricade for the living. Dead battery-horses were utilized in the same way.

Whenever our men endeavored to bring in the wounded from the front they were fired upon by the enemy. We, in turn, fired upon them whenever we saw them trying to plunder the dead.

At last our line was relieved by orders from General Sumner, and was withdrawn to the town. I looked at my watch, and found it was only half-past eleven P. M.; yet it seemed an age since we had charged Marye's Heights.

CHAPTER XX.

THE RETREAT.

It was very cold; but the troops were not allowed to kindle bivouac fires in Fredericksburg that night, lest the enemy should open fire upon its crowded streets. By contrast with the uncomfortable position which we had left, our beds on the sidewalk seemed luxurious.

That night I slept a dreamless sleep, but awoke in the morning lame and hungry. After eating ravenously the few crumbs left in my haversack, I started down the street to find something more to devour. While thus engaged I unexpectedly came upon Rolly-Pooly, sitting in a doorway fast asleep. By vigorous shaking I succeeded in arousing him, and in making him comprehend that I was in pursuit of something to eat. He came very near appearing to be interested and glad; and I was repaid for awakening him when he brought out from under the doorstep a basket containing cold chicken and other goodies, together with a few china plates, some uncut crash towelling, and a bar of soap. The reader may imagine that I did not wait for ceremony, or to make my toilet then, but began an attack on the good things at once. Sergeant Addison Key, who came along just as I was beginning, brought me some hot coffee, and afterwards volunteered to assist, as he termed it, in driving in the pickets on the grub line. And soon nothing remained of Rolly's provender but bare bones and crumbs. Afterwards, when I was inclined to get out of patience with Rolly, the remembrance of that excellent meal inclined me to be more lenient of his trespasses than charity really demanded.

Another surprise was in store for me when Rolly, indifferently making a motion with his woolly head towards a house, said, " De Gigabreer in dar, sar."

" Who ? " I asked.

He vouchsafed no explanation, but it flashed upon me that he meant General Blusterson.

On this supposition I entered the house, where I found a large number of our wounded. It was the same dwelling where Add and others held the carousal on the night before the attack.

How changed the conditions were may be inferred when I say that I found surgeons at work in the hall, and the piano removed from its legs, and set edgewise as an amputating table.

The surgeons were busy at their painful but necessary work. As soon as one subject had been operated upon another was brought in; and they were following one another in such quick succession that there was barely time between cases to cleanse with a sponge the protecting poncho blanket.

Shattered limbs were being · amputated with wonderful dexterity. A sponge saturated with chloroform was thrust to the nose of the patient; the keen knife flashed; there was a faint rasping of the saw; the blood spurted in sharp jets, and was checked at once; the insensible patient was removed by one set of attendants, while another disposed of the bleeding member sacrificed to his country. The limbs were carried out of the back door, where bloody water was also poured, the ghastly refuse crimsoning the small bank of snow at the corner of the fence. I entered the room, and was greeted by Crandall, who lay near the doorway. A fire was blazing on the hearth; and lying near it were General Blusterson and Captain Mason, while fifteen or twenty other wounded men were scattered around the room.

The surgeons had been kept so busy, that the attendant at the time I entered was but just attempting to remove the general's boots, preparatory to an examination of his wound.

The general had insisted upon having the boot pulled off, instead of having it cut away. But when an attempt was made to remove it, although the smile did not desert his face, he grew pale, and ejaculated, "Easy there! easy there." The new boot could not be saved. The general gasped, ceased to smile, and exclaimed, "Cut it off! Cut it away!"

"The old fellow," said Sergeant Crandall admiringly, "is kind of gritty! He made that surgeon attend to me and Captain Mason first."

Meanwhile the boot was cut away.

"There," said the general blandly, but with an expression of pain mingled with his brave smile. "Thank you; that feels better!"

He now saw me, and called out, "Come over here, Alden! How are they getting on up there on the hill?"

I greeted both the general and the captain, and informed them of the situation.

A hospital steward now came in to examine the general's wound. The latter lighted a cigar, and asked me to pass his case to others in the room. The hospital steward began probing the wound in what I thought rather a nervous manner. Once the general removed his cigar, and, taking the probe, said gently to the steward, "By your leave, sir! I'm something of a mechanic myself; the bullet track is downward, like that you see; the shot came from up hill."

There was no wincing; the general, as he looked on, smoked and smiled, and, seeing that bandages were scarce, said, "There's a white shirt for bandages; I've got on a woollen one now," and then, with the old humorous expression on his lips, added, "It's clean; I had it on only a little while

Friday. I wasn't going to be found dead with
dirty linen on, gentlemen!"

The attendant tore the white linen into strips.
The steward continued probing, and finally drew
out a jagged and flattened bullet, when blood
began spurting out in short, sharp jets.

Quickly Blusterson tied the linen bandage above
the wound; the surgeon seized a broken chair
round and tightened it. The patient dropped his
cigar, and sank back deadly pale; for the tour-
niquet had not been applied so quickly but that
he had lost much blood. The young steward said
to the attendant sharply, " Call the surgeon! "

A main artery had been severed, partially by the
bullet, partially by the probe.

" The leg," said the surgeon, after a quick examination, " will have to come off."

" Oh, no," said the general; " not as bad as
that. Can't you save it? "

The surgeon shook his head.

" Well," said Blusterson, " what's a leg? I'd 'a'
given both of them to have driven those rebs out
of their hole with my brigade! Go ahead if you
must! "

The general was carried to the table; the chloroform sponge was held to his nostrils, and the
surgeon, with wonderful skill, cut through the
muscles of the lower joint above the wound, laid
bare the bone, introduced an instrument to hold
back the muscles, drew the saw across the bone

twice, and it was sundered, the foot and lower leg remaining in the hands of the attendant. The ligature of the arteries was quickly accomplished, the flaps of skin drawn down, and stitches put in to hold it in place, and the general was removed to his bed near Captain Mason, before he became conscious. He came out of his chloroformed condition with but little of the customary flurry, and, looking down to his leg, ejaculated, " They've done it, have they? " and sank back, fumbling for his cigar-case.

The cutting and sawing meanwhile went on among the poor men brought to the amputating table. If a man died he was immediately carried out to make room for other patients.

It was horrible; but such is war, and such are the scenes that should be gazed upon by those who contemplate invoking the demon of battle.

Captain Mason shook his head calmly, but gravely, as I turned to him a few moments after the scene described, to ask if there was anything I could do for his comfort. His wound was through the collar-bone and the upper part of the left lung, from which the surgeon had been unable to extract the bullet.

" How," he inquired, " does it look up back of the town now? "

" It looks bad," I said, as I almost involuntarily took his hand; "and it ain't over yet. I wish the army was well out of it."

"Trust in God," he replied gravely. "It is all a part of his plan,— part of the price that must be paid for the country's redemption, Jack. God is over all, the same now as before the battle."

Captain Mason's trust in God never faltered, and to him a belief in his loving-kindness seemed to require no effort.

The general, who was now lighting his cigar, overhearing my despondent remark, said faintly, but in his old confident tones, "Don't croak, my boy; I've wasted lots of good stuff in my day, trying to make models for a new machine, but it always came out right after enough whittling. We made a good fight; there's chance for failure in anything."

"It's my opinion," growled Crandall, his shaggy brows meeting in a scowl, "that old Burney had better get this army out of town kinder quick, before the rebs come after him."

"Tut! Tut!" said the general confidently; "they don't want anything of us on even terms, Sergeant!"

After writing several letters for the general, I went out to send them across the river to mail.

The town was one great hospital and morgue. Even the front yards and kitchen gardens of the houses were occupied by pieces of men, who on the Saturday previous had gone into the battle whole.

It was a gloomy Sunday, such as I hope never to see again. There was no movement made by either Federals or Confederates during the day. It seemed to me that, as Father Crandall had intimated, if the Confederates should make a descent upon the town, or open with their artillery upon the disheartened men that crowded the streets of Fredericksburg, our army would be doomed to yet more terrible disaster.

I returned to the house, after visiting my company, which was in charge of Sergeant Key, and found my comrades in much the same situation that I had left them.

As I looked over the group, I could not help remarking the faces of my friends; the general's lionlike face, and the set determination in Father Crandall's rugged features, expressed the same thing. The most remarkable face, however, was that of young Captain Elbridge Mason. Its pallor alone indicated his wounded condition. The eyes were calm, the brow serene, and the lips had an indefinable grave smile, which, as Crandall said, was like an angel's.

Add came in to report to me; for I had sent him to make out a list of our dead, wounded, and missing. It was a long catalogue of casualties.

"Well," said one of our wounded men, an ex-printer, "they've knocked the regiment into pi!"

"Yes," said Add, holding up his bandaged digit, "and I've had a finger in the pie myself."

There was a ripple of laughter, even among the wounded, at this sally.

"Gentlemen," said Mason, after Add had gone, "it is the Sabbath Day; we've passed through scenes of great peril together. Shall I read to you from this book," touching his Bible, "a few comforting words?"

"Yes," said Crandall; "I say for one, if there is any comfort anywhere, give it to us."

While the general politely replied, "Certainly, my boy; certainly!"

Mason read with great purity of enunciation from the words of his Master, and then read a few verses from the Psalms, closing with, "Though I walk through the valley of the shadow of death, I will fear no evil."

Then, with clasped hands, still lying on his poor bed, he prayed for the country, for the army, and for his wounded comrades.

I do not know that his prayer was eloquent; but it had behind it something that seldom fails to move men,—a consistent character. It was the man himself; his simplicity, bravery, and the unassuming goodness of his life, his love for his comrades, as deep as it was tender, that affected us most.

There was silence for a time after the prayer; then the old general turned, reached out his hand to his boy captain, and said, "Thank you; I haven't thought much of such things of late, but your trust in God, Captain, is worth more than pluck at a time like this."

With a serene look on his shining, lofty brow
the boy captain replied, " Yes, my General, religion don't need pluck ; it makes courage : for
' Jesus can make a dying bed as soft as downy
pillows are.' Let us sing together, —

> " ' Jesus, lover of my soul,
>   Let me to thy bosom fly,
>   When the nearer waters roll,
>   While the tempest still is high.' "

For a moment all joined in singing the hymn as
fervently as if they were soldiers of the Cross, instead of rough fighters of the Army of the Potomac.

Monday morning dawned upon the hosts around
Fredericksburg. There was but little change in
the situation, except the removal of the wounded
across the river.

It was a sight to move the most callous, to be-
hold the loading of the ambulances. Some of the
wounded had a greenish pallor on their faces, or
the reddish cast that denotes congestion ; many of
them were in a state of coma ; some uttered
piercing cries of anguish, while others died from
the shock of removal.

The regular ambulances of the medical department were inadequate to the task, and various
other vehicles from the trains were used, and went
rolling on with their ghastly loads.

Late Monday evening our advance lines were

pushed up close against the enemy, as if to attack; but in the darkness the work of recrossing the river began.

The pontoon bridges were covered with earth, that no sound of the movement should give warning to the enemy.

Swiftly, sadly, and in silence the troops moved on in one black train, until at two o'clock on the morning of Tuesday the last picket-line of the Army of the Potomac was withdrawn; and by three o'clock the army, with its material, was again safe on the northern bank of the Rappahannock.

The battle had been fought and lost, and with it was lost the confidence of the army in General Burnside.

Its harvest of death and wounds depresses the heart even in the remembrance. Ten thousand of our brave men were killed and wounded in this worse than useless attack.

General Burnside's manly assumption of all blame was worthy of his generous character; but it did not atone for needless loss of precious human life.

Thus ended the campaign against the stone walls of Fredericksburg.

CHAPTER XXI.

DISCONTENT.

THE next forenoon, after the army had recrossed the river, Corporal Osgood approached me, and, saluting, said, "Shouldn't wonder, Lieutenant, if they'd send a burial squad over the river this forenoon to bury our fellers."

"What," I asked, "makes you think so?"

"Well, a reb officer come over just now, with a flag of truce; and I see'd old Burny and he sittin' under a persimmon-tree down by the river, talkin' and eatin' somethin' good. Must be that's what's the matter. Can't be anything else."

It was a shrewd guess of a kind not unusual among our acute soldiers in the ranks, who seldom failed to get wind of what was going on in advance of their officers.

On inquiry I learned that all arrangements had been made for the burial of our dead; and I obtained permission to accompany the party with Add, in order to identify, if possible, those of our number who were missing, and among whom we hoped to find the major.

Arriving on the ground, we found the burial

squads hard at work with picks, digging trenches
in the frozen soil. Most of the dead had been
stripped by the enemy. A woman in a house near
Marye's Heights said, " The night you Yanks left
here the ground was blue, but the next morning it
was white."

These dead, among the bravest soldiers of the
army, were thrown into trenches without even a
blanket for a shroud. The bodies were bloated,
blackened, and disfigured. We were, however,
able to identify most of our men, though among
them I could not find the body of Major Grim.

The Confederate officers and men whom I met
here were grave and courteous, as became men on
such an occasion.

I inquired for Captain Milner, and was told that
his battery was farther up on the hill. Upon my
expressing a desire to communicate with him, an
officer kindly sent word for him; but he did not
make his appearance. I learned, however, that
he had passed through the battle unhurt. I sent
word by one of the officers who was acquainted
with him, that Major Grim was among the missing,
and requested him to ascertain if possible whether
he was a prisoner of war, and to communicate to
me any information regarding his fate.

" I think," said an officer, " your friend must be
among the wounded, although it is hard to recognize the dead, I confess, on account of their naked
and disfigured condition."

Some of our men were heard to make bitter remarks regarding the condition of the dead, when the officer said, "Yes; it is terrible. I don't justify it; but our boys are poorly clad, and they cannot resist the opportunity to get warm clothing."

Groups of the Confederates, rank and file, were to be seen chatting, swapping jackknives and jokes, and trading coffee for tobacco, as if they were neighbors and friends, instead of enemies who but a few hours before had been engaged in mortal conflict.

After lingering until late in the afternoon, I again crossed the river, feeling depressed and sorrowful after the terrible scenes of the day, and was not pleased to find Lieutenant Sinclair in my quarters, carousing and drinking with Captain King.

At the time of which I write, the prevailing sentiment among officers in the army regarding drunkenness was very low. The sale of intoxicants among the rank and file was expressly forbidden. But the commissioned officers were permitted to draw on the commissary by order. Thus among those whose morals had not been moulded by healthy family influences, or who had not the instinctive feelings of gentlemen, the brutal habit was considered less a degradation than a subject for mirth.

When the next day I learned that Lieutenant Sinclair had had the company out for drill while he was partially under the influence of liquor, I understood the half-smothered, discontented remarks and sullen looks of our men.

A morning or two after this, when Sergeant Add Key, who at this time was the acting orderly sergeant, came to my quarters with the morning report, I said rather stiffly, "Sergeant, you must not countenance such insubordinate remarks as I've overheard among the men lately."

"I'll do the best I can, Lieutenant," he replied; "but I can't make men over, so they'll think white is black. The best way to reform the men, is to reform some of the officers."

I did not reply for a moment, for the remark cut to the marrow of the subject. The conduct of men in the ranks is usually what officers make it, and good officers make good men. But I said, "Frown it down, and punish such men if you find a good excuse, Sergeant."

Add made no direct reply, but turned the subject to the list of dead and missing on his report; but before he left my quarters he said in his droll, dry manner, "A reb over there on 'tother side told me yesterday that whiskey is sixty dollars a pint in Richmond, an' I tell you that that's where the rebs have got an advantage."

"Why do you think so?" I inquired.

"Why, don't you see?" said Add with a queer twist to his face, "there's five hundred chances more for one of our men in a responsible place to be laid off by whiskey than for a Confederate officer? Why, a week's pay of one of them fellers wouldn't give him a smell of a pint bottle that had had the critter in it before the war!"

I made no reply, and did not smile, but said, as stiffly as I could, "Sergeant, take your morning's report to your quarters again."

Just as Add, with his report book under his arm, was pushing aside the entrance to my tent, Lieutenant Sinclair came in, and with a flushed face and an excited manner, exclaimed, "Do you encourage the orderly sergeant to make insulting remarks about an officer?"

I made no reply to his question, but made him feel by my manner that I was displeased.

"I heard the talk," he continued more moderately, "that you had with Sergeant Key!"

I was now angry, and, rising, faced him, saying in very frosty tones, "If you have been listening to my remarks, and heard anything which you interpret as insulting to you personally, I cannot be responsible for it!"

"I am not blaming you, Alden," he replied with a cringing manner; "it's that d—— sergeant!"

"I allow no profanity in my quarters, Lieutenant," I responded; "and I allow no sergeant or under officer to speak disrespectfully of officers in my presence, no matter how much to blame they may be. You must be on your guard not to occasion disrespect hereafter!"

The lieutenant was from that day a bitter enemy of Sergeant Key, and took every opportunity to injure him.

The general spirit of the army after Fredericksburg was one of discontent and gloom. The men of the company of which I was the commanding officer respected me, and were kept in subordination by that respect; but they could not be kept from being disrespectful to one whom they believed had shammed sickness to avoid the perils of battle. They also growled that an incompetent general had been allowed to blunder away the lives of their comrades in a fruitless attack on an unassailable position.

The soul of an army is its *morale* — that quality which is so undefinable; made up of prejudice, passion, and inference, but to which is attributable, more than to its members, its failures and successes. This soul of the Army of the Potomac was tinged with dejection, discouragement, and want of confidence. It had the blues.

Fortunately for the country, however, it was made up of intelligent and patriotic elements, — citizens who had left their homes to defend the flag, and who deeply loved the cause they had taken up arms to defend. It was a great body of patriotic men, who unselfishly served, with expectation of neither reward nor preferment other than victory for the cause and consequent abiding peace for the nation. The world had never seen

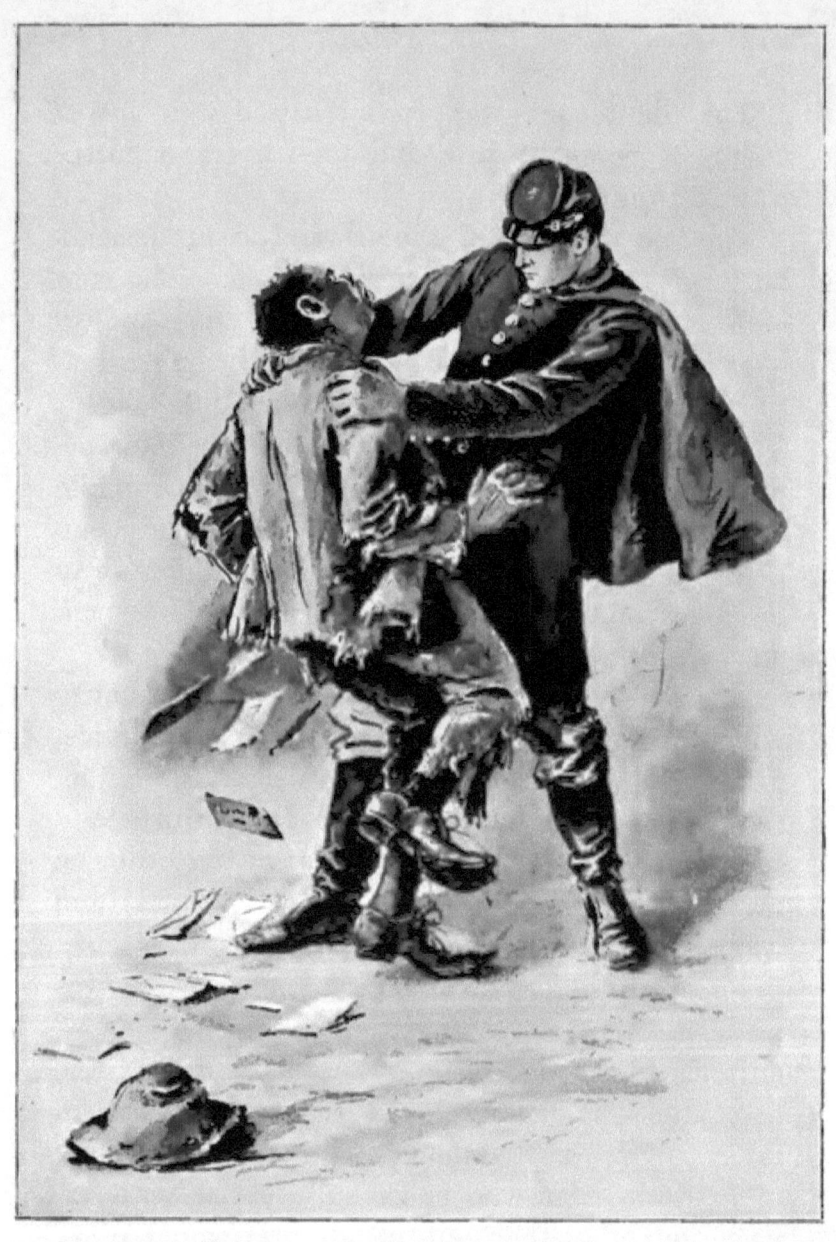

"I pulled him to his feet, and angrily shook him."
— Page 245.

such men in the ranks before; and it was their faith and devotion to the cause of their country that formed a bond of cohesion when those of discipline failed.

But such men also loved their homes and families; and when furloughs were refused to those who had sick children, or aged parents, they sometimes walked off to see them, on French leave.

Distrust, discouragement, and want of confidence are among the malign influences under which an army is destroyed more surely than by the bullets of an enemy; and such were the disintegrating influences that prevailed after the battle of Fredericksburg.

I visited the field hospital a day or two after the battle, to see Captain Mason and General Blusterson, both of whom had been mentioned for bravery in general orders.

I found General Blusterson amusing himself by whittling at a model of an artificial leg, for which, he told me, he intended to secure letters patent.

"Do you think," I said, "a man who has lost a leg will want a contrivance like that?"

"Want it?" exclaimed the general, "they'll run after it and howl for it!"

Captain Mason's wound was not progressing as favorably as the general's. The bullet could not be found; and although he was very cheerful. there was a sunken look about his temples that showed that his vitality was seriously impaired.

Mrs. Grim had written to me regarding her husband. It was one of the phases of womanhood which I did not understand, that, notwithstanding the uncertainty of her husband's fate, she expressed the utmost confidence that he was still alive.

"If," said Mary Grim in her letter, "he was not coming back again, I should know it and feel it: he is not dead." Such intuitions are not uncommon among women; and although I cannot explain them, my experience tells me that they seldom fail to be justified by after events.

"That's right," said General Blusterson, in his most confident manner after I had read the letter to him; "there is no doubt but that Grim is living. The Confederates seldom take pains to capture badly wounded men, and never send dead men to prison. By the way," said he, "have you got those notes of hand that your uncle gave me for the pegging-machine patent yet?"

I told him I expected to hear from my brother, but had received no letters from him lately.

In a few days many of the sick and wounded were removed from the field hospital to Washington, and among them were Captain Mason and General Blusterson.

Two weeks had passed, and I still received no letters from home, nor had anything been heard of Major Grim.

About this time I began to superintend the

building of a log hut for winter quarters. I had got the walls chinked with adhesive Virginia mud, its clay floor pounded hard and smooth, a combination of sticks, mud, and a pork-barrel for a chimney, and was putting up a bunk and shelves.

I seldom sent Rolly after anything of a special character, he was so provokingly deliberate and uncertain. This time I was in a hurry, however, and so sent him to buy some nails at the sutler's. As he did not return, I went to the sutler's myself, and on the way discovered Rolly sitting on the sunny side of a pontoon, in companionship with some of his mates, lazily and leisurely eating from a huge chunk of molasses candy.

Angrily I asked him where the nails were that I had sent him for.

He deliberately removed the candy from his mouth, and in provokingly slow tones replied, "Nails, boss? I hasn't seen no nails!"

"Didn't I send you," I sternly asked, "for nails, and tell you to hurry?"

His manner of assumed forgetfulness was so exasperating, that I pulled him to his feet, and angrily shook him, when there fell from some pocket or other recess in his ragged jacket, a shower of dirty letters and other odds and ends. Among the letters, which were most of them directed to me, was one from Mary Milner, several from my brother, and one for Mrs. Grim addressed to my care in a strange handwriting.

I was so much interested in the contents of my letters, that I forgot to give Rolly a much-deserved thrashing, or to question him, until he was moving off with his mouth glued to his taffy, when I shouted after him, "Where did you get these letters?"

"I dun forgot, boss," he replied, and went on.

The letter was an open one to Mrs. Grim, and proved to be one written two days after the battle, by a private soldier of the regiment, informing her that Grim was a prisoner, and had been hurt. This letter probably came through our lines under a flag of truce, before Grim was sent to Richmond.

In the letter it was simply said Grim had been stunned by an injury during the battle, and that when he became conscious he was in the hands of the enemy. Also that he was now all right except that his head still gave him trouble, and that his memory was not good enough to write, but that the rebel surgeon had assured him that there was no fracture of the skull.

My letters from home were some of them nearly a month old. I of course sent Major Grim's letter to his wife at once.

Among those from home was one containing the notes of hand that I had sent for, which I at once sent to General Increase Blusterson, Washington, D.C., for his indorsement and return.

After finishing my letters I started out to find Rolly, that I might punish him sufficiently to keep him away from my quarters thereafter.

CHAPTER XXII.

A VISIT TO WASHINGTON.

SHORTLY after finishing my winter quarters, I applied for a pass to go to Washington. Certain equipments of the company, such as tompions to muskets, bayonets, and musket-straps, as well as muskets, were missing. I, being in command of the company, must make such affidavits as to what had become of them, as Add said would blister an ordinary paper, or else have my pay stopped to make good the deficiencies. I wanted to go to Washington to explain this, and also to see Dr. Milner and Captain Mason.

While awaiting the slow winding and unwinding of red tape incident to obtaining this pass, I had discharged Rolly several times ; but, like a gun heavily loaded, his indifference had recoiled and sent him back on my hands again.

I was giving him a long-threatened thrashing, and discharging him once more, when Sergeant Addison Key came in with his morning report.

"You lick that little nig too much in the Italian style." he said, laying down his report. "He don't mind it one bit."

"I don't understand what you mean, Sergeant Key," I replied stiffly.

"Why," said Add, without venturing a smile, "the Italian style is where the heavy strokes are upward and the light ones downward."

My leave of absence had come that morning, and I, consequently being in good-humor, replied to Add that I thought Rolly would stay discharged until I could return from Washington.

There were a number of reasons besides those given that made me desirous of visiting the capital, and among them was the desire to secure for Sergeant Key the position of second lieutenant of the company. He had made a good orderly sergeant, and had developed some qualities in managing men that would make him a desirable commissioned officer. He could get more drill and work out of the men, and that in the easiest manner, than any other non-commissioned officer in the regiment. The men respected him for his soldierly qualities, and began to say, "Sergeant Key is full of nonsense; but he has got lots of good sense too, and is no shirk in a fight."

I started by way of Aquia Creek; and when half way to Washington I was very hungry, no meals being served on board the boat. To my astonishment the irrepressible Rolly here appeared with chicken and hot coffee, which he had prepared in the engine-room of the steamer, making me feel by his forgiving manner that he was the better Christian of the two.

On the afternoon of my arrival in Washington, I went up town to the —— Hospital, where I learned that my general and captain were under treatment. Rolly followed with my satchel.

On going to the office to get permission for my visit, I found Dr. Milner in charge. The doctor seemed very glad to see me, and sent at once for Miss May to come to the office. While waiting I wondered to myself how, as I had not mentioned her name, he knew that I wanted to see her.

I must here confess that I found my heart fluttering and my throat growing very dry, at the anticipation of seeing her. When she came, the sight of her beautiful face did not remedy the matter, and I was forgetful of everything but her presence. My pleasure was, however, soon interrupted by the appearance of a black-eyed, bearded young fellow, in the uniform of a medical cadet, who came in, saying to Miss Milner, " I must see you just a moment."

A flash of recognition passed between me and the cadet; for it was none other than the aristocratic George Raymond of Baltimore, whom I supposed to be far away in the Confederacy.

It was like a wet blanket, — a kill-joy to me; and I angrily determined to see Miss May once more, and then to leave Washington that very night. She went out for a moment, but returned again with a deep flush on her face, explaining that one of her patients had required her attention.

" How came that Raymond fellow here?" I said, with the lump in my throat settling down on my heart. " I thought he was in the Confederate service."

" Mr. Raymond? Oh, don't you know? Hasn't papa told you that he was captured at the second battle of Bull Run, and that he has taken the oath, and is a good Union man now? It would make your blood run cold to hear Mr. Raymond tell how he suffered when he was in the Confederate service. He told me with his own lips that he went for a number of days without tonics or washing."

I must have turned green internally, and some of the color must have shown in my face, for Miss May began to inquire in regard to my welfare, and of my promotion and expectations so pleasantly, and allowed me to hold her hand so willingly, that I forgot my displeasure, my errands, and everything else, in that ecstatic employment, and should no doubt have been sitting there until this time, had not the doctor come in and dispelled my bliss by saying, " General Blusterson and Captain Mason are ready to see you."

" The general! " exclaimed May. " Do you know him? He's so polite and complimentary, and so cheerful. He is almost always whittling."

My feelings were becoming a little tinged with green once more, and I hastened to inquire about Captain Mason. The doctor replied, " It makes me believe in everything good to know such a man. His piety seems to be the main element in his character. It doesn't chill one, but warms like the sun. In him religion seems exhilarating and genial; but I fear there is no hope for the poor fellow, and he knows it too."

"Why, papa, I asked him how he slept last night." said Miss May, "and he said, 'Like an angel;' I thought he was getting better!"

All this time we were passing through corridors, the air of which was permeated with fumes of chloroform and carbolic acid, while from the rooms on either side came low, tremulous wails."

"There's the poor fellow they brought in last night," said the doctor; "but he's not conscious of pain, — dying, though."

After passing down a long line of beds, from which eyes pleading for sympathy followed us, we came to Captain Mason's room. He had changed strangely. His temples were hollowed, and the blue veins stood out on his almost transparent forehead and hands; but there was the same lofty, commanding look on his brow, and as he grasped my hand his smile was triumphantly spiritual. I cannot express in words the purity of his face and expression. As I sat holding his hand in mine his mother came in; and when he mentioned my name, she at once recognized me, and spoke of my father as a former friend of her husband. Like New England matrons of her class, she showed out-

wardly but little of her feelings. I knew, however, by an indefinable something that the thought
was constantly with her that she must soon lose
her noble boy.

In a corner of the hospital looking out on the
river was General Blusterson's room. As I entered, the general was beetling his brows over a
complicated combination of brass and sheepskin,
resembling in form a human leg. He was so intent on fitting the pieces together that he did not
look up until I called his name. Then he laid the
parts he was adjusting on the bed, and standing on
one leg greeted me with, " Alden, it does me more
good to see you than I can tell. I didn't know,
Alden, but you had forgotten your old uncle."

After mentioning the affairs of the company, I
spoke of Captain Mason.

" If that Lieutenan Sinclair was in Mason's
place I should feel reconciled, and able to consider
it a dispensation of Providence," said the general ;
" but now it seems hard. If I had a son like
him," he continued with a suspicious choking of
utterance, " I'd be proud of him. It's hard to lose
such a fine officer. How's my wound ? Why, it's
all right. I don't worry over it. What you've
lost, you've lost. I don't trouble my head about
it. I'll soon throw those crutches away, and be
walking around as good as any one."

Then the general took up his crutches, went to
the door, looked down the long corridor, listened,

and then, as if satisfied, came back, unrolled the bandage on his leg, inserted the stump into the aperture intended for it, then adjusted his patent leg, let the trousers leg drop, and walked up and down the room with but little limping.

While walking he gave a sharp cry, and I quickly helped him to remove the artificial leg, which had hurt him by bringing an unfinished part in contact with his wound. We had no sooner got the bandages adjusted than Miss May and her father came down the corridor.

"Humph!" ejaculated the doctor, looking at the general's face, and then at the patent leg, which was lying on the bed. "Been at it again? You'll be a victim of science one of these days, General."

"Let me see how much you've hurt it, you bad man, you!" said May, unrolling the bandage, and scolding in her half-earnest manner.

"Humph!" exclaimed the doctor again, "irritated! inflamed!"

"You see," said the general, taking up his artificial contrivance, "the stump of my leg don't have play enough in that socket; needs more play. I'll file it a little this afternoon, and then it will be all right. I was showing Alden how it worked, when that part there gave out, and the stump struck the rough part, and stirred up the sore a little, I guess. Didn't hurt much!"

The doctor looked on with an amused smile, while the general explained.

"Do I think a one-legged man will want to wear such a contrivance? Why, they'll run after them," said the general with his humorous shake of the head. "They can't be made fast enough for 'em, gentlemen!"

After May and her father had gone out, the general said, "That little piece of dry-goods keeps everything bright here. That Raymond chap, he consumes more commissary whiskey than is good for him; nothing bad about the boy, otherwise."

And Blusterson began with a file to work once more on his substitute for a leg, saying, "I tell you, my boy, there's a fortune in that thing! I've got my patent; strong specifications, covers everything, and you'll see a rush for 'em when they are put on the market."

That night, by the doctor's urgent request, I stayed at the hospital, spending most of my time with Captain Mason, telling him about the company, securing his recommendation, with General Blusterson's, for Add's promotion, and also getting the general to transfer to me the notes of hand which were to be sent to my brother.

I went to my room about ten o'clock, but lay awake long, unable to sleep for thinking of Captain Mason, May Milner, young Raymond, and also because the air of a room, to one long accustomed to a tent, seemed stuffy and close.

I had just got into a doze, when a rapping on

my door awoke me. In a moment I was up and dressed, with soldierly alacrity, and had opened the door.

"What is it?" I inquired of Miss May, who stood at the door with a lighted candle in her hand.

"Captain Mason is worse; he wants to see you," she replied. "I fear he will not last long."

As I entered his room, I found his mother sitting by the side of the narrow white cot, which was surrounded with screens.

A triumphant smile wreathed his lips as he took my hand; and, trying to raise himself, he said with a gasping effort, "Jack, old comrade, I've got my marching orders at last." Then after breathing a moment in gasps he said, "Give all the boys my love." He lay for a while with closed eyes, but occasionally pressing my hand. As the long hours dragged on, he would sometimes open his eyes to smile on his mother, and once, with an effort, he said, "God knows best, mother. I don't doubt him." Then his mind began to wander; and just as the sun lit up the hospital wards with a golden ray, he started up, and with clear, sharp tones of command exclaimed, "Forward! to the last charge, boys!" then fell back, and with one more smile of recognition, and whispering, "Mother, Jack," he peacefully and smilingly fell asleep in the arms of Him, his Master.

Oh, how dark the world seemed to me at such a loss! It was sad to see such a sacrifice; yet it was a sacred, beautiful sight, — the death of a Christian soldier, one who loved his country and his God.

Such a character, consecrated to our cause; such a life, rounded out and finished and given to such a service! If it was painful to think of our loss, it was joy to think of what was imperishably preserved in heaven.

There were a few simple rites, and then his sorrowing, saintly mother took his body to her home, to be buried among his kindred.

Mason was a genuine son of New England. Of strong common-sense, rapid of thought and expression, he had never failed to win the love and admiration of all with whom he came in contact. His religion sat gracefully upon him. It was spontaneous — it was himself. Even Rolly felt the sweetness of his character, and I found him weeping in a corner after the service was over.

I was absent from my company less than a week, and then returned once more to my duties at Falmouth, saddened at the loss of my friend, and feeling not a little blue at leaving May Milner under the influences of Raymond.

CHAPTER XXIII.

A COURT-MARTIAL.

ON my return to Falmouth, I learned, to my surprise, that during my absence Add had been ordered under arrest by Lieutenant Sinclair. I sent for the lieutenant, and asked for an explanation.

"What," I inquired, "is the trouble with Sergeant Key, that you have placed him under arrest?"

"I am sorry," he replied, "to have felt obliged, for the good of the service, to have ordered a favorite of yours under arrest; but he was disrespectful, and when I reproved him, he struck me."

"I have known Key for years," I said, "and have never known him to be wanting in respect to any proper person, much less an officer."

"Do you intend," he angrily exclaimed, "to doubt my word, and to insinuate that I am not a proper person?"

"No," I replied coolly; "you made the application of the term yourself. I am simply trying to account for something that I don't understand. Be careful, or this arrest will recoil on your own head."

During the day I received a message from Add, stating that he desired to see me. Later I sent for him to come to my quarters, and then learned his version of the circumstances attending his arrest.

He had taken the morning report of the company to Lieutenant Sinclair at the usual hour, about nine o'clock. The lieutenant cursed him, and angrily accused him of intruding into his quarters at an unusual hour.

"I saw," said Add, "that he was getting up 'wrong end to,' and was spoiling for a fuss, so I got out, and stayed out until about half-past ten, when I saw him moving around his quarters, and again went there with the report book, asking if he was ready to look over the report and sign it. He began abusing me for not bringing the report before. I mentioned that I had been there with it at the usual hour, and had waited until I knew he was dressed before coming again."

Lieutenant Sinclair signed the report; and as Sergeant Key tucked it under his arm, and was still facing the lieutenant, that officer said, "Be more respectful when you come to these quarters again."

"I said," continued Add, "that I tried to be respectful, when he turned on me, and furiously exclaimed, 'Do you mean to insult me, you dog? Do you mean to tell me I lie?' and he aimed a blow at my head that would have knocked me down if I hadn't put up my left arm to ward it off."

" Well," I inquired, " what next? "

" I felt that he meant to get me into a scrape, and I backed out; but," continued Add, with his fist clinched and his eyes flashing, "I would have liked to have knocked him ' end over end.' After I got to my quarters I was told to consider myself under arrest."

Poor Add! One thing was certain, and that was that his arrest would spoil his chance for promotion, even if his guilt was not proved; and such, moreover, was evidently the intention of Sinclair.

After Add had gone from my office I thought over the matter, and the case seemed to me to stand as follows. The charge against Add was supported by the statement of Lieutenant Sinclair alone, and the defence consisted simply of a denial. Unless more positive evidence was obtained, Sergeant Key's chance for an acquittal from the charges preferred would, I felt, be very poor before a general court-martial.

Here let me explain that for a private, or a non-commissioned man, to strike a superior officer, is one of the most serious offences known in military crimes, and that the evidence of a commissioned officer is often final against his inferior.

It is a saying among old soldiers that " a court-martial is convened to convict," and that a person once accused is supposed by such a court to be guilty until proved to be innocent; thus reversing the ordinary dictum of civil law.

Hence, although I was convinced that Sinclair's charges were made with the cold-blooded intention of ruining Add, and the non-commissioned officers and rank and file were of this same opinion, yet, strange to say, there seemed to be no way of securing the acquittal of the accused.

I wrote to General Blusterson, asking him to use his influence to have the charge dismissed. I stated to officers of my acquaintances my views, as given here. Most of them shook their heads, said it was bad form for an officer to take sides with a man in the ranks, and that I'd better not interfere, though some advised me to prefer counter charges against Sinclair.

While this affair was pending, other scenes of national significance, and which dwarfed individual concerns, were taking place on the broad theatre of war.

On the 17th of January it was apparent that an important military movement was on foot. Sixty rounds of cartridges and three days' rations were issued to the regiment on the 18th, and orders were received to be ready to move at a moment's notice.

"This," I remarked to my senior officer, "looks like a winter campaign. What does it mean?" The old captain shook his head dubiously, saying, "More foolishness, I suppose."

On the 19th the men, loaded with baggage, rations, and equipments (about sixty pounds to each

man, which in military terms was facetiously
called "light marching order"), started out on
their new adventures.

I heard one of our men growling about the
foolishness of making a movement at that time
of the year, and others saying that the best
sergeant in the company was now under arrest
when he was most needed, which showed me
that they had decided opinions about Sergeant
Key's affair.

The military situation, meanwhile, was dubious.
General Burnside, who since the fatal battle at
Fredericksburg had lost the confidence of the
army, sought to re-establish himself in its good
opinion by making a movement on the enemy's
left flank, although the confidence of his army
was the first condition by which his success could
be assured. His plan was to cross the Rappahannock at Bank's Ford, six miles above Falmouth,
and with the Grand Divisions of Franklin and
Hooker attack the enemy.

Our corps was meanwhile sent below Fredericksburg, where at the battle Franklin had crossed
the Rappahannock, to make a demonstration of
attacking there, and also for the purpose of guarding the communications of the army.

The weather and roads up to this time had
remained good; but during the night of the 20th
a wild, cold, driving storm of rain and sleet set in.
The roads soon became as impassable as though

they were three feet deep with slightly warmed tar, and all attempts at further movement were useless.

Disgusted, dispirited, bedraggled, leaving behind it a trail of graves and wrecked wagons, dead mules and horses, the Army of the Potomac turned tail, and with sarcastic laughter and jokes, floundered back through the mud, like flies making a tour through molasses, to its old camping-ground.

All through this campaign Sinclair shirked duty, and at one time, while detailed as officer of the guard, had gone to sleep in one of the baggage wagons. As Rolly was notoriously known to be asleep when wanted, the men slyly termed Sinclair, Rolly-Pooly, Jr., which was another cause of grievance to that officer.

On reaching the camp, the mud of the recent campaign seemed to have settled on the spirits of the army. The men criticised their superiors freely, until it appeared that the rank and file considered themselves better soldiers than their commanders. Men in winter quarters were a sort of a committee of the whole on the condition of the army, and the conclusions reached were not flattering or favorable to the higher officers.

At last Add's trial by court-martial took place. In a large tent around a pine table sat the officers composing the general court. Several cases had been tried, and the court was already wearied, when the case of Sergeant Addison Key was called. The charges and specifications were read in a monotonous tone; the Judge Advocate yawned. Sergeant Key, neatly dressed, his boots blacked, and his buttons shining, looking every inch a soldier, stepped forward.

His intelligent, resolute face evidently made a favorable impression on the court as he pleaded, "Not guilty."

Lieutenant Sinclair, as first witness for the prosecution, was called. His handsome but dissipated face, his restless eye, that did not meet those of the Judge Advocate in the manly, straightforward way that was characteristic of Sergeant Key, was I felt, a favorable contrast for the accused.

Lieutenant Sinclair told his story with but little variation from the one he had told me.

" You say," interrogated the Judge Advocate, " that Sergeant Key struck you with his right hand. Do you wish to correct this evidence in any way?"

Sinclair hesitated, glanced around at those composing the court, and then, as if reassured, replied, " No; none whatever."

" Have you other witnesses ? "

" None," said Sinclair.

Sergeant Standish was called for the defence. His testimony was, in substance, that he had heard loud talk in the company quarters on the morning of the 20th of December, at about nine o'clock, and again at about ten in the morning. The first time he recognized the voice as that of Lieutenant Sinclair, who accused some one of disturbing him. The second time he had heard the same voice angrily cursing some one, and at the same time had seen Sergeant Key backing out from the company quarters with the company report book under his right arm, and with his left hand held up in front of his face as if to shield it from a blow.

"Did you see Sergeant Key make any motion with his hand?"

"None, sir."

A look passed between the officers of the court.

Another witness, Private Quinn, was called, who testified to much the same occurrences, and added that there was a good deal of noise at company quarters during this special night; and in the morning he had at first taken but little notice, as he thought the row was of the same kind as those of the night before.

"What," inquired the Judge Advocate, "was the nature of what you term 'the row'?"

Private Quinn hesitated. "Answer my question," said the Judge Advocate sternly.

"Well, sir," replied Quinn, "I should say the whole crowd was drunk."

The answer was so unexpected that a laugh went round the table, and the witness was dismissed. Testimony was then introduced showing the previous good conduct of the accused, and the case closed.

The whole case, that so vitally interested poor Add, did not cover two hours. The court adjourned for dinner, reserving their decision until later.

The next day was one of great excitement, for it was rumored that General Hooker, against whom charges had been preferred in Washington by General Burnside, was about to be placed in command of the Army of the Potomac; and nothing was talked of during the day but the rumor.

The next day I learned the findings in the case of Sergeant Key, as follows: —

"Of the first charge and specification, viz., striking his superior officer, Not guilty.

"Of the second charge, viz., disrespect of his superior, Guilty."

The sentence of the court was the loss of one month's pay, and that Sergeant Addison Key be reduced to the ranks.

Although many, especially of the rank and file, felt that in all justice Add should have been promoted instead of being broken, yet on all sides considerable wonder was expressed at the findings of the court, and because of the light sentence.

Add was very much chagrined; but to my mind he had every reason to congratulate himself, for if Sinclair had lied a little more consistently, he would have undoubtedly been sentenced to hard labor at the Rip Raps for a term of years.

Sergeant Key took up his duties as a private;

but from that day he seemed to have lost his joyous, joking spirit, and was sobered and grave. He, however, performed his duty strictly, but was apparently broken, not only in rank, but in spirit. I reproved him for his demeanor, when he replied, " A man cannot afford any longer to retain a spirit of manhood in the army."

It was not until April that the rumored promotion of General Hooker became a fact.

The army, which since the Fredericksburg battle seemed to have been under a cloud of distrust and gloom, under " Fighting Joe" soon emerged into the sunshine of confidence and hope again. The change would have appeared astonishing, had not the elastic vitality of the army been so often proved.

Under his administrative reforms, desertions ceased, and the absent ones, amounting in all to about eighty thousand men, nearly all returned to duty; but it remained to be seen whether General Hooker would come forth with new laurels from an ordeal of command whence no man up to this time had escaped unscathed.

CHAPTER XXIV.

THE CHANCELLORSVILLE CAMPAIGN.

NEW recruits and absentees filled up the company, and rounded out its proportions to seventy-five members, all told. These men had to be drilled and disciplined. An army is anything but a place for ease and rest. Even its ordinary functions of eating and sleeping keep it in perpetual motion, and it requires an army of clerks and workers of all kinds. Every officer and soldier has to take his turn, about once a week, as eye or guard for his regiment or camp. The long arms of the army, its pickets and vedettes, are stretched out in every direction like those of a devil-fish, feeling for danger; a great interrogation point of inquiry regarding the enemy. All in turn must take a share in this work.

Then the ordinary work of camp duties, although not hard, is constant. In the morning there is reveille, — the army awakes, dresses, and answers roll-call; then there is breakfast-call, sick-call, drill, then the dinner-call, and then two hours or more of drill again. And so on until taps, when all lights are to be put out, and all sounds that may disturb sleep must cease.

So an army is fed and clothed, and kept in health and in condition for its work, through the toil of many hands and the thinking of many brains.

An army is incessantly active, even when not campaigning. It is like a huge machine which must be lubricated by work, and often by hard work too, which is essential to toughen its muscles, and to keep its limbs in order for the quick and unusual work of a campaign. It loses its strength and health just in proportion as these conditions are neglected.

Under General Hooker a new inspiration of hopefulness and interest was infused into the work, and all seemed to participate in a moral renovation which gave to it a new life and vigor.

The army under Hooker, at the opening of the Chancellorsville campaign, numbered one hundred and twenty thousand men, who were magnificently armed, equipped, and disciplined, and were in the best of fighting condition. It was like an instrument in perfect tune, but which gives forth harmonies only in answer to a master hand.

It remained to be seen whether the master who had attuned it to its highest perfection would be competent to sweep its keys with triumphant notes of victory, or would only produce the discords of defeat.

Early in April, General Blusterson had reported for duty, had once more taken command of his brigade, and had enthusiastically begun his preparations for the spring campaign. The first intimation I had of the general's return was the cheering of our men as he rode down the company street. I went out and greeted him.

"You look as good as new, General!" I said.

"Oh, yes," he replied. "A little rusty for want of use, that's all; I came by steamer to Acquia Creek, and rode over just to see how my leg would work on horseback. It goes first-rate."

The men, with whom the general was very popular, began to gather around him, when he said, "I see many new faces here, and am glad to see the regiment filled up again. Everything looks hopeful and bright for us! 'A long pull, a strong pull, and a pull all together,' and we will finish the war and go home."

The men cheered, the general saluted in acknowledgment; and after inviting me to come to his quarters he rode away.

In the afternoon I visited his quarters, and found him busy tinkering his patent leg, fixing some soft leather where it had chafed his wound in riding.

"There!" said the general, adjusting his trousers over the artificial leg, and puckering his mouth into a smile, "when you can drive tacks into yourself like that, you've reached perfection, and bullets won't hurt you either. Science, my boy," said the general, walking around his quarters, with scarcely a perceptible limp, "has reached that point where a man can lose a leg and not make a fuss over it. I'm not sure but a good artificial leg is an improvement over a natural one ; a man's corns don't hurt him, sir."

It seemed to detract from the force of this statement that he shortly afterwards complained of cramps in the toes of his amputated foot.

The general complimented me on what he was pleased to term my well-won promotion.

"If any of us live to get out of this shindy alive," said he gravely, "it will sound well to be called 'captain' or 'general.' It is worth something to be at nineteen a captain in active service, as you are. I'm growing old, however. Such titles ought to be made hereditary." Then smiling in his humorous manner, he said, "It wouldn't do me any good, though. I've got no chick nor child but my daughter Emily to leave it to. Don't think she'd appreciate it."

"I've never heard you speak of your family before," I said, "and I didn't know that you had any."

The general's face clouded as if with painful thoughts; but finally smiling, he said, "My daughter Emily is at a boarding-school. She is a different kind of a feller from her father." Then after a gloomy silence he added, "I had a son ; he was older than Emily — about your age. He's dead, and I've always thought you looked like him, Alden. I sent him to college. He was a bright boy, but the accursed drink habit got hold of him." And the general buried his face in his hands as if at painful remembrances.

I understood now the interest he seemed to have taken in me from our first acquaintance.

In the course of conversation the general said he had called on General Hooker during the day, and expressed great enthusiasm over the prospects of the coming campaign.

"We've got a commander now," said the general, "that's going to wake up them Johnnies!"

"What," I inquired, "is he waiting for?"

"Well, he wants settled weather, and just a trifle more information about the enemy."

Before leaving the general, I spoke of Add Key's degradation, and mentioned his many manly characteristics. "It's a shame," I said, "to degrade one of the best non-commissioned officers in the regiment!"

The general looked up frowning, as if to reprove me, but only said after a moment, with an abstracted look, "He's a man, you say, thoroughly to be trusted, and brave? Well, send him to me. I'll see what I can do for him. Order him to report at once."

Add reported at the general's quarters that forenoon. The next morning he did not answer at roll-call, and I supposed he had reported for some duty to General Blusterson.

During the day I learned from the general that he had offered Key a position as his orderly, but that Key had respectfully declined the place.

"Out of regard for you, I did all I could for him," said the general, and then hesitated, as if inclined to say something more, which I interpreted to be some word of reproof that he withheld out of consideration for my feelings.

"Inspection to-morrow! Have everything in prime order, captain!" said the general. "We are likely to move now at any time."

Two days after it was reported around camp that private Key had deserted to the enemy. I learned later that he had been seen down by the river in the evening; that he had shoved off from shore, and had crossed the river in a small boat; had been fired upon, but was seen to reach the opposite shore safely.

This upset me, for I had believed Add to be thoroughly patriotic and a man of high principle. The most galling part was that Lieutenant Sinclair, with exultant looks, remarked, "Captain, I'm sorry your friend has turned out so badly."

"Yes," I said angrily; "one bad officer spoils a great many good men."

I was sore at heart; for, although by reason of good luck I was Add's superior in rank, yet in point of soldierly qualities, experience, and courage, I recognized Add as really superior to many higher in rank than myself.

It is very sad to lose confidence in the manliness of a friend; but I felt that Add, naturally brave and patriotic, had, by injustice, been driven to betray not only his country, but his own manly instincts.

Association with Sinclair was very distasteful to me; and when the next day the general offered me a position for a time on his staff, I accepted, thankful to get away from my company.

Other scenes soon claimed not only my attention, but that of the army and of the country; for the campaign of 1863 had opened.

On the 26th of April we broke camp, and on the 27th our troops were moving in seeming confusion on all the roads.

At noon I was finely mounted, and on duty with General Blusterson. Our brigade was now attached to the Second Army Corps under General Couch. The roads were good, and the men were in fine spirits; and, although marching rapidly, General Blusterson halted the men for frequent rests.

"What," I inquired during one of these intervals, "are we expected to do?"

"We are expected to march," said the general, "to turn the flank of the enemy. The two corps under Sedgwick, left behind, will cross the river as if to force Lee's position. This will deceive the enemy as to the army's real intention. It is well understood that Lee has an intrenched line from Skenker's Creek, below Fredericksburg, to United States Ford, twenty miles above, on the river. Hooker is too long-headed to blunder in making a direct attack; he is going to turn Lee's left flank."

Such, in reality, was General Hooker's plan. He had set in motion the Fifth, Eleventh, and Twelfth Corps on Monday, the 27th; and these during the night of the 28th, and the next morning, had reached and made the passage of the Rappahannock at Kelley's Ford. These three corps, divided in two columns, crossed the Rapidan at Germania and Ely's Fords; then rapidly marched to Chancellorsville.

Our corps, meanwhile, reached the Rappahannock at Kelley's Ford, where it was directed to remain until the turning column mentioned, moving down the south banks of the Rappahannock, uncovered the United States Ford. This was accomplished the moment the turning-forces had crossed the Rapidan. The same afternoon we threw a boat bridge across the Rappahannock, and arrived at Chancellorsville on the 30th, at about the same that time the other corps arrived. The rank and file were in great glee; for they understood the importance of the march, and on all sides were heard to say that "Pop Hooker" used their legs instead of their arms to beat the rebs.

So far the movement was a remarkable success,

only rivalled in military annals by Prince Eugene's famous passage of the Adige.

The strategy of the movement almost justified Hooker's braggadocio proclamation issued at the time, in which he announced that "the enemy must either ingloriously fly, or come out from behind his defences, and give us battle on our own ground, where certain destruction awaits him."

General Blusterson, with his map before him, read the proclamation with a shake of his head and the humorous pucker of his lips with which we are familiar, saying, "Hooker had better wait until he gets out of the woods before he crows."

At the same time he pointed out on the map the fact that we had already laid hold of one of the only two lines of retreat left open to Lee (that of Gordonsville); and that we were threatening the remaining one (that by way of Richmond), which, if chosen for retreat, would bring the force at Chancellorsville on his flank, and the two corps under Sedgwick on his rear.

"Hooker," said the general, "has got to look out, or Lee will squirm out of it, and get a twist on him!"

The sequel proved that Blusterson's fears were well grounded; for Lee, learning that Sedgwick's threats to attack Fredericksburg were only a mask to conceal the attack on his flank, gathered up his forces, and, leaving behind him only a guard for

his intrenchments at Fredericksburg, hurried forward to give battle.

The clearing at Chancellorsville was only ten
miles west from Fredericksburg. It was a large
field, in the midst of which stood the Chancellor
House, from which the place takes its name.

This field is hemmed in on all sides by a wilderness of thickets, in which manœuvring is impossible ; but towards Fredericksburg there is open
country, affording a fine field for all arms. On
the morning of May 1st an onward movement was
made, to take up a line of battle two or three
miles towards Fredericksburg, preparatory to an
advance.

While in the midst of this preparatory movement, and just as Banks's Ford, by a movement of
a column down the river road, had been practically uncovered (thus shortening our communication with Sedgwick by twelve miles), orders were
received to fall back to Chancellorsville clearing.

Here, shut up in the midst of brambles and
thickets, and refusing to avail himself of the advantage of an aggressive movement, Hooker,
notwithstanding the protests of his generals, determined to fight a defensive battle.

CHAPTER XXV.

THE HAZARD OF BATTLE.

In the advance towards Fredericksburg our brigade had formed a part of the vanguard. This portion of the line had broken shamefully when in first contact with the enemy. When we arrived at the Chancellorsville clearing, General Bluster-son, for this and other reasons, was not in his usual good-humor.

"Captain," said the general, dismounting, and limping to a log, where he sat down, "I don't understand it! The men acted like sheep!"

I did not reply; for I had learned that it was my own company that had first broken, and I had heard that it was owing to a blunder, or worse, — the cowardice of Lieutenant Sinclair.

"Give my compliments to the colonel," said the general, "and ask him to come here." Then in an undertone, "I want to know what the matter is."

The colonel reported; and in course of his explanation it came out that the break in our lines was not the fault of our men, but was caused by an order to fall back given to my company by Lieutenant Sinclair.

" How came he to give such an order ? " asked
General Blusterson, his square jaw closing with
a snap. " Have him sent to me."

"Sinclair was scared, I guess," said the colonel.
" The other officers say he gave the order, and
went back himself so fast that when I rode up
he was not with his company. Acting Lieutenant
Standish straightened up the line. He's one of
the chaps that ain't afraid of bullets. The company ain't to blame, General!"

" Humph ! " growled the general, with a pucker
of his lips, "I guess Sinclair had better resign.
Such men ain't of any use to us. But he's got
some influential backers. I'm glad, Colonel, to
know it ain't the fault of your regiment."

In closing the conversation, the colonel said,
nodding towards me, " It wouldn't have occurred, General, if Captain Alden had been in
command," and then rode away.

The brigade had stacked arms, kindled fires,
and soon the smell of fragrant coffee and tobacco
mingled with the odor of the pine woods. The
men lounged in line, laughing and talking, smoking and eating, and an occasional discordant bray
of a picturesque pack-mule furnished a minor key
to the refrain of merry voices.

The general had had his coffee and supper, but
had not recovered his good nature. He had begun gloomily to tinker at his artificial leg. The
air was quite cool as the sun declined. After

feeding my horse, I had thrown myself on the ground before the fire, and was enjoying the bustling scene around me. " Can I help you, General?" I asked. Then, as he only grunted in reply, I added, lazily yawning, "It's a nice evening; a little cool after so hot a day, but we've got a good fire, and plenty of wood to keep it up."

"Yes," said the general, with a queer pucker at his lips; " too much wood, Alden, too much!"

"Too much in your artificial leg?" I asked, "or too much on the fire?"

"Too much all around," said he, making a motion with his hand which indicated the Chancellorsville clearing. "This clearing isn't over three hundred yards wide; it's too cramped to use our men in. It's no place for an army to be shut up in! We haven't got any cavalry to feel out the enemy with. We don't know what they are up to at this moment. They'll take advantage of us; they are just mean enough to steal acorns from a blind pig!"

"We are fortified, General," I said; "they can't gobble your brigade here!"

The general shook his head, and with another pucker of his lips said, in an undertone, "They have got too much sense to attack us here; that yelling and firing is all a blind. I shouldn't wonder if they were on our flank before morning." I knew enough of my general to be sure that if he thought there was anything very serious in the situation, he would not be cross, but the reverse, very cheerful, for he delighted in danger; and I mistrusted that there was not much prospect of a fight. It turned out, however, that the Confederates were at that moment moving to do just what the general had intimated.

Our position in front was practically unassailable. Our right flank, however, on the turnpike near Dowdall's tavern, was, in military parlance, "in the air," and poorly protected. Only two regiments were faced on its flank, and two green companies thrown out for its outposts.

The able Confederate commander understood the advantages and disadvantages of our position. He knew that really he was in a perilous position. Stuart, his vigilant and alert cavalry leader, had brought word of the exposed position of our right flank; and when Jackson proposed to make a great march with twenty-three thousand men, to strike and overwhelm this flank, Lee consented, as it was about the only movement that gave promise of success against our position.

The next morning at nine o'clock Hooker, as if anticipating this movement, gave orders to Howard, who was in command of our right wing, to strengthen his flank, and to advance his pickets for observation, as the enemy were seen moving in his direction.

But in reality neither Hooker nor Howard believed for a moment that the glimpses of Jackson's movement that had been reported, were anything but a prelude to a retreat of the Confederate forces.

It was chilly and raw, and I did not sleep well; so about three o'clock in the morning I roused myself, fed and saddled my horse, and otherwise prepared myself in anticipation of an early move of the enemy.

The camp was not astir. The monotonous song of the whip-poor-will, the crackling of the replenished camp-fires, the champing of our horses and mules, and the tramp of our camp sentinels, were the only sounds that could be heard in the depths of this tangled forest. Around me lay thousands of our men wrapped in their blankets, sleeping.

The red flush of dawn in the east soon heralded the approach of another fine day. The brigade was astir with active life once more, the men preparing their breakfast and answering to roll-call.

At seven o'clock the enemy began a cannonade as if to attack. Occasionally during the forenoon the yell of men and the explosion of musketry and artillery kept up the expectation that a fight might soon be upon us at this point.

The enemy continued to keep up their demonstrations, as if feeling our position, for a general rush *en masse* upon our barricaded lines at Chancellorsville.

In the afternoon we were ordered to the right

about half a mile, and here the brigade waited in line.

It had been unusually quiet, when just before sundown a faint but ominous sound was heard on our extreme right. It was the long crackle of musketry, yells, and every indication of a conflict. Our right wing had been attacked.

Jackson had burst upon it with resistless impetuosity, taking its defences in reverse, and driving our men in upon one another, so that they could not fight. The dispositions made to resist such an attack were inadequate. The whole Eleventh Corps was soon in utter rout and confusion, running into and overturning the divisions which were formed to resist the enemy. A whirlwind of men and artillery and wagons swept down on all the roads towards Chancellorsville, in direst confusion and disorder.

It was seven o'clock, and in the dusk of nightfall, when we went forward to form a new line.

"Nothing but a little panic; we'll get 'em yet!" said General Blusterson cheerfully. "They won't have anything to brag of soon!"

All the first part of the night there was fighting by moonlight in the woods; and it was not until long past midnight that silence and rest succeeded.

Sunday morning dawned. We still held the point where the roads converged, near Chancellorsville, and had seventy-four thousand men posted

" Two ragged prisoners under the persuasive influence
of my revolver."

—Page 283.

between the severed wings of the Confederate army. Here it seemed we might, with both these roads for a pivot, have delivered some terrible blows upon one or the other wing of our divided foes. But Hooker had lost his head, and was a mere nonentity in the fight thereafter. The sequel proved that Hooker, and not the Union army, was defeated.

From the first blow that fell upon us his faculties seemed paralyzed.

Our brigade was thrown forward to the right. Here we captured some prisoners, and learned that General Jackson of the Confederate army was wounded in the attack on the night previous. The enemy opened fire upon our position, enfilading our line with their artillery, while their infantry attacked us in front. The firing was so destructive that General Blusterson was ordered to fall back nearer the Chancellorsville clearing, which if the enemy reached in its then crowded condition, meant disaster to our whole army.

I, with another aid, was ordered to communicate this command to the brigade. I went to the left, and gave the orders to the colonels, and helped execute them, and then began picking up prisoners and sending them to the rear under the escort of slightly wounded men. I was marching two ragged prisoners under the persuasive influence of my revolver, to report with them to General Blusterson, when I broke through a dense thicket, and came upon a line of ragged gray and butternut tatterdemalions.

"I reckon," said one of my prisoners, "that things is changed a little, Captain!"

They were. An officer stepped out of the line. I reversed my revolver, and presented the butt instead of the muzzle to this officer, who politely requested me to deliver my arms and equipments to him. So at his earnest request I unstrapped my sword-belt, and reluctantly turned it over.

As the line of ragged Confederates did not seem to regard themselves as my prisoners, and as I was not naturally contentious, I didn't insist upon their surrender to me. It naturally followed that in the irrepressible conflict of arms one or the other had to yield, so, as I believed in the rule of majorities, I became a prisoner of war.

CHAPTER XXVI.

A SOUTHERN POINT OF VIEW.

So quick had been my transition from the *rôle* of picking up grayback prisoners, to being a picked-up Yankee captive myself, that I could scarcely realize that I was a prisoner of war.

I was conducted to the rear without ceremony, under guard of a Confederate, who had but one suspender for his dilapidated trousers, and no shirt to hang out at the hole which ventilated them at the rear.

The Confederate privates, as well as many officers I met, were an ill-dressed, ragged set of vagabonds ; but they had beaten us in a fair fight, with inferior equipments and numbers, and I could not withhold my admiration for their unflinching bravery.

The comparative quiet of the fields and woods around me, after the rage of battle from which I had emerged, impressed me strangely. The calm of which I speak was one of contrast, rather than one of reality.

As we went on through the wood and field, around us could be seen the dead and wounded of both armies. There was the appealing look or gesture of our own wounded, or a muttered curse from an injured foe, as I passed; or mangled horses gave almost human-like cries, and struggled in their harnesses, to remind me that over this field had swept "the battle breath of hell."

I was soon beyond these nearer evidences of conflict; yet still in the clearings, under the shade of large trees, there were groups where the Confederate surgeons were engaged in their bloody but merciful work.

We finally came to an open space, about two miles in the rear of the battle-field, where were about a thousand or more unfortunate captive Federals.

"A pretty good crap o' Yanks," said my guard. I gave him, for he had in the main been respectful, a small piece of silver, at which his ragged comrades gathered around him, and it was passed from hand to hand as a curiosity. I noticed that their horses were half-starved, and in some cases were tied to their wagons with strips of raw hide or rope; that their supply and ammunition trains looked as if they had been crippled by an attack of old age, or a cyclone of poverty.

I confess to humiliation that under all these adverse circumstances they had fairly beaten us. I was satisfied that, man for man, our soldiers were superior to those of the enemy. In what, then, consisted the superiority of their army?

They believed in their cause; they had the *morale* of victory on their side, and a distinctive class for officers, who had learned the lessons of government of masses of men on plantations, a government which was similar to that of military control.

Our men were all of the same station, — citizens of an average class.

Before I turned my toes towards Richmond, I was permitted to write letters to my friends. I had written to them while on our march to Chancellorsville, that I expected to be at Richmond in the following month; and here I was, *en route*, sure enough.

I wrote to General Blusterson a short note, explaining my capture, and saying I should probably be detained on business of such a nature that it would make it impossible for me to serve on his staff during the remainder of the campaign.

Among the prisoners of war I found one or two acquaintances, and among them was Sergeant Osgood of my own company. He shook hands with me with a grim smile, and then gesturing towards one of the guards, dressed much better than his comrades, said, " See any one you know out there, Captain ? "

I looked in the direction in which he pointed, and saw a Confederate sergeant major taking the names of the prisoners. I was about to turn away when I recognized him. It was Add !

I was never so heartsick in my life, and, turning my back on him, walked to another part of the gathering. I was angered as well as sorrowful. He had been grievously sinned against; but this did not justify him in being a traitor to his country, and in fighting against his own comrades.

As I reflected, it seemed so inconsistent with Add's character, that I could not bring myself to believe, even though my own senses bore testimony to the fact, that he had willingly taken arms against the old flag.

I turned and walked towards a group where Add stood joking and laughing with his new comrades, in apparent unconcern. I approached the group, and heard him telling an incident of the battle, which he was setting forth with grotesque humor, to the great amusement of his listeners. Once his eyes met mine, and I was sure he recognized me. Was it possible he was so lost to shame that he could still look me in the face?

The list was soon made, and we were marched ten miles to Spottsylvania Court-House. I had no rations; the day was hot, and I sorely missed my horse for an underpinning. I was accustomed to marching, however, and had but little to encumber me, not even a blanket.

At Spottsylvania we were subject to the annoyance of a search. One of the men who aided in this search was Add. I stood, almost unable to control my anger against him, as he approached,

"We were marched through the streets to Libby."

— Page 289.

and in a loud tone said, "Turn your pockets wrong side out!" Then with his head close to mine, said in so low a tone that I could scarcely hear, "Don't trust appearances! Don't doubt me, Jack! If you have money they'd take it from you in Richmond. Turn it over to me, and I will see that you get it there."

He thrust his hand into my breast pocket, as if to search it, and I heard the rustle of a paper.

My heart was lighter from that moment. When embarked on the cars at Guiney's Station, I felt in my pocket, and found on a piece of crumpled paper these words, "I am here under conditions that you yourself would approve if you knew them; I will see you again in Richmond if possible. There is no chance of escape to our lines now, and I have " — Here the communication stopped abruptly, as if he had been interrupted in writing.

It was cloudy all that afternoon, and at dark it began to rain.

I was soaking wet, when at twelve o'clock at night we were embarked on the box cars, on which we remained until morning, when, at about nine o'clock, the train started.

We arrived in Richmond, and were marched through the streets to Libby, where we were halted while another search of our persons was made. Paper, pencils, pens, and even a small book of photographs of friends, were taken from me. A young, profane, strutting, important Confederate in white trousers, named Ross, informed me that the articles were " contraband of war," an expression which he constantly mingled with his profanity, as if both were needful to his importance.

After this search we were escorted up three flights of stairs into a room about one hundred by fifty feet in size, filled with Union officers lying upon rude bunks, and in their blankets upon the floor.

We were greeted with the exclamation, " More Yanks ! "   " Fresh fish ? "   " More Yanks ! " and then they crowded around us to inquire the news from the army.

I soon found friends, and with four other officers formed a mess, which was henceforth known as Mess 18.

The room was clean, and quite airy. We got half a loaf of good wheaten bread, and about a quarter of a pound of bacon, for a day's rations; and such of us as had money were permitted to buy sugar, eggs, and other food, through a Confederate sergeant who came in each day. Sugar was a dollar and fifty cents a pound, and potatoes a dollar and fifty cents a dozen.

I took turns with others of my mess in cooking at an old rusty stove on the lower floor, and sorely missed the services of Rolly-Pooly; for with all his shortcomings he could cook. Thus it was that I settled down to the common lot of a prisoner of war to the Southern Confederacy.

I had been in prison three weeks, and had seen and heard nothing from Add, when one day an old darky prisoner, whom we called the General, and whose common talk was of a muddled, growling, Copperhead kind, came in and placed an envelope in my hand, containing my money, and turned away without an explanation.

Among the bills was a note, saying, "This is the first time I've had a chance to communicate. This old darky can be trusted. There is going to be an exchange of officers soon; be ready for it." There was no name signed; but I knew the handwriting to be that of Add.

About the 15th of May the exchange or parole began. We were awakened at eleven o'clock at night, and told that we were to be paroled and marched to City Point at three o'clock A. M. When about a hundred or more had crowded out, the prison door was slammed in our faces with the explanation, "No more to go to-day," uttered by our jailers. The next day, when the work of paroling was resumed, there was a good deal of crowding, which, unfortunately for me, I did not feel to be needful, and the door was again slammed, and the explanation, "No more to be paroled," greeted my surprised ears.

Had I known the sequel I should have been more discouraged than I then was, and even more dissatisfied with myself for not crowding and elbowing forward to get out.

CHAPTER XXVII.

THE DEAD ALIVE.

One of the never-exhausted topics of discussion and conversation in prison during July, was that of exchange or parole of prisoners of war.

Some of the new prisoners had informed us that the exchange was soon to be resumed; others denied it.

One morning it was my turn to scrub the floor; and, as I didn't like the employment, I was inclined to consider it a hardship and an imposition. I was giving vent to my feelings, when an Illinois captain who was assisting me said, "You wouldn't fret if you knew how well off you were here. It is a privilege to be allowed to keep clean."

"Yes," I said; "but we only make a sorry attempt at it."

"You ought to be down in one of the cages a little while," replied the captain, "and then you would appreciate this room and its conveniences."

"What are the cages?" I inquired curiously. "It is the first time I've heard about them. Is there any one there now?"

"An underground sort of a dungeon below us,

— there's half a dozen of them, — where they put men once in a while. I was there three weeks once; if I'd been there three weeks longer, I believe I should have gone insane. One fellow lost his mind; he's there yet."

"How came you to get there?" I inquired, pausing, and looking up astonished.

"It's too long a story to tell. I tried to escape; got out; they caught me, and put me there for safe keeping. At first I thought it a great joke; but it wasn't: it wore on me. There were several men there when I came away. Who were they? Why, Union spies; men under sentence of death. I don't want to get there again, you may bet. This ain't a parlor, but it's above ground."

It was Captain Jones's manner, more than his words, that impressed me. His tones were low and hoarse, as if the very remembrance of the cage, as he called it, excited in him terrible remembrances, and made him cautious not to be overheard.

I had a presentiment that my inquiries about the cage would be more fully answered before I got out of Libby.

I belonged to the same mess with Captain Jones; and I think it was about the 6th of July when he came to me, exclaiming, "Have you heard the news?"

"What is it?"

"I guess we are going to be exchanged; all

the captains are ordered down-stairs, and I don't know what it can mean but that. Hurrah, old boy!" and he threw up his hat.

" Well," I replied, "I'll be glad to get out of here."

In a few moments I, with some others, was ushered into Captain Turner's office, which was on the lower floor of Libby, and drawn up in a line.

After some delay we were informed why we were called to the office. Two Confederate officers, we were told, had been tried and shot in Kentucky by General Burnside, for recruiting inside his lines; and we were to select two of our number for execution by drawing lots.

There was probably not a man among us but had faced death more than once in battle, but our faces were pallid and drawn with the strain put upon us by this unusual form of hazard.

Finally the unlucky designation fell upon a captain of the First New Jersey Cavalry and one of the Fifty-first Indiana, and they were marched away. I found myself drawing a long breath of relief, and, looking around on the faces of my fellow prisoners, realized the horrible nerve strain placed upon us.

As these men do not concern my story further, I will simply say that after being conducted to General Winder's office, and taunted by him, they had been turned into Libby again to await their fate.

Our government, on learning of this affair, selected a son of General Winder, and one of General Lee, to be shot the moment that it should be learned that these officers were executed. That settled the question; and the two officers, instead of being shot, were released long before the other prisoners of Libby were.

It was the 7th of July, or thereabouts, before we learned of the battle of Gettysburg. A Confederate sergeant, who sometimes bought provisions for the officers, said while in our room, " I reckon your Yankee army got a right smart lickin' in Pennsylvania t'other day. Our folks hev got forty thousand prisoners marchin' yer."

Shortly after this, the next day I think it was, he told us that Grant had given up the siege of Vicksburg.

This report, as may be supposed, was discussed by my comrades; and how blue we were over it no one who has not been a prisoner of war can understand. A few days after this the atmosphere of gloom produced by this news suddenly changed. Cheering, dancing, and shouting were heard; and then I learned that the (to us) joyful intelligence had come that Lee had been beaten at Gettysburg, and that Vicksburg had been captured, and over thirty thousand men had surrendered there.

This news was confirmed by the old darky, who said in low tones, " We's got 'em shur, sar. The Yanks has done gone an' licked dem Rebs, sar," and he gave me a dirty copy of the Richmond *Inquirer* containing the news.

I was taking my turn at cooking at the stove for our mess one forenoon shortly after this, when there was quite a stir in our room over the advent of some prisoners who had just come in. I was curious as to what the commotion meant, when Captain Jones came up, saying excitedly, " Have you seen those men ? "

" No," I replied; " what men are they? "

" Why, three men just out of the cages below! Here comes one of them I saw there. He's the one that's off his nut. He's worse than when I met him down there. He's a queer old fish! "

The person in question had approached near where I was cooking. He was dressed in the shreds of an officer's uniform. In his unkempt hair and beard was a green mould, the result of the dampness of his underground dungeon. His face was pallid, like that of one long excluded from the light of day.

" How are you, old fellow? " I said sympathetically. " Have a piece of toasted bread? "

He made no reply, but with one hand clutched the bread, and with the other made a pitiful motion to shield his eyes, as if from light. Then, slowly dropping his hand, with his half-closed eyes fixed on me, he came nearer.

" They must have used you pretty roughly down there where you've been," I said, as I

" How are you, old fellow ?   Have a piece of toasted bread ? "
— Page 296.

grasped and shook his hand. Once more he peered at me, with his hand to his eyes, and then for the first time, in high-pitched tones, tremulous with suffering and weakness, he said in long-drawn-out words, "I can't seem to kinder remember." In a moment I recognized him.

I dropped the pan I was holding over the fire, and had him in my arms. It was my brave, dear old friend Grim! But, oh, how changed! "Don't you know me?" I exclaimed, with tears in my eyes, and sobbing as I spoke; "don't you know Jack Alden?"

As if some benumbing influence rested on his faculties, he still peered in my face, and said slowly, in his far-away, high-pitched tones, "Yes, Jack; I remember Jack," and then put his hand to his head, as if it pained him, and said slowly, "Yes, Jack; the blacksmith shop. Jack — Jack" — and began a pitiful sobbing.

"This is Major Grim," I said to a friend who had come up, "a dear old friend of mine."

Again there was the same movement of his hand towards his head, as if it pained him to think, and again the slow, pitiful voice, "Yes, I'm Major Grim;" and then, as if overcome by some great strain of his faculties, with both hands to his head, he gave a sharp, whimpering cry, and staggered.

I got him to my bunk, and said, "Don't talk now."

I soon got his face and hands washed, his beard and whiskers trimmed, and brought him some nourishing food.

That night he slept well, and continued to sleep as late as nine o'clock in the morning. When he awoke, he remembered me perfectly; and I thought his memory and mind were restored, though weak and shaken.

That afternoon I began to speak to him of his wife. He shook his head, seeming to have forgotten her.

I spoke of this to my friend Jones; and he, in reply, called out to an officer of his acquaintance, " See here! This is Captain Alden, — Colonel Brown of the ——st Penn.;" then in explanation said, " Colonel Brown was a surgeon before he got so interested in fighting that he stopped carving legs and arms, and went to making business for them that did." I shook hands with Brown, and told him about Grim's being in the underground cell, and of his curious loss of memory.

" Let me see him," said the colonel; " I can tell better then." The ex-surgeon looked him over, without asking him any questions, but observing what he said; then took me aside, and said, " He has probably got a hurt on his head. If he had fallen and struck on his head, I should say, fracture of the skull."

I then remembered that in the letter Major

Grim had caused to be written after being taken prisoner, he mentioned being stunned by the explosion of a shell just before being taken prisoner of war.

"That's it probably. He may never get over it, and he may suddenly recover. Let him alone ; don't worry him."

Things continued in much the same way for two months, and yet there was no exchange of prisoners. I had, meanwhile, bought clean underclothes for Major Grim, who could by this time talk quite clearly about many things connected with what naturally interested us in prison ; and yet there were a number of subjects connected with his past life which he could not remember ; and, according to my instructions from Colonel Brown, I did not press such subjects.

In September some articles, including a small photograph-album, which it will be remembered had been taken from me when I went into Libby, after repeated requests were restored to me. One of the photographs was of Grim and his wife, taken when he was at the hospital in Washington. The major had taken this album to look at. As he turned over the leaves, I watched him as he came to this picture. He didn't remember. Finally he startled me with his peculiar, shrill cry, which I have described as like sobbing. He had dropped the album, and with both hands to his head swayed back and forth, and then sobbed out,

" Mary ! Mary ! Mary ! " Another blank space in his mind had been filled.

All this I tell as it occurred. I don't pretend to explain these facts; I only try to detail them minutely, because they were matters of astonishment to me at the time, and are still, although I have since heard them explained from scientific data by Dr. Milner and other eminent surgeons.

I do not pretend to follow their course of reasoning, and am inclined to believe that all theories regarding such mental disturbances are guess-work. I simply tell the facts; and as curious and wonderful as they appear, they are but transcripts of what I observed.

The major's general health continued to improve steadily from the time I first met him in prison; but yet his mind was far from being restored to a healthy condition. He was, as Captain Jones said, very queer. There were still many things in his past life which, to my astonishment, he did not remember.

I wrote to his wife, and sent the letter to the prison commandant. with money to have it forwarded through the lines, telling her of her husband's welfare. The letter, however, as we afterwards learned, like many others sent from prison. for some reason I cannot explain, never reached its destination.

CHAPTER XXVIII.

"I CAN'T GET OUT."

IT was October, 1863. I had been a prisoner over five months, and yet there seemed no prospect of the resumption of exchange, or parole of prisoners, by the Confederate and Federal authorities.

I envied even Major Grim's benumbed condition of mind, which made him fret at imprisonment less than myself. I now understood for the first time the pathos of the cry which Sterne attributed to the caged starling, "I can't get out." It is but a natural expression of the impotent impatience of a prisoner. It was not so much hunger or cold that made our life hard to bear; it was the lethargy to which both mind and body were condemned. As the caged bird beats with its wings the bars of its cage in useless endeavor to get out, so the prisoner at Libby spent his time and thought in many unavailing plans and attempts at escape.

Major Grim had made perceptible improvement. His general health was better; and he no longer exhibited that wildness of manner regarding most objects suddenly presented to his mind. At times, however, when I spoke on what I supposed would be a subject of common interest, he regarded me with a surprised, listless look, as though he thought *me* demented. About all matters of our prison life he was exceedingly acute. One of the curious things about his mental condition was that he did not recall the incidents of his capture in battle. There were, as he had said, blank spots in his mind.

In October I saw the surgeon of the prison, who had his quarters on the lower floor, and attempted to interest him in the case. He responded at once, and said, " Where is he ? He ought to be in the hospital."

When I went back to Grim and told him what the surgeon had said, " I won't go ! " he exclaimed. " Don't send me away ; they will put me down there with the rats ! " And he became so excited that I thought best not to press the subject.

A few days after this, meeting the surgeon in one of the lower rooms, he asked me about Major Grim. I explained to him how excited he was when it was proposed that he should go to the hospital.

The next day I got an order to accompany a Confederate sergeant and Major Grim to the surgeon's office, which was on the lower floor, at the east part of Libby.

Upon seeing him, Turner. the commandant, who

was at the surgeon's office, said, " This is the man who was arrested and confined as a spy."

I then learned for the first time the cause of Major Grim's incarceration in one of the dungeons of the prison.

The major had been found under suspicious circumstances in the streets of Richmond, wearing a long linen duster over his uniform. And, on being arrested and questioned, his answers had been unsatisfactory; and as it had been ascertained that information regarding the plans of the fortifications of Richmond had been conveyed to the Yankees, the Confederates naturally concluded that he was a spy. But they had been unable, after investigation, to connect him with any such work, and had, therefore, after a long time released him.

" We have been told, however," said Turner, " that other information of a very dangerous character has, within a few months, been regularly conveyed to the Yankee army."

I thought at once of Add, and the mystery that surrounded him.

I explained to the surgeon, in the presence of the commandant, the peculiar condition of Major Grim's mind when I first met him in Libby; and I must confess the surgeon treated us very kindly.

He questioned Grim : and at the conclusion of the examination said, " It is a very obscure case."

And then suspiciously exclaimed, "I have read in
the books of similar cases; but how do I know but
what this is a Yankee trick of his, in order to
facilitate his escape?"

"If it was," I replied rather stiffly, "would he
not prefer to be placed in the hospital, where his
chances of getting away are better than in the
prison quarters?"

The surgeon shook his head doubtfully, when I
added, "There is an officer in your army who
knows us both, and who will vouch for our honorable conduct." And then, somewhat hotly, I
continued, "We treated him somewhat differently
when he was a prisoner than you are treating us.
Inquire of Captain James Milner if you doubt it."

"Captain Milner!" exclaimed the surgeon; "I
am well acquainted with him. He's in the city
now; he's a very distinguished officer, sir, and
has just been married to a young lady of our
city — one of the first families. We'll take his
indorsement for anything."

When we left the commandant, he very kindly
said, "I will ascertain if Captain Milner is still
in the city; and, if so, I will communicate with
him."

I was somewhat excited, as the reader may
infer, at thoughts of meeting this young Confederate captain, of whom I had formed a very
high opinion.

I did not have long to wait; for the next day

I was called to the commandant's office, and there found Captain Milner awaiting me.

He greeted me almost affectionately, and I had a long conversation with him. He very kindly and generously acknowledged to the commandant his indebtedness to me, and said, " If you are willing to take Captain Alden's parole of honor, I should like to take him out and introduce him to my friends."

" Impossible ! " exclaimed Turner; " it's against General Winder's express orders. I have rather overstepped the rule in this case, anyway. I'm blamed by the Yankee prisoners for being harsh, and General Winder blames me often for treating them too well. He holds me to a very strict account, Captain."

I was more and more impressed with Captain Milner's manly and chivalrous character, and am sure it was not his fault that he did not afterward succeed in his endeavor to get both myself and Major Grim out of prison on a special exchange.

I mentioned Raymond to him, and spoke of his leaving the Confederate service, and of his taking a position as a cadet in the United States medical service.

" Such men," he said, with his face darkening into a frown, " are a disgrace to any service ; he's a traitor to our side, and will turn traitor again if it suits his convenience. He always was a little sweet on sister May, though. I hope she don't encourage him." I hoped so too, but said nothing.

"By the way," said Captain Milner, "one of your men deserted to us at Fredericksburg, who said he knew you."

"Wasn't his name Key?" I said, thinking of Add. "One of my men, by that name, who had been court-martialed and 'broke,' deserted while we were there."

I told him about the circumstances, but of course did not tell him what I was more than half convinced of, that Key was a Union spy.

I did not see Milner again; but several days after his wife sent me a basket containing fruit, food, and clothing, and a note expressing her gratitude to me for kindness rendered to the captain while he was wounded and a prisoner of war; that she hoped some day when "this cruel war was over" to testify in person her gratitude to one who, though an enemy, had saved the life of Captain Milner. There was much more in the same vein, such as might naturally come from a highly cultivated and newly married young woman.

Major Grim was attended occasionally by the surgeon, but there was no marked improvement in his case.

November was rather an exciting month in Libby. Scurvy had broken out among us, and one man had died from it. One of our officers had obtained a citizen's suit in some incomprehensible manner, and had coolly walked by the guard, and into the streets, without hindrance.

Another prisoner showed me a Confederate suit in which he proposed to dress himself, and then escort me, as if under guard, outside the prison. "You've got the money," he explained, "and I've got this suit, and with both together we can get into our lines." In a day or two, however, a Confederate guard came in and searched our part of the prison, and seized the suit.

I had a suspicion at the time that the man was a Confederate spy in disguise, and that this seizure was intended to give us confidence in him. It was about this time, I think, for I haven't a record of dates, that a Confederate sergeant came through our rooms, as often happened, saying, "If there is any one here who has any greenbacks, I'm paying five dollars for one in Confederate money!" When he came near me, he stopped, lifted his hat, which had been pulled down over his eyes; and I could not wholly restrain an exclamation, for it was Add. He gave a warning shake of his head, slipped some crumpled paper into my hand, and then began fumbling some Confederate money in his fingers, as if he had made an exchange with me. He then passed down the room, uttering the same cry, "If any one here has greenbacks, I'm paying five dollars for one, gentlemen!" I got near the window, and examined the note. It began abruptly, —

"Since I was here last I've seen General Blust. Exchange is no go. Your folks are well; they are very anxious, though. I could help you escape, but it would endanger more important service I'm concerned in. Keep this number, 32 —— Street. If you can get outside, go there; give them this password, ' Lincoln's friends.' " The note was written in a hurried manner. I could not make out whether the last figure was a seven or nine; and as I had no immediate hopes of getting away, it did not interest me then as much as it did afterwards.

During November and December there were whispers and covert allusions to· tunnelling out of Libby; but I could not discern that they were anything but rumors, and that loose kind of talk that is common among men similarly circumstanced with ourselves.

One day, soon after this, Captain Jones came to me, and said in a whisper, while brushing some dirt from his uniform, " Keep mum if I'm away nights; don't say anything. Grim is in it too! "

" In what? "

" Tunnelling," he replied. " Mum's the word."

As the major had not said anything to me, and as I had never heard him even discuss plans for escape, I concluded Jones had either been dreaming, or was simply pretending to know something of which he had possibly heard rumors.

CHAPTER XXIX.

THE AIR OF LIBERTY.

DURING the larger part of the winter of 1863 there were twelve hundred prisoners in Libby, mostly crowded into the six rooms of its two upper floors. These rooms communicated with one another, and, by means of a stairway below them, with the room used as a kitchen.

At the west end of Libby, next to the kitchen, was the commandant's office; and at the east end the hospital, both of which were separated from the kitchen by heavy blank walls without doors or other means of communication except from the outside.

Under the whole length of Libby was a cellar separated into compartments by blank walls which corresponded with those we have mentioned. This, with the isolated position of the building, made it easy to guard. At first glance it would seem impossible for its prisoners to " make a break," or find any means of escape.

During the winter months I had been one of seventy men who had participated in an attempt at escape by means of the central cellar, which

had been reached by taking up two floor boards
in the kitchen.   From this cellar, on the basement
side, was an open doorway leading to the street.
This was unguarded except by two sentinels on
the sidewalk.

At the north end of this section of the cellar
were the padlocked dungeons, which I have before mentioned as the place where Major Grim
had for a time been confined.   At this time,
however, they had no occupant.

The plan for escape had been abandoned, because it was believed that some one of our
number was a rebel spy in disguise, who had
communicated the secret to the prison officers.
Whether this was true or not, we had one night
almost been caught while in the cellar, by the entrance of the Confederate guard into the kitchen
above.   We had got out without being detected;
but it was, as Captain Jones called it, "a very
close call."

It was decided by our leader that the attempt
had better be abandoned, as it was impossible to
overpower the guard without creating an alarm,
which would lead to detection and punishment,
and thus spoil any future plans of escape.

A few days passed without anything more being
said, when one morning Jones informed me that
he and others had been trying to tunnel out of
the east cellar into a sewer; but after breaking
their knives, and wearing themselves out, they

had encountered such formidable obstacles that it had compelled the abandonment of the plan.

" I guess," he added, " that it is the last tunnel that will be attempted for some time. I'm all worn out, and I guess the rest of the men are in the same fix. So you didn't lose anything by being out of it."

After this, both Jones and my old friend talked their tunnelling exploits over with me, but refused to divulge how they had reached the east cellar, saying they had promised not to tell; and as I supposed they reached it in some way from the middle cellar in the old manner, I did not exhibit a great deal of curiosity. My imagination, however, was excited by these events, and I often said if there were again any plans formed to escape, I for one was anxious to take my chance in it.

Grim said, " I shouldn't have gone out without you, but you couldn't have stood it, digging in that tunnel; I almost gave out myself."

After this, talk of escape for a time ceased. I, like many others, resigned myself to the fate of awaiting the tardy exchange of prisoners. My health, which up to this time had been very good, began to yield under the strain of imprisonment.

It was more than a month after, if I remember rightly, that I awoke one night and turned to speak to Captain Jones. All the lights were out; but he was absent from his accustomed sleeping-place.

At first I thought he was absent in some other room, visiting friends; but when for several nights in succession the same thing occurred, I began to wonder where he spent his nights.

This wonder was not decreased when one night not long after I heard Major Grim get up and softly creep away. The next night the same thing occurred again; and I got up and followed him down the stairway to the kitchen. To my astonishment, here he disappeared; for, though I called to him, and groped all around, he was not there.

I went back to my sleeping-place, wondering what new scheme was on foot, no less than at his mysterious disappearance from the kitchen. When at dawn I awoke, I found both Grim and Jones in their accustomed places, sleeping heavily. Major Grim looked haggard and tired, while on Captain Jones's clothing there was evidence that he had been in some underground place.

Here let me say, that though Major Grim had what we called "blank spots" in his memory, he was sharp and keen regarding what was going on in the prison. The surgeon told me that under sudden excitement he might regain his lost power, or by the same means be thrown into a worse condition.

Captain Jones yawned when I shook him, and said, "What's the matter, my boy? Can't you let a fellow sleep a little longer?"

"I suppose I ought to," I replied; "you get so little sleep nights now."

Sitting upright, he exclaimed in evident surprise, "What's that you say?"

"You seem," I replied, "to be away from your bed and board all night; and too much dissipation and excitement are apt to wear one out, you know. There's Grim! Look at him; he looks like death."

"Well, I'll tell you," said the captain, coolly yawning. "My bed itself is a board; and the attractions and amusements of this place are so numerous that, like Artemus Ward and his twins, I have to get up nights to laugh. I don't want to disturb you, bunkie; so I seek out secluded spots in which to do my laughing."

"Underground, I suppose," I said; "but it seems to me you might find secluded spots that don't leave such a smell on you."

"Sh-h-h-h!" ejaculated Jones between his teeth. "Don't speak so loud." Then, significantly nodding towards our slumbering comrade, said, "The old boy is pretty well played out with digging; but you can't keep him out of it."

"What is it?" I exclaimed. "Why don't you trust me?"

"Well," said Jones, "we are sworn into it ourselves; we've asked leave to take you into the secret. I'll see the leader to-night, and tell him what you know. You wouldn't have me violate my word, would you?"

Finally all plans of escape ceased to be talked of, and February, 1864, came. The weather was cold, and our food was insufficient for proper nourishment. I had received food and notes from young Milner's wife twice since the times mentioned, and was deemed very fortunate in having friends in Richmond with whom I could communicate.

I mention this fact; for little things, in themselves insignificant, count for so much among prisoners of war.

In conversation with the Confederate surgeon, I learned that an exchange of prisoners between the Confederate and Union authorities was practically impossible since the appointment of General Butler as Commissioner of Exchange.

The surgeon was polite, and very much interested in what he called Grim's extraordinary lapse of memory. The days dragged their slow length away, when, on the night of the 9th of February, I was awakened by Major Grim, just as I had fallen asleep.

"Get up," he said in a hoarse and excited whisper, "and scramble your traps together to go out."

I sat up and rubbed my eyes, and perceived, as if in a dream, that both Grim and Jones were equipping themselves for a journey.

"What is the matter? Have you gone wild?" I said in a low and astonished voice.

"Sh-h-h-h!" said Captain Jones hoarsely. "This

is a chance in a thousand; get your things together
and follow us. We've no right to tell you anything, but 'twill pay to follow us."

I was now all excitement; and soon, equipped
with my blanket and haversack, softly stepping
over the slumbering forms of fellow prisoners, followed them down-stairs and into the kitchen.
Here, near the Carey-street door, I found fifty
men or more silently but excitedly struggling for
precedence.

I wonderingly held on to Jones, waiting my
turn, and was pressed by the door to the fireplace, which I was very near before I saw what
was happening. Men were disappearing down a
wide hole in the rear of the fireplace, where brick
-had been removed. Without question I followed
Jones down this hole, which led to the east cellar;
and here, after some delay, reached the mouth of
a tunnel which had been dug under the street,
and, almost before I could realize it, was crawling
through a dark, damp hole underground.

When I stood in the free air, sheltered by a shed,
which I had often noticed from the prison window,
on the opposite side of the street, I was almost
bewildered. We saw the sentinels pacing their
posts; and in the interval while we stood waiting, their cry, " Ten o'clock, and all's well," rang
out like a voice of prophetic assurance.

" We'd better get outside of city limits," whispered the captain, " as soon as possible."

"No," said Grim in a low voice, but in a tone of command, more like his old self than I had heard since meeting him in Libby; "we'll stay in the city till the pursuit and cry is over. Come on."

And then in his old manner of commanding, that reassured me, without hesitation he went with firm tread down the street leading in a northerly direction out of Richmond, as if the air of liberty had reawakened and invigorated his faculties. In the partial darkness we passed people on the street; and then, through alleyways and back streets, went toward the northern suburbs of Richmond. For some time we went on in this manner, when at a narrow alley Grim began counting the doors; and then, turning back, began to count once more.

"This is the place," he finally said confidently, stopping at a low door in the narrow alley; "but I'll make sure of it." And, turning, he retraced his steps, and came back, counting the doorways once again.

"Yes; I kinder thought I was right."

He was about to knock at the low door, when Jones caught his hand, and said doubtingly, "Major, you know you ain't just right in your head always."

"Step to the corner," said the major in a tone of assertion, "and watch and listen if you doubt."

He knocked at the doorway in a peculiar manner. We heard the doorway unbolted.

"Who come dar?"

"Lincoln's friends," said Major Grim.

"Always true," said the other voice in reply, as if by agreement.

The old colored man beckoned to us; and I then remembered that "Lincoln's friends" was the password Add had given me, and I had no doubt it was the same place he had mentioned in his note. We were soon escorted to a small room, apparently the servants' quarters of a large residence.

"Clar ter goodness! Whar dus you uns come from?" he exclaimed.

"You remember me, don't you?" said Grim. "I came here with Sergeant Key. Have you seen him lately?"

"Yes; I 'member," said the black man. "You war not right here," touching his head. "Massa Key, why he was here a right smart time ago ter send Steve thro' to de Lincoln folks."

"The streets are full of Yanks," said Grim. "Guess you had better hide us for a while. The rebs will be kinder wild when they find out about it."

"You bet," agreed Jones; "they'll be wild tomorrow."

Seeing me give Captain Jones a warning look, Grim said, "Don't doubt this black man. He's all white inside, if his skin is black."

In fifteen minutes the colored man returned, bringing a basket; and with the basket in one hand and a candle in the other, conducted us through a passageway, and, after cautioning us to remove our shoes, conducted us up a pair of back stairs of the main building into a low attic room. In this room there was a large bed, several packing-boxes, trunks, and a clutter of other such material as is found in the store-room of a large house.

After cautioning us once more, the colored man set the basket inside the doorway, and then saying, " Will see you right smart soon, sar," bowed, and I heard him lock the door.

I lay down on the bed, and fell into a heavy slumber; and when I awoke, though it was broad day, both Grim and Jones were still slumbering.

The attic room was lighted by a half window, to which I went, and looked out upon a broad street, where there were residences devoted evidently to the better class of the people of Richmond. When Grim had awakened, I commented on this fact to him.

"Yes," he replied; "we entered this house by the servants' quarters from the rear."

The street seemed deserted during the morning hours, and but few people passed. After Captain Jones awoke, Major Grim set out some food from the basket, such as bacon, sweet potatoes, cornbread, and a bottle of cold tea. We all ate a very hearty meal.

"The air of liberty," said Jones, smacking his lips over the last crumb, "gives one an appetite like a wolf's. I could eat the basket!"

CHAPTER XXX.

UNDER GOD'S FLAG.

WE remained in the room described for four days, during which time we were visited several times by Sam Brent and his wife, who brought us food, and news from the outside world. In this way we learned that when it had been discovered that one hundred and forty prisoners had mysteriously disappeared from Libby, the greatest excitement prevailed in Richmond.

General Winder was furious, and had caused the entire guard detail of the prison to be arrested and searched for greenbacks, believing that they had been bribed. After two days of conjecture and mystery the tunnel was accidentally discovered. Scouts had meanwhile been sent out in every direction to capture the escaping prisoners.

Sam thought it was best for us to lie still in our present place of concealment until the active chase was over, and then our escape could be made with comparative ease. This plan was not destined to be carried out.

On the evening of the fourth day of our concealment, Sam Brent, with a candle in one hand

and a basket in the other, entered the room, carefully closed the door, and said, "Time y's gwine away fro' heah. Massa Robert wor heah ter-day, and says, 'Sam, der ye know whar dem Yanks is?'"

"Guess he was joking," said Grim, "wasn't he?"

"Massa Robert mighty fon' of me. We's raised togedder," said Brent, "but Massa Robert neber joke."

It was about ten o'clock at night when we went down the narrow stairway, and halted in the kitchen to fill our canteens. Sam suddenly exclaimed in a hoarse whisper, "Get inter dat closet dar, quick! Dar's some one comin'!" and with this, Sam blew out the candle and went to the door.

"Sam! Sam!" said a feminine voice, "are you there?"

"Yes, missus," answered Brent; "jus' blowed out de candle ter leab!" Then the door opened, and a young and beautiful lady, with a lighted candle in her hand, stepped through the doorway.

We had been unable to fully close the closet door on account of our number, and therefore were in much fear that we should be discovered.

"I have rung for you twice within a half-hour, Sam," said the young lady imperiously; "where's Milly?"

"Beg pardon; didn't hear yer," said Sam

humbly; "'spect I's gettin' deaf. Milly's gone
ter bed, missus!"

"Master James will be here to-morrow, and
you must be particular about the dinner." Then
she gave Sam directions about a dinner that made
my mouth water, all the time looking toward
us, but standing with the light shining in her
face.

She was certainly very beautiful, but of a different type from our New England girls; and I
could not but admire her graceful habit of command, her self-possession, and that certain something which gave to her an air of refined dignity
and distinction, which blended very sweetly with
her every attitude, even when speaking to her
servant.

Had not the light been shining in her face, and
throwing the place where we stood in shadow, we
must have been discovered.

She was gone when Sam came back into the
kitchen, saying, "You gemmen were powerful
near ter trouble. Dat yer lady's sister been married lately, and dey's powerful towsey, dey is,
when Massa James comes home fro' his regiment."
And Sam shook his head gravely when he said,
"Better be gwine by dat do' while I locks up
de house." We stepped outside, and Sam soon
joined us.

As Sam had by the questions of his master
been hurried into preparations for our departure

sooner than was contemplated, our supply of rations was not large.

We hurriedly passed through the streets of Richmond, and then, keeping clear of the roads, went eastward across the fields and through the wooded country and its by-paths for an hour or so, when Sam intimated that he must be going back. He gave us before leaving, however, very clear directions as to the course we had better take.

On parting we tried to give him what money we had, but he would accept of no reward.

We shook hands with him, gave him our names, and asked him, if he ever got his freedom, to come and see us.

We were now in the vicinity of Fair Oaks, not far from the Richmond and York Railroad, and Grim was familiar with the country between us and the Chickahominy. Sam had told us that the roads were being watched at all the crossings.

After he left us we travelled in a north-easterly direction, and just before daybreak stopped in a piece of swampy wood on the south side, and about a half a mile from the Chickahominy.

This was, as Grim said, not far from where the bridge had been built in 1862, during the Peninsular Campaign.

"I know the ground here," said Grim; "I was all over it in the Peninsular Campaign, and we have got some advantages in that."

During the day we lay concealed in the thickets, where we could see those who might approach, but could not be seen. Once during the day I saw two Confederate soldiers going towards the Chickahominy; and again a colored boy, apparently a servant, passed near to our place of concealment. When night came we moved towards the river, thinking it best to cross at the first opportunity.

"The engineers had a pontoon bridge here in 1862," said Grim, "and just below we helped to build a log bridge through the swamp." We went down the river bank, under the shadow of the bluff, until we came to a corduroy way, which, Grim said, was the approach to the Woodbury bridge.

"S-h-h! what's that?" whispered Jones.

It was a sound like the measured tread of a sentinel walking his post. We threw ourselves upon the causeway; and, after a whispered consultation, it was determined that Grim should reconnoitre the position.

It was some fifteen minutes before he came back, and, giving a signal for silence, beckoned us to follow him into the thickets which were on all sides of the corduroy approach leading to the bridge.

We halted in a place where we were out of the wet of the swamp; and not until then did Grim inform us that we had been near running into the guards of the Confederates. "The rebs," said Grim, "are guarding the bridge. It's a sort of home guard from Richmond," he said, " and we must have come kind o' close to their encampment. I heard one of the sentinels asking another if it wasn't time they were relieved, and the other said he had heard the relief coming at the other end of the road. They must have mistaken the noise we made for the relief. These logs are too good a conductor of sound, I guess."

After some debate we concluded to move down stream to a narrow place, and then swim the river. But this brought out the unpleasant fact that Jones could not swim a stroke. In the course of an hour we came to a portion of the stream which was narrow; and it was opposite here, Major Grim declared, that Sumner's corps had been encamped in 1862, just before the battle of Fair Oaks.

After some debate, it was agreed that either Major Grim or I should strip, and, with his clothes on his head, cross the river. As Major Grim knew best the surroundings on the other side, we thought it best for him to do this. He waded in to see if it could be forded, and then with a few strokes reached the northern side.

After full half an hour he came back, pushing before him three pieces of board and a cracker-box; but he was very cold and shivering. The boards, he said, had probably been used by our men for flooring to a tent, and by their aid Jones could swim the river.

After Grim had got warmed up by exercise, we stowed our clothes in the cracker-box, constructed a kind of raft, and then, by wading and swimming, safely reached the other side of the narrow river. We were soon dressed and on our way eastward, travelling single file on what the Major declared was the Williamsburg road.

It was not far from twelve o'clock at night when we crossed the river. We met with no accident or hindrance worthy of mention thenceforth, except being frightened by the barking of dogs at a house near which we had passed about daylight.

Grim thought we were now near New Kent Court-House, and about twenty miles from Williamsburg, near where we had been informed there were stationed United States troops.

"We are through the worst of it now, but we've got to keep our eyes peeled," said Grim, who seemed to have recovered all his old-time *vim* and courage. "If we are seen by a single white person, especially a woman, we'll be gobbled. The women are the worst rebs there are in this country, by a long chalk."

"You can reason with a man," agreed Jones; "but a rebel woman is the very devil! there ain't no reason in 'em.

"I was out on picket here once," said he,

"and a nice-looking young lady, all smiles, invited me to dinner. Well, I hadn't eaten four mouthfuls before I smelt a rat, and found that some rebs were close onto me. I barely got out of the door with my six-shooter in my hand, before they were at the house, and then for a minute or two you could have played dominoes on my coat-tail.

"Afterwards, when we had advanced our pickets beyond her house, that young woman jeered at me, and said, 'Ye wus right smart in gettin' out, I reckon, Yank, that day. What made ye suspect me?'

"'I saw the devil in your eye, and I knew you had signalled,' I replied; 'and before I had got out of the door I saw the Johnny Rebs skulking towards the house.' "I tell you," said Jones emphatically, "the best men they've got here are the women; they are clear grit."

During that day we had taken refuge in a piece of wood, and we did not sleep much, as it was rather cold. We had eaten all our provisions, and started out at night hungry, but not dispirited; for we thought that in twenty-four hours we might be able to obtain food in some way. And so it proved; for during the night we came to a corn-crib, from which we obtained several ears of corn apiece.

Soon after this we halted near the crossing of two roads, one of which Jones declared led to

Charles City, and the other to Williamsburg.
We were suspicious that there might be pickets
here, and Grim said he thought that we would
probably find them on all the cross-roads here-
abouts until Williamsburg was reached.

It was therefore agreed that we had better
keep away from roads, and, travelling north-east,
endeavor to reach the York River, where it might
be possible to obtain a boat. In any case, as
Major Grim represented, there could be found
along the shore of the river at low tide oysters
and hard clams for sustenance. If we could obtain food, time was of less consequence than
safety. We therefore adopted his suggestion, and
travelled all that night across the fields and
through the woods.

We finally halted for rest in a dense growth
of scrubby trees. Here we kindled a fire, and
parched corn and ate it; for we were ravenously
hungry. We had but a small quantity of water
left, for we had not been able to refill the two
canteens.

We took the precaution of concealing the place
where we halted by cutting limbs of trees, and
sticking them into the ground around us; and it
was well we did so, for while I was on guard and
my comrades were sleeping, I saw three Confederate soldiers, with muskets at "right shoulder
shift," coming through the wood.

"I seen them Yanks in yer' not over two hours

ago," I heard one of them say. I was so much excited that I almost held my breath. They passed near where I was; then I awoke Grim and Jones, and told them what I heard.

"There must have been another party of Yanks in the wood here, then; for we have been here since morning," said Grim, looking at the sun, "and it is now nearly four o'clock. We'd better lie still, however, as the chances are they won't come back this way."

But there was no more sleeping; and we were very anxious until darkness came on, as a safe shroud for our concealment when we attempted to travel farther. Even then we advanced with unusual caution, moving silently, in single file, through the fields and woods.

It was quite light when, in the early hours of the morning, we reached a creek running nearly north and south, and were moving down its easterly bank, when we came to a whitewashed log structure, at the sight of which Grim gave an exclamation of glad surprise.

"I know this place like a book!" he exclaimed. "We used to get oysters and fish of an old black fellow here in '62. I wonder if he's about here now." We reconnoitred the hut carefully; but there were no signs of life, not even the dog which is usually found at such huts.

Major Grim knocked at the door, but there was no answer. We pushed aside the cotton cloth stretched over a hole for a window, and looked in, but saw nothing but darkness. We were just turning away from the place, by a narrow path, when we almost ran over a black man coming towards the hut with a basket on his shoulder.

"Who am dat?" the man inquired, halting. "What are yer doin' yer'?"

"We are Yankee soldiers," I replied; "we want something to eat."

The old black man stood peering into our faces, when Grim said, "Uncle, don't you remember me? I used to buy oysters and fish of you, and I wouldn't let the boys steal your chickens. Don't you remember Captain Grim?" The old negro advanced doubtingly, peering into Grim's face, and led the way to the cabin, struck a light, looked at Major Grim by the light; and then, as if satisfied with the inspection, said joyfully, "Yes, sar; I's 'member you, Captain. Golly, sar! ye's powerful peaked, do'."

"We've been prisoners of war, and are escaping," said Grim confidently. "We want something to eat now, and then we want you to help us down the river. We'll pay you all the money we've got, and try and get more money to you when we get into our lines."

The old darky said nothing, but started a fire, cooked corn-bread, a tin pailful of oysters, and some coffee, and we sat down and had a

"We almost ran over a black man."
— Page 330.

square meal before we inquired where he got the coffee.

"Down ter York," he replied. "I sells fish, and gets what provisions of coffee and Yankee traps I want foh the grand folks." This allusion was to his master, whose house was about half a mile from his hut.

We remained in the vicinity of the hut all day; and when night came we ate one more hearty meal, and then got on board the old man's scow boat, went down the creek to the York River, and before morning, without incident worthy of note, were landed at Yorktown, and thanked God for his infinite mercy, that through many trials he had brought us once more in safety under his flag.

We were warmly received by a young officer of the guard, who escorted us to his quarters.

We were royally entertained at Yorktown, and in course of another twenty-four hours were sent to Old Point Comfort.

CHAPTER XXXI.

IN WASHINGTON AGAIN.

ON arriving at Fortress Monroe, we learned that several prisoners who had escaped by the Libby tunnel had preceded us.

This daring escape, coming at a time when there was a comparative dearth of military news, was caught up by the newspapers, so that some details of this adventurous affair were known at almost every home in the North.

Illustrative of this, before I took the steamer for Washington, I had written to my mother of my arrival within our lines, incidentally giving some of the details of my escape. Three days afterwards — even before I had heard from her — I saw in the telegraphic news of the Associated Press some of the contents of my letter, which had been caught up by enterprising news-gatherers, and repeated almost *verbatim*.

After our arrival in our lines, Major Grim, who up to this time had shown much of his natural power of decision, courage, and brightness, relapsed into a condition similar to that in which I first found him at Libby.

The surgeon at Old Point Comfort attributed this to over-strained nerves, and said, "I think with rest and nursing he will come out all right in the end."

We remained at the fort about twenty-four hours, and then took the steamer for Washington, where we arrived the next morning.

I was hurrying, with Major Grim, towards Pennsylvania Avenue, when a mounted officer, with an orderly at his heels, apparently from the Arsenal, cantered by us. I had taken no particular notice of this officer, until I saw him halt, and then wheel his horse and come back to us. At first I thought he was an officer of the provost guard of the city, and had mistaken us for deserters, or men on "French leave." It was not until he came up to us, stopped, and was extending his hand, that I recognized General Blusterson.

It is needless to say I was very glad to see him.

After shaking hands with me, he turned to my superior, and said, "Major Grim, I am glad to congratulate you on your safe arrival within our lines."

The major shook hands with the general, returned the greeting with a dull, apathetic look, saying, "You've got the advantage of me, sir; I don't remember where I've met *you*."

"He seems to go back on me," said the general in a low tone, half in anger and half in inquiry. "Is he miffed over that Fredericksburg affair?"

I explained the major's condition by pointing to my head, and saying in an undertone, "Not quite right here, General."

The general walked his horse by our side until we reached Pennsylvania Avenue. There, almost forcing upon me the loan of some money, saying I would need it before I got my pay, he invited me to visit him at Willard's Hotel, where he informed me he was quartered with his daughter while on sick leave, and on business connected with the manufacture of artificial limbs.

He had, so he said, sold his patent to a stock company, but still retained a large interest, and also a handsome royalty, therein.

"I've got quite a pile out of it already, Alden," said the general effusively, "and there are fortunes in it still."

As the hospital where Dr. Milner had charge was at quite a long distance, I called a carriage, and rode to the place, as I was anxious not only to give him tidings from his son, but also to interest him in Major Grim's peculiar case. Besides this, Mrs. Grim was probably there, and — well, never mind.

On my arrival I went to the office door, where a young black boy, the whiteness of whose collar was only equalled by the whiteness of his eyes, answered my summons.

"Is Dr. Milner in?"

"No, sar," said this conglomeration of white

collar, brass buttons, and blackness; "de doctor
am out. Will you leab your card, sar, or, " —
Here a surprising transformation in this important
personage took place, which at first I was at a loss
to understand. His eyes bulged out of his head;
he began to hop up and down excitedly, exclaiming, "Hi! hi! hi! Golly! Golly! Glory! It am
de boss! It am de boss! de captain! de captain!"

"Well!" I exclaimed, astonished in my turn,
"it's you, is it, Rolly?"

"I 'clar' ter gracious, Cap'n! you's so power-
fully peaked, I done gone forgot yo' when yo's
com' ter dis do'."

The doctor soon appeared; and, after recognizing in the shabby persons before him Major Grim
and Captain Alden, greeted us in his very kindly
and friendly way, seated us in his comfortable
office, and without ceremony invited us to make
our home with him during our stay in Washington.

I called the doctor's attention to Major Grim by
a gesture; for he sat apathetically looking around
the room, and did not apparently evince any interest in the doctor or the place. Evidently he
did not recognize the doctor any more than he
had General Blusterson. But when the doctor
set down his case of instruments, which he had
brought into the room when he came to us, opened
it, and began to carefully cleanse and readjust
them, I saw a change sweep over Major Grim's
face. He started, rose to his feet, stared — then

with one hand to his head, and the other extended, with the sharp cry which I have described elsewhere, exclaimed, "Dr. Milner! — Doctor! — I'm glad to see you!"

The doctor gave an inquiring look. I explained to the best of my ability in pantomime; and in a moment more he was excited by professional as well as friendly interest in Major Grim.

I relate the incident of Grim's associating Dr. Milner with his instruments and his old wound minutely, as it occurred, because at the time it seemed to me very curious.

The doctor took me aside; and in a few words I told him of Major Grim's injury and of his lapse of memory, and besought him to do his utmost to restore him.

"Does he know that his wife is here?" asked the doctor, his dark eyes showing his interest, while his reddish hair seemed to bristle with increasing energy at the prospect of so interesting a case. "Does he remember about his wife?"

"Apparently he does remember about her," I said hesitatingly; then added, "It is curious, however, that he has not inquired for her since we came here."

"I will step over to her ward," said the doctor, "and bring her in. And you, meanwhile, prepare his mind for it the best you can. She has always been sanguine that her husband would return."

While the doctor was absent I took out my

pocketbook of photographs, which I have before mentioned, and called Grim's attention to the picture of himself and wife.

"Yes," he said, nodding and smiling; "it's Mary's picture. She's a good sort of a girl."

"She is here," I explained. "She's been here, my dear Major, ever since you were taken prisoner at Fredericksburg!"

I saw a look come to his face, as if there were something he did not understand; but at that instant the doctor came in with Mrs. Grim, who rushed with almost frantic pleasure towards her husband.

The major recognized her; but his manner was embarrassed, and showed us that there was something in his mental attitude that we did not yet comprehend.

During the interview between the major and his wife, it came out, bit by bit, that he remembered her as Mary Crandall, but had no remembrance of ever being married to her.

"Leave them alone together," said the doctor in a low tone, shaking his head doubtingly, "and perhaps some chord of association will be touched which will restore his memory of her, as it did of me."

So we left them together, and retraced our steps to the office. I then asked a question which had been on my lips a dozen times since my entrance into the hospital.

"Doctor," I said, and my throat was very dry and my voice husky, "where is Miss May?"

"May!" said the doctor, facing me, "oh, didn't I tell you? She's in Baltimore, visiting the Raymonds. They are making a good deal of fuss over her; but I guess they won't spoil her. Raymond, you know, lost his money, but has lately, by the death of his uncle, come into a large property again; and he is also home for a while on leave of absence." Then he added with a laugh, "Guess he won't come back till May does."

My heart sank within me as the doctor added, looking at me, "Let me see, — May is about three years older than you are. She's thinking of getting married perhaps. Raymond is no match for her in anything but family and property; but his folks put on a good deal of style, — old family, you know, — women like that, — well, — humph!" and the doctor turned away to some duty to which he was called.

Every word of the doctor had pierced me like a knife. I knew, however, that what he had said was true, and that May Milner was a person likely to be influenced by fine and luxurious surroundings.

I then proudly determined to dismiss her from my thoughts, a determination more easily made than kept.

In two days I had discarded my rusty prison clothes and got a new uniform, which had been fitted to me, and which, by contrast with the clothes I had discarded, made me feel very well satisfied with my appearance.

In the evening I called at Willard's Hotel to see General Blusterson. Here, also, I met Miss Emily, his daughter.

Miss Emily Blusterson was about fifteen years of age, with grave but sympathetic manners, and a demure, Quaker-like face, that made her appear older by several years. At first glance I was inclined to think her very plain; but after a few hours this plainness seemed to disappear in an attractiveness which I cannot express.

Afterwards, in endeavoring to recall what she had said during the evening, I found that she had talked but little, and that she had expressed more interest in me with her eyes, which were very large and earnest, than by any verbal utterances. She had, however, led me to talk of myself, of my escape from Libby, and of my other military experiences, and had been a very attentive listener. What young man is not interested in a young lady who leads him to talk of himself?

The general smoked, discussed the military situation for a while, and then, as I talked of myself to Miss Emily, took a nap in his easy-chair.

When at a late hour that evening I left Willard's, in spite of the shock which my feelings, or vanity (calling it by no more serious name), had sustained by learning of Miss Milner's visit to Baltimore, and the possibility of her engagement to Raymond, I found that I had not only passed a very pleasant evening, but had scarcely thought of Miss May during that time.

My visit was so pleasant, that during my stay in Washington I was a constant visitor at the general's — ostensibly to inquire about a leave of absence I had applied for, but in reality,— but that's another story.

Once when I had spoken to the general of my former comrade, Addison Key, he became enthusiastic.

"He is just the kind of a boy you told me he was," said the general in his positive manner, — true as steel; and he has rendered very great service to the army."

"Where is he now?" I inquired,

"That's something I don't know; he's gone beyond my control. I haven't heard from him for two months. That Sinclair? Humph! he ought to have been dismissed the service; but he's on special duty, I understand, somewhere here in Washington, — got transferred after the Chancellorsville fight. Influence saved his bacon, my boy;" and the old general shook his head in his humorous manner, as he added, "Influence can't make a mule of a brass button, but it can make an officer of 'most any kind of poor stuff."

"What do you think Addison Key is up to

now?" I inquired. "I don't like the idea of his being a spy."

"I offered the boy a lieutenant's position, and represented that it might be risky if the rebs caught him. But he said, 'General, 'I guess 'most everybody that ever was caught by them rebs has found it risky, whether he was in the secret service or any other. It's in the rebel blood to make themselves disagreeable to people they don't like.' I've heard," said the general, "but I won't vouch for the truth of it, that Key has lately passed an examination for promotion in one of the new colored regiments; and like as not it is true, — can't tell."

At last my leave of absence was granted. I had accounted for the last missing tompion, which, as captain of the company I was held to be accountable for while in active service, having obtained affidavits which would blister ordinary paper to account for their non-appearance.

I went several times to bid good-by to the general and Miss Emily. I had settled my accounts, obtained my ration money and back pay, amounting in all to what I considered a large sum of money.

After bidding good-by to my friends in the hospital, I paid one more good-by visit to the general and Emily, — Miss Emily, I should have said, — and took my departure for home.

Rolly insisted on carrying my satchel to the

depot; and then, in spite of my protests, I found he had made all his arrangements to accompany me, even to buying a ticket to Boston. I was so touched by this evidence of the boy's attachment to me that I had it not in my heart, and probably not in my power, to repulse him.

When I arrived in Baltimore, and had to wait for a train, after a transfer across the city, I wondered at myself because I had no inclination to wander around the city, as I might have done at another time, in the hopes of catching a glance of Miss Milner's face.

As I meditatively drummed on the car window while *en route* for New York, I remembered a saying of Sam Slick, that a woman's heart was like a turtle's egg, and that one dent in it remained only until another was made. And I wondered, as I meditated, if sex had anything to do with the truth of the application.

CHAPTER XXXII.

AT HOME, AND OFF AGAIN.

WITHOUT incident worthy of note we arrived in Boston; and before taking the train for Center-boro' I went up to call on Ivory Rich.

I found that person with his feet elevated on his desk, smoking a clay pipe as if he had taken a contract to make smoke by the square yard, and had but little time to fill the contract.

He rose to his feet as I entered, and said, "Waiting for the boy to come in; time to shut up; I'm only waiting for him. What can I do for you, sir?"

Then I held out my hand, and for the first time he recognized me.

"You've changed a good deal," he said; "taller and thinner, and some older."

I was indeed so worn and haggard by hardship, that though I had recovered somewhat from the strain of prison life, I still bore traces of it that made me look older than many men of thirty.

"Better go out home with me," he said heartily; "I want to talk with you about your mother's estate and that pirate, Richard Alden. Better go out."

Seeing me look at Rolly, he added, "Oh, he can come along; we can take care of him. He will amuse the girls."

I learned from Ivory Rich that a lawsuit to recover the value of the Blusterson notes, as he termed them, was then pending in the Court of Common Pleas of Pilgrim County, to which Richard Alden had put in a counter plea of their being obtained by fraudulent representations.

"He's got an up-hill row to hoe," said Rich aggressively; "the burden of proof is on him, and not on us. He hopes, I guess, to compromise by having us throw out those conditional notes. We can prove, if we have to, that these conditions have been fulfilled; and we have ordered him to bring his books into court to prove it. If he tampers with them, we'll fix him."

"You think," I said, "we've got a pretty sure case, then?"

"Beautiful!" he ejaculated; "clear as daylight! — Your uncle knows it. He's contrary, but not stupid; and since we've begun it, I have heard he's been taken sick, and that's a pretty good indication he feels bad over it."

"I'm sorry for him," I said. "I have no ill-will."

"S'pose you haven't," said Rich. "By the way, how's Blusterson? I see he's quite a general — see him mentioned in the papers."

I told him all I knew about the general, and was warm in his praise.

"Oh!" said Rich, "he's a pretty good man unless you attempt to drive him. He won't stand much of that; he turns on it like a tiger. Get such men in a corner, and they'll hurt somebody besides themselves. He sent me word some time ago to make a fair settlement with those State-street sharks, and he's settled all his 'industrial rat-trap' business too — paid up like a man. He's honest enough when he's prosperous. I've got an affidavit from him, too, about those notes."

"Isn't it better to make a settlement with uncle Richard if we can," I asked, "rather than have the case come to trial?"

"Of course," said Rich, "if he will make a proposition for a fair settlement; but we are the ones to be conciliated, and not he. It isn't good policy to offer a premium for cussedness; there's enough of that article in the world without that."

During the evening I had to narrate my experiences in prison, and my adventure in escaping therefrom.

Rich was very much interested; and when I told him of Major Grim and his condition when I met him in prison, he began to get excited, and to walk the floor of the room, as he said hoarsely, "What men! You've suffered; it was rough for your friend Grim;" and his strong features worked, and his very hair seemed aggressive as he added, "The country can never repay men for such work and suffering. Republics are ungrateful, they say: but I envy you your experiences; they are something any men might be proud of."

In the course of the evening I told him that I had drawn about a thousand dollars of back pay and ration money, which I was going to put into the bank for my mother; to which he said, "Well, that's the way you should do. Your mother has not been able to do so much for you, but she's a good woman; and I've noticed that boys who have a hard time, and look out for themselves, often do more for their parents than those who have been pampered. When my father died, my mother had a hard time to give us a chance. That chance wasn't much. I came down here with not more than a common-school education, and studied law; but I never let her want for anything I could get for her after I got to earning money." There was a moisture in his eye, and he cleared his throat as he said it. "She was good. A good mother is the greatest blessing a boy can have, or a man either."

The next morning Rolly and I arrived in Centerboro'; and I am not sure that Rolly's appearance did not create more of a sensation than did "the Alden boy."

There had been decided changes in Centerboro'. Such had been the impetus given the shoe busi-

ness by the demands of the war, that it had grown
to be a large village.

Richard Alden, so I was told before I had been
there long, had, with the push for which he was
noted, been employing a large number of men
in his new factory, but was then sick, and that,
too, at a time when the business most needed his
attention.

It is needless for me to relate how joyful was
my reception by my dear mother and sisters and
brothers, or how the neighbors came in to get me
to tell my prison and army experiences, and to see
"that genuine contraband that Captain Alden had
brought from down South."

The village *Gazette* magnified my army service by a very flattering "personal notice," which,
though in the main correct, in some way grated
upon me.

I found the disposition to make a pet or hero
of contrabands was common here as in some other
places in New England during the war.

Before Rolly's appearance in town, a black
man, who claimed to have been Jeff Davis's
coachman, had been lionized by the good town's
people; and this disposition to make much of
"real Southern niggers" was soon illustrated by
the treatment of Rolly in the village.

Even the minister was not proof against this
temptation, and asked Rolly to "speak in meeting."

One evening I happened into the village grocery, and found Rolly seated on a cracker-barrel,
surrounded by an admiring audience of villagers.
Silas Eaton, who was supposed to know a great
many "pints" about war, was interrogating him.

"Why don't you enlist," said Silas in his dogmatic, querulous manner, "and fight for your race
and kintry?"

"Why doesn't I want ter fight?" and Rolly
showed his teeth and rolled up the whites of his
eyes as he craned his person towards Silas, like
a black interrogation point. "Does yer take me
for a mule, sar? You doesn't know nothin' 'bout
fitin'! 'Clar' ter gracious, gemmen! I reckon ye
neber see dem rotten shell, big's this bar'l, come
along fro de air, jus' like a big catch dog, wif
a smoke tail, and his head down, and growlin'
and worry, worryin' along, jus' sayin', 'Get out of
this! I'm after y-e-r-r-r-r, sar-r-r !' 'Pears like
yer neber seen de po' white trash toted 'way fro'
de fitin', wif der han's and legs and heads mashed
off, like chickens ready fo' de stew? No, sar, yer
isn't, or yer wouldn't 'spect a colored man ter
mix wi' sich foolishness, sar!"

"But," interrupted the more thoughtful proprietor, Tinkham, "you black men who want
your freedom must fight for it; you mustn't expect others to do all your fighting."

"Golly, sar!" said Rolly, "I'se got *my* freedom
by runnin'; I neber gets freedom by *fitin'*, sar.

Neber liked der sound ob dem bullets, sayin', ' *Sur-r-r, git!* ' Mighty dangerous, foolin' round mules, too; dey's powerful 'structive, sar, dem mules is; but de bullets hiss like snakes, dey does. I'se seen 'em; and dem shell, when dey come fro de air, keep a worry, worryin',' as if dey was lookin' for a nigger; and when dey 'splode, fright'nin' a man ter def 'fore dey kill him. No, sar; got freedom 'nuf tendin' to de captain, I is ! " And Rolly tipped his hat on one side and looked aggressive.

My coming, when perceived, put a stop to the conversation, but not to the interest with which many in the town regarded "Captain Alden's nigger."

My eldest sister, when I expressed the belief that Rolly would be spoiled, teasingly said that she believed I was jealous of poor Rolly.

He made himself handy around the house; but he annoyed my mother by waiting on me at the table during meals. This was so contrary to her simple taste, and to the usage of an ordinary New England household of that time, that I had to put a stop to it. Rolly expressed his disapproval of this by saying in a disgusted tone, "Dey all works here, jest like common trash, sar."

While at home, my regiment, of which there remained scarcely enough men for one company, was ordered to be mustered out on account of expiration of term of service. Those who had re-enlisted were to be consolidated with two other regiments, the senior officers of them to take command. This threw many officers of the regiment, including myself, out of a command.

While I was debating what course to pursue, and whether I should re-enter the service, my friend Crandall, who had been commissioned in our old regiment, and who by the new disposition had, like myself, been left without military employment, came to see me.

He represented that a good many of our men were ready to re-enlist, but objected to being consolidated with old and rival organizations.

"I'd go if I knew about the other officers," I said; "I don't want to fight under a man who knows less about it than I do."

"Didn't I tell you? I forgot! Major Grim got home a week or so ago. He's chipper and bright as ever. He's all right, and has agreed to go out as colonel if they'll commission him. He'll be a good deal better at the front than when reading about it in the newspapers, and fretting because he can't take a hand; 'twill do him good!"

I was glad to hear of Grim's recovery; and, as a man's wishes give color to his judgment, I agreed with Crandall.

I also entered heartily into the work of helping to form the new regiment.

I was offered a commission as its major, but finally accepted that of senior captain. Major Grim was commissioned as its colonel, and the positions of lieutenant-colonel and major were filled by men of comparatively little experience.

Before I left Centerboro' I was one day passing my uncle Richard's house, where he was confined to his bed by sickness. My aunt, for whom I still retained affection, ran out to greet me, and with tears insisted that I should go in to see my uncle.

"He isn't so bad as he sometimes seems, and is fretting because you are in town and he can't see you."

. I was not a little suspicious; but my anger disappeared when I saw him but a shadow of his former self as I had known him.

After talking with him for a while, he said, as if the subject was uppermost in his mind, "I wish that lawsuit was out of court. Why can't we settle it? It's going ter cost us both a lot of money, and the lawyers'l eat us up alive."

I finally told him that I was willing to accept his proposition; namely, that he would give us his mortgage against the estate for the unconditional notes. The value of the conditional notes should be settled by three referees, of whom Ivory Rich should be one.

"I ain't afraid of the law, Jack," he said, with a cold glitter in his eyes; "but you've got the best of me, and I might as well acknowledge it. I never thought you'd make so much of a man."

I inferred from this that the reason Richard

Alden was so humble in his acknowledgments, was that he thought it cheaper than fighting. In this opinion I found, long afterwards, that I had done him injustice, and with all his natural hardness and sharpness, he had a sort of liking for me, because I had always resisted instead of yielding to him.

I communicated with Ivory Rich, and he came to Centerboro'. With some unimportant changes in the agreement the suit was taken from court, and settled without further cost.

"I ought not to allow the suit to be taken from court," said Ivory Rich sharply. "Your uncle would have gobbled the whole estate if we hadn't been too much for him. It was by no good will towards you that he hasn't, either. Under the circumstances, it's best to settle it, however."

Our land was nearly in the centre of the village, which made it valuable; and one of the circumstances that to Ivory Rich's mind made a settlement best, was that a large manufacturing establishment, unknown to my uncle, had offered a large price for the Alden place.

The sale was finally made, the house, orchard, and garden being reserved for the family home. This large sum of money, with my back pay, was by Rich's advice put into United States government bonds, where it brought over seven per cent interest, and finally, by the appreciation of gold, made the family quite rich.

While this was taking place, recruiting for my company went forward in Centerboro' and in the surrounding towns; and at last, in June, the ranks of the regiment were full. During the same month we went into barracks at Readville, where the colonel joined us.

Mrs. Grim anxiously confided to me the fact that Dr. Milner had advised her husband against going into the service again.

"Mr. Grim," she said, "is gloomy and queer at times, and I dread the excitement, which Dr. Milner says may prove too much for him."

I learned that Miss Milner had returned home before Mrs. Grim left Washington, and seemed very sorry, when she learned that I had been there.

I confess it gave me a flutter around the heart when Mrs. Grim said, "I think she cares more for you now than she does for that Raymond feller."

CHAPTER XXXIII.

IN FRONT OF PETERSBURG.

ON the 21st of June we landed at City Point, on James River, which at that time was Grant's base of operations, and where was gathered the material of his vast army.

The weather was dry and hot, and we marched over roads knee-deep in dust. The boom of cannon and the shriek and groan of shell which exploded above and around us, showed that the enemy was in position nearly parallel to our line of march.

On arriving before Petersburg, we encamped in some woods, back from the main line of works.

About sundown, and before we were well settled, we were ordered to relieve men in the rifle-pits. Thenceforward we alternated forty-eight hours off and forty-eight hours on, in this duty.

As we marched down a sheltering ravine, in the mellow light of a Southern sundown, we were saluted by exploding shell and hissing bullets. Looking towards the enemy, we caught glimpses of yellow ridges of earth, right and left, which told, to men accustomed to soldiering, of the nearness of our own to the enemy's intrenched lines.

I have said glimpses advisedly; for even then we knew that a full view of the enemy was perilous, hence were not seeking for minute particulars.

The intrenchments, behind which we were soon sheltered, were wide, dry ditches, with the soil thrown out towards the enemy, of whose presence we had plenty of evidence, though we could not see them plainly.

Our breastworks were from eight to ten feet high, with head-logs on top, and loopholes underneath these logs, made by removing the soil.

Peeking through these I could see one mud heap more prominent than the rest, which showed to my practised eye a heavy fort in our immediate front.

Back of this salient, or fort, was an elevation of land from behind which I could see the spires of Petersburg, which, though a mile and a half away, was within easy reach of heavy artillery.

Meanwhile, shot and shell, and occasionally the hiss or hum of a bullet, came like angry protests to our presence. On the other side of our intrenchments, limbs of trees, with the brush end towards the enemy, had been thrown, forming a rough abatis as an impediment to the enemy, should they adventurously attempt to charge our position. These had not been fastened to the ground,

as is customary; for a man's life in such service
was not likely to be of long duration, for, as
Colonel Grim said, "It was kinder unhealthy
over t'other side of the dust-heap."

That night was starlight and warm; and as I
passed down my company line, I noticed with
satisfaction that our new men had lit their pipes,
and were vigilant and soldierly. They were
assuming their new duties without excitement,
and in a matter-of-course manner beyond what
is usually seen in new recruits.

"The men," I said in an undertone to Colonel
Grim, "seem to take to it pretty well."

"Yes," replied the veteran; "pretty good set
of men, I guess."

"Intelligent farmers' and sober mechanics'
sons," I suggested, "are good material."

"Yes," assented the colonel, withdrawing his
eye from a loophole, where he had taken, as he
called it, "a peek at the rebs;" "but I kinder
think it is because we've got a good sprinklin'
of old vets here." Then added reflectively, "I
don't know but a few old soldiers added to a lot
of new men is just as good as a lot of new men
put among old vets. They need a little welding
together in either case; fightin', good officers, and
pride 'll do that after a little while."

"We are rather comfortable here as a whole,"
I said, "and we are likely to get fighting enough
for educational purposes; near enough to the rebs,
anyway."

"Humph!" growled Lieutenant Crandall, who overheard the remark, "guess we be, — rather too neighborly, if anythin', for me."

"Crowded up to 'em rather close," said Grim with a grin; "hope they won't get too sociable before we get broke in."

As Grim hitched his sword farther to the front, and, after giving clear instructions, walked down to the left, I could not but admire his soldierly carriage and manner, which carried confidence to all who came in contact with him.

"This soldiering is doing him a lot of good," said Lieutenant Crandall. "It's all nonsense thinking it was likely to throw him out of balance again."

Colonel Grim seemed, in fact, very much improved; his eye had its old fire, his manner a wonted something it had lacked for weeks. Yet I thought of Dr. Milner's suggestion as to the uncertain effect excitement might have on him.

During the night there was but little exchange of shot, though the enemy's artillery kept up a "growling and a barking," as my lieutenant termed it.

The course of the solid shot could be traced in lurid lines against the background of the darkening sky, while the shell traced lines similar to those of rockets.

As daylight came on, the big guns "let up," as Lieutenant Crandall called it; and presently bullets began to drum against the head-logs and throw up little smoke-like splashes of dry dust, and whisper, and *yur*, and *zipp*, around us ominously.

Our new men began excitedly to crowd to the loopholes, disputing for a chance to shoot.

I heard Mike Conlin, the former drummer of our company, but now a corporal, remonstrate with them, saying, "Oh, now, don't be crowdin'! Faith! it's fierce ye fellers are now for fitin'; but ye'll get your bellies full ov it, or it's Oi that am a raw recruit. Toime ye've been at it a month or so, ye'll wish ye was at home, under yer mither's bed."

I could not help smiling at this; for Mike, from the first of my acquaintance with him, had shown so much of an Irishman's fondness for a fight, that it seemed to me he ought not to censure any one for a like disposition.

Our breakfast, which was cooked in the rear, was brought up to us; and about that time there was a lull in rifle practice, as if the enemy were similarly engaged.

While the men were eating, Rolly cautiously crept into the trench with my breakfast, and some of our new men laughed and jeered at him for being "scared."

"I'se no 'casion ter get hit, sar!" said Rolly to one of them. "I'se seen heaps better'n you alls killed. De boss and me seen mo' fitin' dan

" The man reeled and fell into the trench."
— Page 359.

eber you alls heard on. We's at Freds'bug, we
war, and a right lot mo' fights whar de rotten
shell an de big shot an de small shot killed a
heap o' trash like you alls. Seen 'em wifout dar
close on, like dead dogs, sar! Duz yer heah me?
I takes care myse'f, I duz."

During the lull in the firing which for a time
followed breakfast, one of our, what Crandall
called, "high-priced bounty men" jumped on the
parapet, and swung his hat towards the enemy
with a shout of bravado.

"Git down!" I heard Colonel Grim half hu-
morously order. "Git down, I say! You cost the
government a thousand dollars apiece, and I'll
be plagued if I'll have you shot! You're too
expensive!"

Before the words were fully out of the colonel's
mouth, and, as if to emphasize them, the man
reeled and fell into the trench with a crash. He
had been shot through his head. "There," said
Colonel Grim severely, "the government has lost
a thousand dollars, and we have lost a good man
— all for nothing."

It was not long before our men learned that
while shot and shell could be seen by keen-sighted
men, and dodged, as Lieutenant Crandall said,
"almost as easy as a base-ball" the death-whispers
of bullets were not heard by their victims until
too late for safety.

During the day two of our men, who had carelessly exposed their heads above the top-logs, were shot; and when, after forty-eight hours' duty in the trenches, we were relieved from duty, we had lost eight men. This loss was not many for one day; but a loss correspondingly large along the whole line would have soon destroyed the army.

Here let me say, that the loss among new men on any line of dangerous duty is always larger than among veteran soldiers, and that with less effective service. An old soldier learns to protect himself, does not expose himself to danger needlessly.

At last, after forty-eight hours, we were relieved from duty, and then for the first time got a good opportunity to refresh ourselves by "washing up," and by more sleep than could be obtained by what Crandall called "cat-naps."

I have chronicled thus minutely our first experience on duty in the trenches, because first duty in such a place is most vividly remembered, and also because all subsequent duty here generally resembled that I have here described.

As the reader may suppose, on my arrival on these lines I hunted up my old army acquaintances. On inquiry, I learned that General Blusterson had been transferred to duty with the Fifth Corps, and was in command of a brigade. I had written to him of my arrival, and was attempting to obtain leave of absence long enough to visit him, when, one afternoon in July, he rode into camp, inquiring for me, dismounted, and came into the colonel's quarters, where I happened to be, "for a rest and a smoke," as he said,

"Very comfortable; good cigars too," said the general complacently, after the first greeting was over, and he was seated on a barrel-chair, and had lighted his cigar. "Well," he continued, "glad to see you at the front, gentlemen. We are having lively times enough; but it's better than marching all night, and fighting all day, as we did in the Wilderness. I came into the army expecting to do my share of the fighting, but the overland campaign suited me too well."

"I suppose," I ventured to say, "the enemy were just as sick of it as our army was, General."

"I don't know about that. It was a failure," said the general, shaking his head, smiling in his old manner of decision and humor. "We lost in the battles from the Rapidan to the James nearly sixty thousand men; many of them our best officers and best soldiers. You remember Lieutenant Standish? As good and as brave an officer as there was in the army. He was killed in an attack on the enemy's fortified line at Cold Harbor. It was little short of murder in the first degree. Such men can't be replaced. It's against common-sense, and the rules of war too, to attack positions reconnoitred and intrenched by an enemy, as we did in that campaign."

"What are we going to do here, General?" I

interrogated; "we don't seem to get anywhere as I see."

"Here?" ejaculated the general, and his brows beetled and his jaws came together with a satisfied snap, which showed me before he spoke that he was well pleased with the situation. "See here, we've got the vice turned on the rebs;" and the general, taking out a pocket-map, and pointing to it, said, "There, don't you see those turnpikes and railroads running into Petersburg like spokes to the hub of a wheel? Well, Lee feeds his army by those. Grant has got hold of some of these roads already, and when he gets all of them, Richmond will fall; for the Confederate army will starve, or come out from their intrenchments, and retreat or fight us. Our system of strong defences is to enable the front to be held with a part of the army, leaving a large portion of it for manœuvre or attack on their left flank. Meanwhile, you may see their lines forced right here in your front soon."

"I've heard a good deal about a mine our men are digging near us," I said. "I know several officers who say they are old Pennsylvania coal-mine bosses and superintendents, who are at it."

"Supposed you'd heard of it," said the general, blowing out a puff of smoke like an exploded shell. "Burnside's officers don't keep very close mouths."

"Heard one of 'em say," I continued, "that

they had it mined under that fort in our front, — the Elliot Salient, they call it, — and that when at work they could hear the rebs tramp and rattle things, and throw planks down above their heads in the fort."

"Humph!" grunted the general, blowing out another puff of smoke still more emphatically. "Well, I've just been up with some other officers to look over things. The mine's a good one; but they'll need some picked troops after it's exploded, to act decisively, in order to gobble Petersburg! Burnside's a good man, brave as a lion, but too slow and muddled for such work." Then, as if he had said too much, he added, "Mum's the word!"

I turned the conversation by asking if he knew where Add was.

"No," he said; "but he came to me about two months ago for recommendations for a commission. I don't know where; haven't heard from him since."

The next morning after this conversation, when we went on duty, I examined our front with some speculative interest, and saw that if a breach was made in the enemy's lines, a force might be lodged on the crest of a hill, behind which, as I said before, I could see the spires of Petersburg within ordinary cannon range.

Our lines, at the point at which we were on duty, bulged out in a curved form towards the enemy. Under the Elliot Salient before mentioned a mine was almost in readiness to be exploded or "sprung."

Two weeks passed, and I had several times seen the mouth of the mine, the soil excavated from it being concealed from the vigilant enemy by bushes stuck into the ground.

Our advance line was on the crest of gradually ascending ground, and this ascent continued towards the enemy. In our rear was a ravine, and back of this the wood in which was our encampment. A covered way was constructed from the wood to this ravine, which enabled us to approach the front without exposure to the Confederate artillery.

In front of the covered way, on the opposite side of the ravine, was the mouth of the mine.

For two weeks following the conversation with General Blusterson, which I have given, but little was said about the mine; and I supposed at last that, like many other experiments in the army, it had been abandoned.

During this time, however, the regular routine of the army went on, — pay-rolls were made out, requisitions for clothing and food made, camps policed, men drilled, descriptive lists made out and forwarded, with sick and wounded men, to the hospitals.

The *morale* of the army was good, and our food was improved by the attention paid our men by the Christian and Sanitary Commissions.

About the 25th of July there was much riding of orderlies; and once I saw General Grant and his staff, on their way, it was said, to General Burnside's headquarters.

"I really think," I heard one of our vets say, "that they are fussing about that mine some more." I thought, too, that it might be so.

We were formed for an assault on the morning of July 30, before dawn. Colonel Grim walked down the line, his eyes gleaming with excitement, and his whole attitude that of a man ready to act quickly. At about half-past four there was a dull, jarring explosion which shook the ground.

"There she goes!" exclaimed Colonel Grim excitedly, "right up under Johnny Reb's fort, sure's I'm alive! We'll toast them now!"

A dense cloud of smoke, through which blazed ignited powder, sprang hundreds of feet into the air, hung suspended for a moment, and then fell back. A black, sulphurous smoke overhung the spot, and then slowly drifted away.

The terrible force of the explosion was such that fragments of cannon and gun-carriages from the rebel fort were hurled several hundred feet within our lines.

"That's a good one, for the Confederacy!" I exclaimed.

Colonel Grim turned slowly towards me, without remark, with a puzzled look on his face, and with one hand to his head, as, simultaneously with the explosion of the mine, our artillery (which had been greatly strengthened at this part of the line) opened on the enemy as if with a roar of anger! Every brazen throat belched and thundered.

We expected orders for an immediate assault, for the enemy seemed stupefied, and for a long time made no demonstration for a defence. We learned afterwards that the utmost consternation and confusion had been produced on the foe, and that they had abandoned their guns in the intrenchments for several hundred yards in the vicinity of the mine.

An hour elapsed before they recovered sufficiently to plant artillery on the right and left of the crater made by the mine. It was an hour before getting orders for a forward movement; and by that time the enemy opened with artillery on the right and left of the position, besides opening a plunging artillery fire from their front.

CHAPTER XXXIV.

THE ASSAULT AND TRUCE.

THE Confederates on our front were paralyzed for a time by the terrible volcano-like explosion beneath their feet. Had our battalions rushed forward at once into the breach made in their lines, the result must have been decisive. But a vexatious delay followed the explosion, in which precious time and opportunities were lost.

"Burney is a good and brave man," said one of our veterans, "but it always did take him a good while to turn over."

Meanwhile the enemy, after an interval of silence, opened a gradually increasing fire on the right and left of the "crater," or big hole caused by the explosion.

Then we heard the hurrahs of our men going forward to the assult.

While we were awaiting orders to charge, Colonel Grim, pulling at his beard and mustache, walked in the rear of our regiment, as Sergeant Osgood said, "like a caged lion."

"He's narvous," said Crandall, looking towards him with an anxious look; "kinder shook up, I guess."

Finally Colonel Grim with a few sharp words
gave the order, and the regiment moved forward.

I saw, as we moved at double-quick, the ragged
" crater " sixty feet deep and a hundred yards long,
in which a confused jumble of our men had taken
refuge.

The shot from the enemy meanwhile struck our
ranks on both flanks, while a plunging fire burst
from their front.

They had recovered from their panic, and we
had missed the time for profiting thereby.

Amid the bursting of shell and *ping* of bullets,
we sheltered ourselves on the reverse side of the
enemy's intrenchments, and the fragments of the
" Elliot Salient," which had mostly been blown
into the air.   The shell and shot made dismal
music, while whispering messengers of death from
rifles were constantly thinning our ranks.

" Keep the men at it," I said to First Sergeant
Osgood.

" Well, they are doing well. See, they are doing like the vets, trying to make over this side of
the breastworks, and they keep up a popping at
the rebs on t'other side too."

" Yes," I replied; " pretty sharp work, fighting
men within arm's length."   For by this time the
Confederates had got on the opposite side of the
intrenchments, and muskets protruded through
every opening, almost in our faces.   But we soon
made it too hot for them, and the fire in part died

down, but broke out spasmodically here and there along the line.

It was about seven o'clock in the morning when the black division charged. I have since heard much said of the cowardice of these men. But although I was at that time, like many others in the army, prejudiced against their employment, I must confess that their conduct was good.

"They're going in in pretty good style," I said to Crandall.

"Ain't no use denying that," said my lieutenant, who didn't like what he called "nigger equality;" "shouldn't wonder if they'd got there, if they'd gone in first. See that," he continued; "that flag's been down twice; there it goes again! I didn't think they had it in 'em! They are well led."

They had met the converging fire of artillery, under which they still went forward for a while, and then, like those who had preceded them, went to pieces bit by bit under the terrible fire; and finally the men, every one for himself, began, like a scattering flock of sheep, to seek safety. Some took refuge in the crater, others behind the same breastworks as ourselves.

"They did well," said Colonel Grim. "Whenever I see a brave thing, something comes up in my throat and chokes me, as it did when those black fellows went in."

I looked curiously at my colonel. There was

something unusual in his manner; what did it portend?

The fighting was again becoming fierce in places along the intrenchment.

"They can't drive us out," said Lieutenant Crandall decisively; "they haven't got it in their boots;" and then exclaimed, pointing to the right, "Them black fellows stand up to the rack pretty well there! Jerusalem! that young feller's seen fighting before!"

I glanced in the direction he had pointed, and saw near an embrasure a stalwart young officer with drawn sword, directing his men. His cap, from which escaped curly blond locks, was on one side of his head, his face was blackened with powder.

As I looked, a rebel officer sprang out on the other side of the opening, pointing a revolver close to the young fellow's curly head, and, as I learned afterwards, called on him to surrender.

With lightning rapidity he struck up the revolver with his left hand, and with his right ran the Confederate through the body with his sword. The brave Confederate fell back with the sword on which he was impaled on the other side of the parapet, beyond reach.

Our division general, who had seen the act of the brave young officer, in a spirit of chivalry unbuckled his sword, and said, "Put it on; you are as worthy to wear it as any man I've seen to-day!"

All this occurred in less time than I've taken to tell it, and was but one of the kaleidoscopic changes of the fight.

The young officer turned towards the general when he was addressed; and then I saw that it was my friend Add Key. I had only time to exchange salutations.

Our men were calling for cartridges, and fighting hard to hold their position. We held the line until night, and then in the darkness got out of the intrenchments as best we could, and were glad to get to the rear. We had lost very heavily.

Add came with me to the rear, and halted for a time near by us, while collecting some of his men.

"What is your regiment?" I inquired.

"The Massachusetts ———st; and they are mighty good men, if they are a little off color," said Add. "I led the regiment; lieutenant-colonel, you see; and I ain't ashamed of the boys or their work, if they be black!"

Lieutenant Crandall, who was present, said, as he shook hands with his former comrade, —

"Well, you went in in good shape; but I prefer white men in mine."

"'Tain't what's outside of a man," said Add; "it's what's in him, that makes a good soldier. A darky can stop a bullet."

"Yes," I said bitterly; "'most any color is good enough for that in such a miserably managed affair as the one we've been in. I'm glad you have distinguished yourself, Add; and whatever your men are, no officer in the line was braver than you. I wish you were in command of white troops, though."

"Well, I ain't; and some of the men in the white regiments are mighty poor stuff now. There's that regiment Colonel Cross used to command; used to be one of the best regiments in the field: it's filled up with trash. They desert so fast that the rebs sent word over t'other day, that as they had most of the men over there, they'd better send over their regimental flag."

"Yes," said Sergeant Osgood; "I was over there once when they had a roll-call, and some of them fellows had enlisted under nigger names too, such as 'Johnnie Boker' and 'Jim Crow,'— names they couldn't remember themselves, for I saw them look in their hats to make sure to answer to the right names."

"I'll admit," growled Crandall, "that a man who don't wear his own name hain't got pride enough to make a good soldier."

The reader will see that Add was much the same as ever; yet there was a change. Under the jovial exterior there was a stratum of more earnestness and resolution, and his face in repose showed more dignity and thoughtfulness than it had formerly expressed.

There was something besides intellectual development in this, — something which I did not understand.

I mentioned to him this change; and his reply was, "The change that you see in me is the greatest one of my life. I had been through many perils thoughtlessly, and had never acknowledged God's hand in it. I now see that he has preserved me, and every day of my life I acknowledge him."

This was said in a low tone, doubly impressive for its simplicity, and was so free from affectation and cant, that it impressed me very deeply. It showed how Christ gave all the transfiguring influences of manhood and sweetness and dignity to those who caught but a spark of his true spirit and love.

The day after the "mine fiasco" the dead were still unburied and the wounded uncared for between the hostile lines. During all the night we had heard the wounded moaning piteously for help, and calling for water.

A flag of truce at an early hour had been sent out to gain consent of the enemy to the burial of the dead, and to caring for our wounded. It only succeeded so far as to allow us to give the wounded water, for which we could still hear them piteously calling. A few of them had, however, been stealthily removed during the darkness of the night.

August 1st my regiment went into the trenches

once more. At dawn General Burnside sent in another flag of truce, which was met by one from the Confederates.

The truce being arranged, officers and men met midway between the intrenchments. I was one of the officers from our side to meet the Confederates who had come forward for the purpose proposed. From the unburied dead there came a terrible effluvium.

Our men dug two trenches side by side, for their burial. The negro prisoners, captured by the Confederates in the recent fight, then brought our dead on stretchers to the trenches.

The blacks were buried in one trench, the whites in the other. The colored stretcher-bearers looked, meanwhile, with pathetic wishfulness over the narrow line which separated them from friends and freedom.

While this was taking place, our officers entered into friendly though constrained conversation with the Confederates.

Among the striking features in the group was General A. P. Hill, dressed in the uniform of a Confederate major-general.

He was full six feet in height, black-bearded, and with strongly marked features, presenting a striking contrast to the quiet manner and slight and graceful figure of General Dick Taylor, and the thick-set, stolid, but dignified person of General Bushrod Johnson.

Among this group of Confederates, a tall officer in the uniform of an artillerist arrested my attention. I could scarcely believe at first that he was, as it proved, Captain James Milner.

We greeted each other like old friends, rather than enemies.

"I suppose," I said, "you've had great rejoicing on your side over our failure in this affair."

"No," he very gravely replied; "we fight for our homes, and defend ourselves, but it is no pleasure for us to kill men of our own race."

Captain Milner introduced me to the Confederate officers, with very complimentary remarks on the services I had rendered him while wounded and a prisoner in our lines, and a very pleasant conversation took place.

I gave Milner intelligence of his friends, and I do not think he was much more pleased than I was when he heard of Miss May's visit to the Raymonds.

We pointed out to each other as near as possible our quarters within our respective lines; and Captain Milner said earnestly, "I shall never needlessly fire a shot in your direction."

While this exchange of civilities was taking place, the men of both armies stood on their respective breastworks, as lookers on, two hundred yards apart.

On the right of our group of officers, meanwhile,

were gathered a hundred or more privates of both
armies, joking and trading, without the reserve
manifested by their superiors. Their manner soon
became very friendly. "Just as if," as Captain
Milner said, "they hadn't made it a business shooting at each other for weeks."

"What did you think," I heard one of our men
ask, "when that there fort went up, Johnnies?"

"Why, Yank," said the Confederate, "we did
just reckon the Confederacy war goin' with it."
"You 'uns are right smart for diggin', Yanks," said
another; "but we uns can lick you uns right smart,
I reckon."

Both sides expressed a desire to see the war
close.

"The men seem very friendly," I said to Captain Milner.

"It is not probable," said an officer near us,
with a grave smile, "that a similar number of
non-combatants on either side could meet each
other on as pleasant terms. This war has taught
us to respect each other, if nothing else."

The pleasant exchange of courtesies and jokes,
tobacco and hard-tack, among the rank and file
was soon stopped by the officers on both sides.

"They are getting too friendly for practical
fighting," I heard one of the Confederate general
officers say.

"Yes," said one of our officers; "important information may be divulged by them unawares."

When I parted from Captain Milner, it was with many expressions of good will, and with the wish for a more pleasant meeting "when the cruel war was over." I little thought how soon such a meeting would be possible!

After the truce, a sentiment of disgust over the needless butchery, and of fighting in general, was expressed by men of all ranks on our side.

"When I am killed," said Lieutenant Crandall, "I want to count, and not have my life thrown away by that kind of blundering. I don't want to be led by an officer in a bomb-proof, a quarter of a mile in the rear, either."

Up to this time, firing had been, as I have said elsewhere, fierce and constant on this line; but for a week following, scarcely a shot was exchanged between the contestants.

During one of these days a Confederate soldier had jumped upon the parapet opposite, and, swinging his hat, exclaimed, "I say, Yanks! doggone it! let's go home!"

It was as if the meeting of the contestants had vividly brought to both sides a renewal of the feelings of kindred.

Hostilities were never waged with such continuous fierceness thereafter.

The two months that followed were, however, wearing in the nerve-strain and friction that such duty produces.

I saw Lieutenant-Colonel Key occasionally, until

in November he formed a part of Ord's movable column.

In one of the conversations with me he said, "Our old friend Grim seems strangely changed. In some way he don't seem the same man."

This was true; for though he neglected no duty, he was gloomy, unsociable, and strange.

CHAPTER XXXV.

THE LAST CAMPAIGN OPENS.

SPRING had come, with its promise of leaves and flowers, singing birds, and the fragrant sweetness of beautiful Virginia.

The two armies still confronted each other in their formidable intrenchments, extending for miles to the left.

Add had come over to my quarters from Ord's command, then near Petersburg.

There were present Colonel Grim and Lieutenant Crandall, besides Add and myself, sitting at a pine table. There were two rude bunks on the sides of the hut, which was built of logs, chinked with mud, and surmounted by a tent for a roof. In the wide fireplace, built of sticks and mud, there blazed a cheerful, crackling fire; for the evenings were still chilly.

Crandall was smoking his pipe in a semi-reflective and contented attitude. We had been talking about the opening campaign and its possibilities.

"The spring campaign," I ventured to say, "will finish the war."

"Can't remember one that wasn't goin' to!" ejaculated Crandall. "I guess this war will last forever."

"Rather think 'twill hold on a spell longer," said Add; "and that puts me in mind of Silas Eaton when he got the Millerite bee in his bonnet. You know some of them fellows prophesied that the world was coming to an end; and they went so far as to set the day for it, same as you would for a big boil to come to a head, and was just ready to break, — like that mine explosion."

"Yes," ejaculated Crandall; "I remember that dummed foolishness."

"Silas was digging potatoes," laughingly continued Add, "and I stopped by the fence, and said anxiously, for I was a little scared about it, 'Mr. Eaton, do you think the world is coming to an end soon?' After looking at the sky, as if it was a question of the weather, Silas rested his chin on his hoe-handle, and said in his most sepulchral tones, 'Well, it may hold on till spring.'"

"You don't think, then," I interrogated, "that the war will hold on much longer than spring?"

. "Don't look so," Add responded. "I know something about the Confederate army. No braver and more determined men ever fought. I've sometimes felt so much admiration for them, that I couldn't see their wickedness. But I believe the old Confed is on its last legs now."

"Yes," said Colonel Grim, rousing himself from a gloomy mood, and speaking with his old clearness; "it does kinder look like it; for Sherman has cut the Confederacy in two, and Charleston and Savannah have fallen, and Sherman is now, so we hear, not over a hundred and seventy miles from us. Sheridan has cleaned out the Shenandoah Valley, and is about coming here to take a command; and Hood's army has been scattered by Thomas."

"That," said Crandall reflectively, "does have a bad look for the Johnnies; and we know that Lee's army is short of rations, even for them, and that the people are sick of the war, and that their men are deserting all along these lines. Grant, I am told, is afraid they'll get away before he is aware of it; they always could out-march us."

Such was indeed the situation; but the brave men of the "Army of Northern Virginia," which had so long confronted us, and had fought us on so many battle-fields, were yet capable of great deeds.

On the 24th of March, we were on picket-duty at the front. A part of our instructions were that we were not to fire on any Confederate deserters coming into our lines with their arms. These instructions were issued for the purpose of encouraging deserters to bring their rifles and equipments with them.

Before dark, two deserters had come in on my part of the line, saying that a lot of men were coming over as soon as it was dark enough.

" A right smart more of our men are comin' in," said one. " We don't have a heap of work drawing rations over yer now."

I sent these men, after disarming them, to the rear under guard.

No more deserters came in during the night; but about three or four o'clock in the morning I heard Sergeant Osgood say, " Here comes their whole picket-line, I guess."

I saw, indeed, by the dim early morning light, from my place in the rear of the company, from twenty to thirty Confederates leisurely coming to our lines, bringing their muskets at a trail, and still more following.

I was about hurrying to the scene to take their guns and send them to the rear, when a struggle took place. Arms were wrested from our men, and a tall Confederate made a rush at me. I struck him with my sword, and he fell. I felt my arm grasped, and found Lieutenant Crandall urging me to the right, saying, " It's time to run, Jack, not to fight."

All around us we heard, as we crept away, confused sounds of a fight.

On the left, through the gap made by the capture of our line of pickets, the Confederates were pouring like water through a broken dyke.

We got into a ditch, and crept along on all fours until we saw a strong earthwork looming up before us, and knew we were under the mud walls of Fort Stedman. Even as we lingered and listened, curses, shouts, and shots were heard in the fort; then silence, as if the conflict was over.

"Hush!" I whispered; "what is it?"

"The rebs have been trying to take the fort," whispered my lieutenant, "but I guess they are gobbled."

In a moment more we were in the fort, only to find ourselves prisoners of war, and that the Confederates were just manning the captured guns and turning them on the neighboring intrenchments.

A big Confederate, seeing my high-topped boots, made me remove them, went through my pockets, and expressed disgust at not finding more money.

The gray of morning had now brightened into full day, and the sun was up, when a terrible converging fire was directed upon the fort from our batteries.

Crash followed crash; and then, for I was under guard, I heard the Confederates exclaiming, "Here they come! The Yanks are charging us!"

The hissing of shot hummed and blended into one roar like the sound of machinery in motion, and then a great yelling and cheering as our men came on over the works and took possession.

I recovered from the reb who had made me come out of my boots, my money, my boots, besides some other things not my own.

Among the things was a cigar-case and a pocket-book which I recognized as Colonel Grim's.

"How did you come by these?" I inquired of the bearded Confederate from whom I had made reprisals.

"From a Yank outside of yer," he replied; "he was wounded."

I was all excitement. Crandall joined me in the search; and we finally found the dear old fellow with three dead Confederates near him, one of them apparently killed by a sword wound.

The colonel was not dead, but fatally wounded. Before he died, he rallied for a time as we gathered around him, recognized me, and his face had on it a brighter expression than for many days, as he said, while pressing my hand, "Tell Mary I understand now; things look clear, the clouds are all gone."

These were his last words. The brave and simple soldier and friend had passed away into unclouded daylight.

Tears from many a rough soldier who had known brave Colonel Grim fell on the coffin, before Lieutenant Crandall, with a guard of honor, took the body to his old home.

CHAPTER XXXVI.

THE RACE FOR LIFE.

ONLY fifty-eight men of my regiment had escaped capture, wounds, or death on the line before Fort Steadman. The remnants of its companies were therefore ordered to be consolidated with older organizations, and I would soon in all probability be once more without a command.

I was down-hearted and gloomy over these prospects; for I had hoped to win promotion, when General Blusterson offered his influence, and had me transferred to his command as a member of his staff.

"One of my staff, a first-rate man too, went home during the holidays and got married," said the general. "He hasn't been good for anything since. The fact is, a married man has no business in the army, unless he has been married so long that he'd just as lief be killed as not."

"Do you think," I said, after laughing over the general's joke, "that Grant will open the spring campaign soon?"

"Bless you," said the general, wagging his head, "it *is* opened already. Grant's got 'em in

a vice. They tried to wrench away from it at
Fort Steadman, but failed; and now the orders
are given for a final twist that will finish 'em."

"Yes," I replied, "but we've been saying something like that ever since the war began. But
my chances for promotion seem poor, whether it
is true or not."

"Tut, tut," said the general reproachfully,
"I'll see to that."

I went on duty as a member of the general's
staff on the 27th of March, and on the same day
orders were issued to be in readiness for a movement on the 29th.

"This looks like a general move," I ventured
to say.

"Yes," said the general; "I understand that it
is a flank move to the left with the whole army,
except your old corps, which is the pivot of the
movement."

Each day saw evidences of the gigantic struggle
about to begin. On the 29th the division, which
was then near Hatcher's Run, broke camp and
moved towards Dinwiddie Court House.

The country was densely wooded, broken here
and there by clearings, traversed by ridges and
ravines through which rushed deep and narrow
streams.

It shows the difficulties of the campaign, that
soon after beginning our march I was directed to
convey orders to the officers of a flanking-party

that had penetrated the thick woods, and was obliged to dismount in order to make my way through the wild vines and thorn bushes, and even then had my clothes and my flesh torn.

On the Boydtown plank-road there was heavy fighting, in which the enemy had been pushed back after heavy loss.

At ten o'clock that night we made our head-quarters in an abandoned farmhouse, the barn and out-buildings of which were being torn down and piled up as the foundation for a heavy line of defence. Dark masses of clouds overcast the sky and rendered the darkness intense, relieved, however, by the crackling camp-fires.

Before daylight I was awakened and went out to convey orders. The rain was falling in torrents. It was wet, cold, and cheerless; but long lines of our soldiers, rolled in their blankets, though drenched with rain, were sleeping the sleep of tired men. Through the mists of the morning, officers of the pickets discovered an intrenched line of the enemy not a hundred feet from us.

I went back and reported this fact to General Blusterson.

Rolly, who was now master cook for the staff, was cooking, in the house we occupied, breakfast of bacon and chicken before a blazing fire in an open fireplace. The other members of the staff were asleep in their blankets, and the general was just adjusting his artificial leg.

I reported; and several other reports having come in, the general said, "Plenty of time; their works are light, probably their advance;" and then stumping to the door and looking out on the drenched and muddy ground, for it was now full daylight, he added, —

"The best either Johnny Reb or we can do, just now, is to sit down in the mud and look at each other for awhile.

There was no fighting until later in the day. At three o'clock that afternoon I rode forward with orders to the different colonels, preparatory to driving the enemy out of their works on our front.

Fighting began at four o'clock. Our men went forward with a shout that rivalled the Confederate yell, and captured their works.

The Confederates fell back, evidently to a stronger line of intrenchments in their rear. The rain still continued to fall in torrents.

Another advance was soon ordered. The skirmish-line was formed for attack, but the enemy opened a heavy fire; and it was so evident that they would give us a hot reception, that we fell back on the first lines we had captured, and then strengthened them.

Our skirmishers were driven in about dark, and the enemy were reported to be moving forward a heavy line to recapture the intrenchments we had wrested from them.

The general was seated on his horse under a severe fire. As I rode up to report, a musket-shot struck his new saddle. The general, with a scowl, looked down to see how badly his property had been injured, and then said, "My compliments to Captain Black, and tell him to place his battery on the right of the line and to keep it dressed with the brigade. Give them canister at short range!"

With the mud flying, the men cheering, the horses galloping like mad, the battery went into place on the battle-line, and poured canister and shell into the yelling column of the advancing foe.

The soldiers at this time but little resembled the holiday men of a dress parade. Privates and officers were smeared with red mud, in which many of them had been lying, their faces blackened with gunpowder or dirt, their uniforms faded, torn, and drenched. The muskets of the men and the side-arms of the officers alone showed care.

We remained in the Confederate works during the cold, cheerless night, wrapped in our wet blankets, on the muddy ground, where we soon forgot the conflict in restful sleep.

In the morning the brigade was relieved by other regiments.

The general, with myself and two others of his staff, had begun to eat our dinner of chicken, which Rolly had procured the day before, and had

now prepared with great care. The brigade had
stacked its arms in an open field. The men, in
groups, were eating, boiling their coffee, cooking,
and spreading their blankets to dry, for the storm
was over, and the sun had come out again.

To a soldier exercising in the open air everything tastes good. The general was in good
humor, for he liked good eating; and fighting was
likely to be had at any moment. In the midst of
our repast we were almost brought to our feet by
an awful roar of battle not a mile away on our
front. The remains of the stew — grease, gravy,
and all — were hurried into our tins and haversacks, while sound of cannon, musketry, cheering,
blended in one terrible, indescribable roar of
battle, swept towards us.

We mounted our horses. The general gave
quick and decisive commands, which I, with other
members of his staff, rode forward to communicate
to the different regiments. The bugles rang out,
" Fall in! fall in! " Officers shouted commands,
the weary men caught their guns from the stacks
and sprang into line, and, with glistening muskets, and by the right flank, rushed forward.

Soon we encountered groups of men, galloping
batteries, drivers furiously lashing their horses —
the broken fragments of defeated divisions closely
pursued by the enemy.

We took possession of a ridge where we could
look down upon a ravine, through which rushed a

swift, dark stream, while shot from the enemy's artillery smote our ranks.

The enemy's lines were checked at the stream, and our brigade soon occupied the position from which a division had been driven.

Away beyond, on our left, we still heard the crash of cannon and the roar of musketry. It was Sheridan fighting near the Southside Railroad, being driven back by the foe.

During the night we found ourselves too near the enemy for comfort, and fell back.

The morning of April 1st dawned clear and cold. The whole corps had meanwhile come up, preparatory to capturing the Southside Railroad, the last line of road by which Lee received supplies for his army, and by which he communicated with the heart of the South.

If we could wrest this line from them, they must abandon Richmond in any case, no matter what other plans Lee had formed, because no army can exist without food supplies.

A long line of breastworks had been built parallel to this road for its defence.

We moved towards Five Forks, near where Sheridan had fought with his cavalry, but had been driven back, the day before.

We silently formed in a wood on a hill, where we could see the enemy's intrenchments below us, and then, with a dash, were upon them before they could fire a shot.

So complete had been their susprise that they had no time to resist, and surrendered in masses.

The number of prisoners embarrassed us, and we were obliged to detail a large number of our men to send them under guard to the rear.

I had been sent to our officers with orders to accomplish this with as little delay as possible, when, in the midst of its execution, a terrible conflict began. The Confederates had rallied again.

The fight was at its height when Sheridan's cavalry came to our rescue, but none too soon. We then pursued the fugitives, and gathered up their arms. It was a great victory.

The sun went down on many dead and wounded men; but the Southside Railroad, the life-line of the Confederacy, was in our hands.

The bugles rang out the recall; our shattered brigade reached the battle-field, and again encamped for the night. But there was no rest for our wearied men. Our wounded must be cared for, and our dead buried.

Late at night I found my general sitting by a blazing camp-fire, tinkering at his artificial leg. He said, with a scowl, " that a bullet had seriously stirred up its internal economy. The scoundrels! " said the general crossly, "I'm all worn out with them. " So was I.

General Blusterson had been caught in the very maelstrom of the fight I've mentioned as having

been resumed by the enemy, and had escaped from
the "row," as he called it, "by the skin of his
teeth."

"I don't see that you escaped, my dear General,"
I ventured to say. "You'd have thought so," he
answered, "if you'd seen two of the scoundrels
shoot at me, and then try to pull me off my
horse."

On the 2d of April we learned that Richmond
and Petersburg were evacuated, and that Lee was
in full retreat. We were ordered to press forward
again to support Sheridan in his attempt to head
off the retreating Confederates.

From that time to the 9th of April we were in
the saddle night and day, and the brave men of
the brigade were marching with but little rest or
food.

Meanwhile, on every side were indications that
Lee's army was going to pieces. Prisoners poured
in by thousands; Confederate flags were numerous;
while Confederate mortars, cannon, and baggage-
wagons, abandoned by them or captured, lined the
roads along which they were retreating.

As they fell back, they turned again and again
in furious sallies, showing even in defeat and retreat, while harassed by outnumbering foes, that
they were worthy to be named as soldiers of the
"Army of Northern Virginia."

The Confederates were making their last campaign. Who can repress a thrill of admiration

for the brave veterans of Lee's army in this, their last struggle? Bleeding with wounds, worn by marches, hungry and hopeless, they were yet dauntless in the face of famine and despair. One must have lacked the feelings of a soldier and a man, who did not feel admiration and pity for these brave men in that last great struggle.

The roads over which our wearied columns marched were poor; but the foraging, if they got time to forage, was good.

With a short rest at sundown, we were again urged forward, and, with short intervals of rest, marched all night.

I was ready to drop out of the saddle; General Blusterson nodded and reeled, he was so tired. We had reached the division, and had dismounted, when an officer rode up with orders for our brigade to hurry forward.

On the 8th of April the brigade marched thirty miles, and that, too, over poor roads.

Once during the day Sheridan, with his staff and several scouts dressed as Confederate officers, passed us. They carried numerous captured battle-flags of the enemy. General Blusterson and staff rode forward and saluted Sheridan. I saw Sheridan with gleaming eyes, excitedly emphasizing every word of command as he spoke a few sharp, decisive words to General Blusterson, and then with a peremptory order to his staff rode away.

"General Blusterson and staff rode forward and saluted Sheridan."
— Page 394.

"He is a hurricane in cavalry boots," said the general."

Night came, and yet the whole division was again urged forward. "Sheridan has headed off Lee's army," said the general; "and if we hurry up they must surrender. Pass the word down the line!"

With a cheer the devoted men, who, with scanty rations had been marching almost continuously for forty-eight hours, once more pressed forward, staggering with fatigue and hunger, as they marched. They marched all night with another short interval of rest, disputing the right of way with cavalry and artillery.

The sun came up, and shone in a cloudless sky; it was the sun of Appomattox.

We could hear firing on our front now and then. Our column was soon halted in a field, and their arms were stacked as if for a rest.

The men broke ranks, and pulled down fences for fires. I had dismounted, and the general sat on his horse, nodding, when heavy firing was once more heard.

An orderly rode up; a staff-officer from Sheridan followed; a few hurried words; the bugle once more sounded, "Fall in!" A sharp command, "Forward! Double-quick, march!"

Reaching a piece of wood, we met cavalrymen singly and in groups, excitedly shouting and gesticulating to us.

The wearied men, who had been promised rations at that time, caught a glimpse of Sheridan and staff, and with a half groan and laugh, shouted in chorus, "Here's that darned little Irishman, *Pat* Sheridan! Plenty of fighting where he is, but no rations!"

On reaching an elevation near at hand, I could see with my glass the yellow earthworks of the enemy on the opposite hillside, and their artillery back of them, with their skirmish-line in little rifle-pits at the foot of the hill.

A few orders; officers galloping down the line; the charge was ordered, and the men were advancing to attack, when a white flag among the artillery of the enemy's intrenchments appeared.

"What's that?" said the general excitedly, as it came down the hill towards our line; "a flag of truce?"

We rode forward, when an officer, swinging his hat like a madman, riding forward exclaimed, "Halt! halt your men! Lee has surrendered!"

CHAPTER XXXVII.

THE END.

WE lay for three days on the hillside, encamped and fraternizing with our former enemies, foes no longer, but fellow-countrymen. We shared with them our rations, and, though rejoicing that peace and the Union were restored, did not exult over them.

General Chamberlain's brigade received the formal surrender of the Confederate arms on the 12th of April, 1865.

I inquired for Captain James Milner; but though I met several of his acquaintances among the Confederate officers, and learned that his battery was one of those that surrendered here, I did not meet him until later.

The morning of April 12, 1865, was balmy and bright. The last act in the drama of surrender was about to take place.

"Here they come!" "Here they come!" was the exclamation, as down the little valley we saw a line of men in gray advancing. They arrived opposite, and halted a few yards from the blue line with burnished steel.

The order rang out to salute the last of the brave army of Northern Virginia — "Present, arms!"

The gray line returned the salute, then stacked arms, laid on them their equipments and tattered battle-flags, and sadly broke ranks, never again to follow the flag they had surrendered.

They were thin, wearied, earnest-looking men; and some of them cut away pieces of the weather and battle-stained flags which they had followed, oh, how faithfully! through so many battles and vicissitudes.

We respected these manifestations of sentiment, and did not hinder them. But one of these, an officer, went farther than this. I saw him bowed over a small battery guidon; and when he turned, the flag had disappeared, leaving only its staff.

I sprang towards him, he confronted me: it was my friend and former enemy, James Milner.

I extended my hand, and said, "The war is over; let us be friends. Come with me." He was my guest for a while, and was entertained like a brother.

That same day our brigade began its march towards home.

"I have forebodings about my wife," said Captain Milner; "for I've heard our men say that the order was to set fire to the city when they abandoned it."

Captain Milner, by the terms of surrender, was

permitted to retain his horse, and by my invitation and that of General Blusterson was an honored guest. He accompanied us until just before we reached Farmville, when becoming impatient to see his family, with many friendly expressions he rode hurriedly away.

In the afternoon we crossed the Appomattox and rode into Farmville, and there learned that our beloved President Lincoln had been assassinated. The feelings against the Confederates was, for a time, so very bitter that I was glad Captain Milner had left us before we heard the news.

On the 9th day of May we reached Richmond. We found the lower portion of it almost in ruins from a fire. Its huge piles of brick, and crumbling granite, charred wood, and blackened chimney-stacks, stood as monuments of the cruel spirit of the Confederate War Department, that had ordered the city, which its soldiers had so bravely defended, to be fired.

As we rode through the town, the people gave us a cordial greeting. The sidewalks were crowded with people, both black and white, who cheered us. The day was very hot, and at the northern part of the city we had ordered a halt.

The ladies came out in large numbers, filling the canteens of our soldiers with cool water. On the left of us was a large mansion where two beautiful ladies had filled the canteens of General Blusterson and members of his staff. I reached down to take my canteen from the hand of one of these, when in the upturned face before me I recognized the lady I had seen at my hiding-place after escaping from the Libby tunnel. Yet another surprise was in store for me.

A young fellow, in the uniform of a Confederate officer, rushed down the steps, and in a moment I was shaking hands with my friend James Milner. He introduced us to his wife and her sister, Miss Gertrude Austin, and invited us to make his house our home while in Richmond.

The ladies excused themselves for waiting on us, and for the character of the food, as they said their servants had left them, and they had no food except United States' rations.

For the reasons given above I did not again see Sam Brent, who had concealed me in that very house, after my escape from Libby Prison almost a year before.

Marching by way of Fredericksburg, we reached Washington in season to take a part in the final "Great Review" of all the armies of the Union.

There, as our corps ended its march, I was accosted by Dr. Milner and his daughter, Mrs. May Milner Raymond. I was, however, ordered North before I had a chance to visit them.

I was soon mustered out of the United States service, by general order of the War Department, and arrived home June 9, with Colonel Addison Key and other army friends.

We were received by the enthusiastic citizens of Centerboro, the fire company, the brass band, the ringing of church bells, and the firing of an old rusty cannon in charge of the war-like Silas Eaton.

I learned that my uncle had died since I last heard from home. With what seemed to me singular inconsistency, he had left by will all his estate to me, reserving for his wife a life interest.

There remains but little to be written.

Dr. Milner died a short time after the war, widely known, and honored as an ornament to his profession.

Raymond died soon after, and left his widow, it was said, very rich.

Mrs. May Milner Raymond uses her wealth as if she held it in trust for the poor and needy. Wherever there is sickness or poverty near her, she is known as a ministering angel of mercy.

The sick, poor, and distressed bless her beautiful presence, for her care for them has become her highest happiness.

Crandall, with his daughter, Mary Grim, still lives in Spindleville; and here the brave Grim is buried.

General Blusterson retired from business a few years after the war. So much does he dwell on his recollections of his army experiences, that my son, Jack Alden, Jr., has confidentially expressed to me much indignation that his grandfather had so little help in putting down the Rebellion.

As I write, I hear Rolly talking to Master Jack on the broad stairway. " I 'clar' ter goodness, Massa Jack, de Cap'n an' I fought endurin' de wah. I procured an' cooked de chickens, an' toted de stuff, an de Cap'n do de fitin' right smart."

Captain James Milner visited me the summer after the war closed, when Colonel Key, who had already become a successful business man, invited Miss Gertrude Austin (Captain Milner's sister-in-law) to become his wife. She protested that she would never marry a Yankee; but Colonel Key, as persistent in that as in everything else, at last compelled a surrender.

We have both grown old since the days I've here recorded, and, as Add insists, are among the "have beens." We never cease to render thanks to Him who brought us safely through so many perils.

With whitening locks, like flags of truce to life's conflicts, we now await the roll-call of our great Commander, who will soon write under our earthly records,

FINIS.